All the best wishes.

Randall Silvis

The Luckiest Man in the World

Winner
of the Drue Heinz
Literature Prize
1984

The Luckiest Man
in the World

RANDALL SILVIS

University of Pittsburgh Press

Published by the University of Pittsburgh Press, Pittsburgh, Pa., 15260
Copyright © 1984, Randall Silvis
All rights reserved
Feffer and Simons, Inc., London
Manufactured in the United States of America

Library of Congress Cataloging in Publication Data

Silvis, Randall, 1950–
   The luckiest man in the world.

   I. Title.
PS3569.I47235L8   1984   813'.54   84-4217
ISBN 0-8229-3476-0

The writing of this work was supported in part
by a grant from the National Endowment for the Arts.

For Rita

Contents

The Luckiest Man in the World

The Luckiest Man
in the World

WHEN Emiliano Fortunato returned to Torrentino after being wounded in the war, he found his small village still in mourning. Of the twenty-eight men who had marched off happily a month earlier, vowing to destroy the oppressive federal regime, only Emiliano, a thin, hazel-eyed youth of seventeen, survived his outfit's first encounter with the enemy. Ironically, the men of Torrentino had suffered no previous oppression at the hands of the government. So remote and insignificant was their mountain village that most of the inhabitants could not even name the politicians then in power. But the revolutionary soldier who happened into Torrentino had told such eloquent stories of repression and taxation, such tales of brutality, of rape, torture, and decapitation, that the men of Torrentino felt a long-neglected national pride stirring deep within them, and all were subsequently moved to march against the faceless capitalist tyranny that was threatening to usurp their birthrights.

That their birthrights consisted of little more than a dusty garden plot and an earthen-floored shack for each of them did not seem to deter their enthusiasm. Any opportunity to escape the monotony of Torrentino was welcomed. And as a consequence, every Torrentino male between the ages of thirteen and sixty-five was wiped out. Only Emiliano Fortunato survived. Perched thirty

3

feet up in a treetop, he had been acting as lookout for his regiment but fell asleep cradled in the fork of two branches. He awoke to the sound of gunfire, only to discover that federal troops had already passed beneath his perch and were swarming over the resting revolutionaries. The men who were taken prisoner were lined up almost immediately and shot. The entire encounter could not have lasted more than fifteen minutes. Emiliano huddled in his treetop cradle, weeping and vomiting, and watched as the federal soldiers tossed his dead neighbors into a shallow ravine and covered them with a few shovelsful of dirt.

When the soldiers departed Emiliano attempted to climb down out of the tree. But so weakened and dizzied was he by what he had witnessed that he lost his footing and tumbled down through the branches, shearing off limbs as he fell. Landing on his right side, he struck the earth with a heavy thud and lay unconscious for several minutes. Finally he staggered to his feet. To his amazement Emiliano discovered that a twig approximately an inch in diameter had been rammed through the triceps muscle of his right arm. There was no pain, though he could see clearly where the skin closed around the twig at its point of entry, sealing the wound, and where, on the other side of his arm, the twig's sharp point distended the skin.

As though in a dream Emiliano watched a trickle of blood drip from his arm. Then, regaining some of his senses, he removed from around his neck the green bandana, symbol of the Regimiento Torrentino, and tied it tightly around his upper arm, tugging at the bandana end with his teeth. He then walked in wide circles around the battlefield for several hours, pivoting in a daze past the pit in which his slain neighbors lay like fishing worms in a tin can. Toward nightfall his legs gave out, and he fell asleep beneath an huisache tree. Inhaling the rich fragrance of its yellow flowers he lapsed into unconsciousness. For the next eighteen hours he slept, his sleep haunted by mocking, accusative visits from his dead neighbors.

Early the next morning Emiliano awoke, his arm throbbing and burning, swollen to three times its normal size. After breaking off the protruding twig so that only a fragment extended outside the skin, he began the long hike back up the mountain to Torrentino. He was afraid to go home, but at the same time afraid to go anywhere else. For the first time in his life, he was alone. As the only child of his widowed mother, Emiliano had been coddled and pampered, and at seventeen was still very much a boy.

He filled the tedious walk with self-denigration and chastisement. He called himself a coward, a little girl, a shivering puppy. On the third day he reached the depths of self-humiliation and stood on the rim of a high rock ledge, wanting to jump. But he could not force himself over the edge. Aloud he prayed: "Dear God, I am a gnat, a mere pimple on the face of the earth. I don't deserve to live. If You will give me a little push I won't in any way attempt to hold myself back. Send me hurtling down into purgatory where I belong. I am ready to die and am awaiting your assistance."

But although Emiliano stood poised on the ledge for a full ten minutes, not once did he feel the hand of God upon his shoulder, giving him that necessary shove. No dark wind came sweeping down upon him to carry him off into space. There was not so much as a breeze to ripple his torn shirt.

Emiliano stepped away from the edge and sat down in the dirt. Apparently God did not want him dead. Maybe, Emiliano thought, it was not by accident that he had been perched in a treetop while his neighbors were dropping like flies. Maybe it was more than chance that had landed him on his shoulder rather than his head when he tumbled out of that tree. The sharp twig could as easily have pierced his heart, couldn't it? But no, it had been directed into the muscle of his right arm, to an out-of-the-way place that would not prove to be life-threatening.

Maybe God had plans for Emiliano Fortunato. He certainly had not gone to all the trouble of keeping the boy alive only to help him kill himself in a fit of self-loathing.

Reasoning thus, Emiliano quickly overcame his depression and turned his attention to his wounded arm. The arm had, thankfully, ceased its intolerable burning. Emiliano took this as a sign that God was looking after him from moment to moment. The only discomfort Emiliano now felt, aside from his hunger, was an occasional prickliness in the tips of his fingers and a bothersome itch around the mouth of the wound itself. Throughout the rest of his arm he felt nothing. It dangled from his shoulder like a wet cloth.

On the fourth day after the battle Emiliano staggered into a small village in which there was a doctor. Dr. Sevilla was a slight, heavily perspiring man who lived in a large white house, its screened porch alone as big as the house Emiliano shared with his mother. The doctor appeared quite touched by Emiliano's wound. He even stroked the boy's chest reassuringly while, between strokes, he gingerly removed Emiliano's shirt.

"You don't have to be so careful," Emiliano told him, affecting the stoicism of a hardened warrior. "My arm no longer hurts. In fact I can't feel a thing."

Dr. Sevilla cut away the green bandana and exposed the arm. "Oh, you poor beautiful child," he said, and he actually began to weep. "Who tied this scarf around your arm like that?"

"I tied it myself," Emiliano said, a bit too proudly.

"But much too tightly," the doctor said. "And you never loosened it to let the blood flow, did you? The wound itself wasn't serious; the muscle would have healed in time. But you cut off all the circulation to your arm. Oh, my poor stupid child."

Emiliano did not quite understand. Wasn't the purpose of a tourniquet to prevent the blood from flowing? Nor was he certain just what Sevilla had in mind when he prepared a hypodermic syringe and then swabbed Emiliano's shoulder with alcohol.

"Will that help my arm to heal?" Emiliano asked.

"Your arm is no longer an arm," Sevilla said, shaking his head and not bothering to wipe away the tears as they trickled down his cheeks. "It's just a tail on a chicken now. It's just an old snot rag that you used to wipe your nose on."

Emiliano was confused, but he said nothing. Without feeling he watched as the syringe needle punctured his skin, as the clear fluid in the hypodermic was gradually injected into his shoulder.

"You never even tried to clean the wound, did you?" Sevilla asked. He placed some frightening-looking instruments in an enameled basin, then poured over them a full bottle of alcohol.

"Do you know what gangrene is?" Sevilla asked.

Emiliano shook his head. He was beginning to feel very sleepy.

"Oh, you poor child," Sevilla said. After preparing his instruments he came back to sit beside Emiliano and to hold the boy's good hand, his thin finger's stroking Emiliano's wrist.

After a few minutes Emiliano slumped forward into the doctor's arms. Sevilla held him upright, his smooth-shaven cheek against the boy's as he caressed the back of Emiliano's neck. Then very gently he eased the boy down on the table. He lifted Emiliano's dangling wounded arm, truly as lifeless as a wet cloth and as useless as a tail on a chicken, and laid it flat on the table. Then he went to the enameled basin to retrieve his instruments. He came back to the table and spread out the instruments in a row. Then, weeping softly each time he looked into Emiliano's handsome, youthful face, he began to saw off the arm.

For three weeks Emiliano recuperated in the doctor's comfortable home. He wore Sevilla's clothing, slept in Sevilla's bed, ate at Sevilla's table. The doctor pleaded with him to remain permanently, to become, Sevilla said, his assistant. But Emiliano did not feel at ease in the huge empty house. The servants looked at him snidely, and he had the feeling they talked about him behind his back. Also, Sevilla was constantly wanting to touch him—under the pretext of examination, of course. But sometimes in places which, the boy thought, could not have anything to do with his amputated arm.

One day when Sevilla was attending to another patient, Emiliano gathered a bag of food from the doctor's kitchen and resumed his journey home to Torrentino. His village was approximately a five-hour hike away, situated on a remote mountainside well off the main-traveled roads. He walked half the distance that first afternoon, and then, still weakened by his operation and three weeks of inactivity, spent the night beside a shallow, fast-running stream. He slept until noon the next day, and in mid-afternoon finally caught sight of the low buildings of Torrentino.

The villagers of Torrentino, all of whom were now women or children or very old men, were preparing for their siesta when one of them looked down the road to see Emiliano trudging toward them from fifty yards away. From that distance he appeared lopsided and hazy, his body seeming to shimmer in the heat. As soon as his face was recognized, the assumption was made that Emiliano, thought to have been killed with all of the other village men, was a ghost.

Argentina Neruda, a wrinkled, shrunken, and smelly old woman who practiced Aztec shamanism, chanted and shook a small leather pouch of animal teeth at the approaching figure. She warned her neighbors to remember the federal soldier who had come to gleefully announce that the entire Regimiento Torrentino had been killed, snuffed out like a weak candle flame in a windstorm. The pathetic little rebellion had been squashed, the messenger had said. Ground like a tarantula beneath the bootheels of the magnificent General Cruz. He had spoken as eloquently as the revolutionary who had earlier led all of the men to their deaths. How could they not believe him?

The villagers gathered in the dusty street in front of Father Vallarte's Mother of the Holy Infant church and watched Emiliano approaching. As he came nearer they stood their ground but huddled closer together. Father Vallarte, his glaucoma-plagued eyes squinting to make out the hazy figure, feebly made the sign of

the cross and began to mumble the Lord's Prayer. Halfway through
the prayer he lost his place and was forced to clear his throat and
begin again. Argentina Neruda chanted ancient indictments and
rattled her pouch of animal teeth.

What could the ghost of a seventeen-year-old boy want of them?
the villagers asked themselves. Hadn't they been lighting their
votive candles nightly for the souls of the departed? Hadn't they
been reciting their novenas and attending religiously to their
mournful thoughts? Why was this specter coming to haunt and
grieve them even more?

Emiliano Fortunato approached the villagers and stopped just
five feet short of their huddled group. A layer of reddish brown
road dust clung to his eyebrows and lashes. His face was streaked
with dirt, his hair tangled and uncombed. The clothes he wore,
clothes that had once belonged to Dr. Sevilla, were a bit too small
for him and made him appear as though, swollen with death, he had
grown a few inches. The clothes too were painted with a fine veneer
of brown dust. Overall he looked as though he had only recently
climbed up out of his grave. His beautiful hazel eyes were dulled
and cloudy with fatigue, and he had only one arm.

Teresa Fortunato, Emiliano's mother, stepped out of the crowd
and faced her son. Before marching off to war he had been her only
source of comfort, her reason for enduring a hard life. She did not
recognize the clothes he wore, but as he stood there, slouching and
unwashed, Teresa thought she saw in his tired smile a true-to-life
vestige of her son.

"Emiliano," she said hesitantly, almost afraid to open her mouth
to speak. "Is that really you, or are you a ghost?"

Standing lopsided, smiling crookedly, Emiliano answered,
"What would a ghost be doing with only one arm?"

His mother rushed forward to embrace him.

In the ensuing weeks it became all too easy for Emiliano to lapse
into an infantile laziness. His mother tended to his every need: she

washed his hair and scrubbed his back and shoulders when he bathed; at times she even fed him like a baby while he reclined against a thin mattress propped up in the shade of the gabled roof against the outside wall of their house.

To answer the barrage of questions with which his return to the village was met, Emiliano fabricated an elaborate story about being left for dead on the battlefield, about later regaining consciousness only to discover all of his comrades slain. He had dragged himself from body to body, he said, saying a prayer over each man and gathering some small momento to carry home to the grieving family. From Juan Volutad he had recovered the tiny penknife with the mother-of-pearl handle. Hadn't he watched Juan on innumerable occasions use that very knife to carve up a piece of fruit, and didn't he know how much the return of such a souvenir would mean to Juan's bereaved wife and children?

From Carlos Gutiérrez he had secured the gold coin with the hole punched into it so that it could be hung from a string and worn about the neck as a good-luck piece. And from Pablo Márquez, the devout, soft-spoken Pablo, he had recovered a medal of the Blessed Mother.

From each of the twenty-seven men, Emiliano said, he had salvaged some momento certain to bring comfort in the empty days ahead. All of these treasures he had wrapped carefully in his green bandana to carry home to the grief-stricken families. Unfortunately he had been accosted by bandits along the way, beaten and robbed.

When he told this story he bowed his head and wept and begged forgiveness for his failure. All but a few of the villagers comforted him when he grew sad or recounted for them his nightmares peopled with specters of slaughter and death. Argentina Neruda and a few other bitter old women wondered aloud why Emiliano Fortunato alone had been saved, why a skinny, lazy boy had been returned to them while good men with large families had been struck down.

All but these few women paid a certain deference to the boy. This was especially true of those women aged approximately fifteen to thirty-five. More than once Teresa Fortunato was forced to shoo away a crowd of women who with their solicitous attention threatened to smother her son. What thick dark hair he had! they told him, each wanting to run their fingers over his head. What beautiful and sad hazel eyes! they cooed. How he must have suffered from the loss of his arm! How truly brave he was! What a good brave husband he would make one of these days!

Emiliano, of course, did nothing to discourage such kindliness. He luxuriated in the attention as a well-fed cat luxuriates in the warmth of the sun. He teased playfully and even stole a kiss or two when no one was looking. Late at night he would sometimes slip out his bedroom window and not return until dawn was already creeping up the mountainside. This latter activity became so habitual, in fact, that by the time Emiliano had been home for only twelve days his mother was remarking how wan and lethargic he had become.

"Don't you sleep well at night, my little soldier?" she asked.

"I am haunted by dreams," he told her while lying on his mattress propped up against the outside wall of their home.

"Dreams of the battle?" she asked.

"You will never know, mama, how horrible it was for me. You will never know how bravely I fought. And all to no avail. I sometimes wish I had not been successful in keeping myself alive."

"You must never say such things," she warned. "It's a mockery of God's will."

"If only I could forget how terrible it was."

His mother clicked her tongue sympathetically. "Such awful scenes you must have witnessed."

"They are etched into my memory," he replied. "Even my arm, shot off as it was at the very height of the battle, even it will not allow me to forget. Each night it burns and pains as though it were still attached. Consequently I am forced to crawl out of bed to take

long walks through the darkness, hoping to wear myself out sufficiently to snatch an hour or two of rest throughout the day."

Emiliano quickly discovered that such wounded-hero posturing
was very effective in eliciting his mother's sympathies, and equally
effective on many of the widows he visited covertly each night. This
self-pitying attitude was best with the older women, women who
had lost sons of their own, while the braggadocious swagger could
be counted on to produce the desired effect in the younger girls.

One warm afternoon Emiliano awoke from his siesta to realize
what a fortunate man he was. He may have lost an arm, but in many
respects he was truly blessed. He had a loving mother who doted on
him, who dragged his spare mattress back and forth, who placed
herself at his beck and call. And there were several warm, lovely
women who each night waited anxiously for him, waited naked and
eager beneath soft sheets, their hearts fluttering like tiny birds
learning to fly. And there were several other women who, while not
quite lovely by the light of day, were soft and solicitous and whose
murmurs in the thick syrup of darkness were just as sweet as those
of the prettier ones.

There were, of course, those few women who could not bear the
sight of Emiliano Fortunato. To see him lounging on his mattress
reminded them that their husbands or lovers or sons, once as virile
and handsome in their eyes as was this boy, were now dead. Why
couldn't Emiliano be dead and the lost husband or lover or son here
in his place? The women who entertained such thoughts frequently
gathered together in the evenings to condemn the boy. Argentina
Neruda encouraged their enmity; she cracked eggs and pointed to
the spoor of blood, she read viscera and threw her bones and
regularly pronounced Emiliano an evil spirit raised from the
battlefield to haunt their village. After all, hadn't he been spotted
more than once slinking between the small houses in the dead of the
night, slithering through the shadows like a thief? And didn't it
seem that he had cast some kind of spell over the younger women,
so that they fondled and caressed and cooed over him as though he

were a newborn baby? He was behaving as though he was Christ Incarnate, and not just a lazy, shifty-eyed boy with one arm and a huge supply of sexual energy.

Emiliano knew very little of the machinations of his detractors. He ate well and was well looked-after and was practically lionized by three-quarters of the women in town. He slept throughout the day and indulged himself sumptuously each night. He had participated in a raging battle and had managed to escape with the loss of only one arm. As far as Emiliano Fortunato was concerned, he was indeed the luckiest man in the world.

Nearly a month had passed when Dr. Sevilla came riding into Torrentino on horseback. He sat stiffly astride his well-lathered gelding, jouncing along like a small boy on a merry-go-round. He wore leather riding breeches and a pink silk shirt, and over the shirt a rebozo of handwoven wool. The first person he met was Argentina Neruda, who, when Sevilla came riding down the narrow street into the village, was returning from her daily scouring of the mountainside for dead wood for her oven.

"Which is the house of Emiliano Fortunato?" the doctor asked, reining back his horse and peering down at the wrinkled old woman. She had a face like an ancient cat's, small and round and suspicious as she squinted up at him.

"Who are you?" she asked, her arms full of dead branches and twigs.

"My name is Dr. Sevilla. Emiliano is a patient of mine."

Argentina did not like this man with the thin face, hawk's nose, and large, piercing eyes. Why would a man in a pink silk shirt—she had caught a glimpse of the shirt when the doctor raised his hand to shield his eyes from the sun—come all the way to Torrentino to see a patient who could not afford to pay him more than a compliment? Besides, what right did he have to sit there peering down at her so disdainfully, as though she were some kind of an animal, a bug he would like to step on and squash?

"Six houses down," she finally told him. "On your right. You'll find him where he always is—sleeping on a mattress outside his house."

The doctor nodded his thanks, shook the reins, and urged the tired horse forward.

The clopping of a horse's hooves against the dry earth stirred Emiliano out of his slumber. Shielding his eyes he peered up the street, uncertain of what he was seeing until the doctor grinned happily and waved.

Now Emiliano stood and went inside the house. His mother, surprised to see her son moving so quickly in the middle of the day, asked him what was wrong. He did not answer. Hurrying into his bedroom he pulled the already lowered shades down over the windowsill, then sat on the edge of the bed in the tepid dimness.

Out front, Dr. Sevilla introduced himself to Teresa Fortunato. A few minutes later he lifted aside the blanket that hung across Emiliano's doorway and, like a prairie dog peeking out of its hole, poked his head into the bedroom.

"Emiliano," Sevilla said, holding back his emotions for the sake of the boy's mother in the next room, "I've come to have a look at your arm."

"There is no arm to look at," Emiliano said dryly.

Now the doctor came into the room and sat on the bed beside the boy. He laid his medical bag and another small package against the pillow.

"May I unbutton your shirt and take a look at your arm?" Sevilla spoke softly, his voice timid and almost whining.

"Everything is fine," Emiliano told him. "If you've come all this way just to examine me, you've wasted a trip."

"Please let me look at you," the doctor said. He raised his hand to Emiliano's shirt and undid the top button. Emiliano seized the doctor's hand.

"I have to examine you," Sevilla said, speaking firmly now, "in order to determine that the wound is healing properly, that there is

no infection, and that I got all the gangrenous flesh. Now please
don't be a stupid boy. You don't want to have another operation, do
you?"

Hearing this, Emiliano submitted and allowed Sevilla to unbutton the shirt. Afterwards Sevilla raised the window shade, then
turned the boy by his shoulders so that the amputation faced the
inward-slanting shaft of sunlight.

"It's healing nicely," Sevilla said, probing the scar tissue. "All
the pus is drained out, isn't it? That's what I like about you young
boys; you all heal so quickly."

The doctor's hand slid from Emiliano's shoulder down across his
chest and over his waist. "You've put on a little weight, haven't
you?" Sevilla said. "Somebody must be taking very good care of
you."

Emiliano reached for his shirt and draped it over his right
shoulder, then drew his left arm through the sleeve and began to
fasten the buttons. Quickly the doctor stood again and lowered the
shades. He sat lightly on the bed, leaned toward Emiliano, and slid
his damp palm beneath the boy's shirt.

"My poor dear boy," Sevilla whispered. "Why did you sneak
away from my house the way you did? You know you broke my
heart, don't you? I couldn't see any patients for a week, I felt so
miserable without you."

Emiliano tried to stand but Dr. Sevilla grasped him by the belt
and held him firmly. "Please don't walk out on me," Sevilla said. "I
came so far just to see your beautiful face again." He sniffed, his
own face held close to the boy's, his breath smelling of cloves.
Sobbing quietly, he massaged Emiliano's wrist.

"If you'll only come back with me you can have everything you
want. You'll have new clothes and a fine big house to live in. Why
would you want to stay here when I can give you all that?"

"This is my home," Emiliano said archly. "This is where I
belong."

"Who is to say where each of us belongs? And what makes you

think you belong here, in a village full of women, rather than in my village living in a handsome white house? What can you accomplish here? From what I have heard, you do nothing all day long but lounge in the shade on your mattress."

Emiliano drew himself up straight. "I sleep in the day because my services are so much in demand at night."

Now the doctor understood. "So that's what keeps you here, is it? No wonder you're acting like a rooster in a henhouse. But how long do you think this can last before you tire of it?"

"I will never tire of it. When I don't have it I spend all my time thinking about it."

Dr. Sevilla emitted a soft click from the back of his throat. A pout formed on his lips and he looked as though he might weep again. Then he turned and reached for the small brown package that lay on the bed. He stripped off the paper and handed the contents, a neatly pressed and folded pink silk shirt, to Emiliano.

"It's just like the one I'm wearing," Sevilla told him, and lifted his shawl in evidence. "Touch it; feel how smooth it is. Your skin is so delicate, especially here, at the amputation; you should have a material that will caress and soothe your skin instead of chafing it. What woman here could give you a shirt like this?"

Emiliano held the shirt in his lap and fingered the cloth. It was as slick and sensual as the skin of a woman's breast. Emiliano was only remotely aware that, while he stroked the soft cloth, Sevilla had slid his hand along the inside of Emiliano's thigh.

"I will give you a whole closetful of shirts like this," the doctor whispered. "As well as silk trousers and silk socks and silk pajamas. And silk sheets to sleep on every night."

Emiliano ran his finger over the shirt collar. He felt each of the small pearl-like buttons. While the cloth had the texture of a woman's skin, smooth and slightly cool as when you first touch it before it becomes flushed with excitement, the buttons reminded him of the small hard nipples of María Castaneda's breasts.

It was this analogy that finally convinced Emiliano to lay the shirt aside. "I'm staying here," he announced. "This is where I'm needed."

"It would be easy enough to inform your admirers of the truth about your injury," Sevilla said. "I remember well how you wept when you told me, knowing that you alone were responsible for the slaughter of your neighbors."

Emiliano's eyes narrowed. "And it would be easy enough to inform your patients of what a maricón you are."

The doctor drew his hand away as though it had been slapped. He stood and snatched his medical bag off the bed. "You'll get tired of them," he said. "You'll get tired of the way they moan and the way they smell. You'll get tired of their flabby breasts and their soft stomachs. And sooner or later, with only one young man in town, there's bound to be trouble, isn't there?"

"What kind of trouble?" Emiliano asked.

The doctor only looked at him, smiled as though he knew a secret, and sniffed. "Keep the shirt," he said. "It's my gift to a poor stupid boy. Maybe in a month or so I'll return to see how you're coming along."

Emiliano found the doctor's jealousy amusing. "Stay a while," he said consolingly. "My mother can make you something to eat before you go."

After Sevilla's departure Emiliano returned to his bedroom. Prostrate on his bed, he wondered if there could be any truth to Sevilla's prediction of inevitable trouble. It was something he did not wish to think about, but Sevilla's words kept returning to him. On the other hand, Sevilla was a capon, so how could he guess what a village full of women might or might not do?

To put the doctor's warning out of his mind, Emiliano turned his head toward the wall and watched a spider constructing a web in the corner of the room. Emiliano had always been fascinated by spiders. They never seemed to rest. They suspended their delicate doilies in out-of-the-way places, then crouched unobtrusively like a dustball and awaited their lunch. But why did spiders never get entangled in their own webs, Emiliano wondered. Because they knew where to step, how to tiptoe around trouble. Just like me, Emiliano told himself. Even so, there was something about the subtle horror of the spider's anticipation that filled Emiliano with a vague unease.

Later in the evening his mother looked in on him to inquire if everything was all right. He answered that the doctor had given him some medicine that made him sleepy, and would she please not disturb him again? He lay on his back and draped the pink silk shirt over his face and imagined it to be the perfumed hair of María Castaneda. So aroused did he become by his fantasy that he was barely able to wait for the fall of darkness so that he could climb through his bedroom window and, wearing his new silk shirt, hurry to María's house.

María Castaneda was only nineteen years old, but she lived alone because her husband, to whom she had been married just two short weeks, had been a member of the Regimiento Torrentino. Before being married she had acquired a reputation as a bold and adventuresome girl. Now she was just another widow, younger than most, but one of the many who prayed fervently each night that Emiliano would choose her window or door to come tapping upon.

This night Emiliano was barely into her bed, his new pink shirt hung carefully over the back of a chair, before María accused him of neglecting her.

"It's been four days since you were here last," she complained. "Do you expect me to be satisfied with that when you promised you would be back the very next night?"

"I'm sorry, I couldn't make it," he said, and allowed his hand to explore the firm fullness of her breasts, the slope of her stomach, and the warm gentle curve of her thighs.

"As you know, María, I have many other things to attend to."

"Things?" she said. "Is that what we are to you? I get awfully tired of waiting here by myself five nights a week while you attend to your other things. I'm a young woman and I need more attention than you've been giving me. Didn't you mean it when you said that I was your favorite?"

"Please, María," he said, snuggling up to her, her jealousy more than a little bit pleasing. "Believe me, I do everything I can to get to you sooner. I'm working myself to the bone."

She giggled at this and allowed him to move his hand in playful circles over her belly. Then she pushed his hand away. "Do you have more fun with any of the others?" she asked.

"Not half as much as with you," he answered honestly. "They all seem to take it too seriously. Some of them even pray afterward. They get down on their knees when they think I've fallen asleep and ask God to forgive them for their sins."

"But one of them gives you silk shirts."

"I have only one silk shirt so far," he told her. "But I've been promised a closetful."

"Who in this village can afford to give you a closetful of silk shirts? Is it Constancia Volutad? Or maybe that old hag, Alissa Márquez? I don't know how you can stand to be with her."

"She's barely thirty years old, María. Besides, when she prays it's not to ask forgiveness for her sins, but to ask for the opportunity to sin even more."

"Then she's the one? She gave you the silk shirt?"

"No," he teased. "But it's someone who likes me very much."

"How can I compete with someone who gives you silk shirts?" she asked angrily, and struck him so hard on the chest that he drew back, stunned, and blinking in the dimness stared down at her angry face. She had struck him as hard as she could with the ball of her fist, her clenched hand thudding against his sternum and causing him to lose his breath for a moment. He was torn between being flattered by her jealousy and wanting to slap her for having dared to strike him. But after a few moments he concluded to himself that her possessiveness was amusing, in fact satisfying; and above all else, it was understandable.

"I pay more attention to you than to any of the others," he told her. He stroked her hair and lowered his head to hers so that his lips brushed against her neck. "I have been with some of them only twice since I returned from the war, and then only because of my sense of civic duty. But I have been with you ten times so far."

"Only nine," she told him. "Counting tonight."

"Everyone knows that I think you're the prettiest," he said. He lowered his head to kiss her breasts. "Just the thought of you brings me running to you."

"So you've thought of me only nine times in over a month?"

"That's not what I meant. Sometimes I have other commitments. But it's always you I'm thinking of, María. When we lie in bed together like this you remind me of a cat, so sleek and graceful, the way you purr and rub yourself against me. And then there's that glint in your eye that reminds me that, like all beautiful cats, you are essentially untamable and perhaps even a little bit dangerous. The truth is, María, I am fascinated by you. I always have been. And no matter who I am with, I always close my eyes and pretend it is you lying beneath me."

"If that's true," she said, sliding her hand between their bodies to grip him firmly between the legs, "it shouldn't be such a hardship for you to marry me."

Her grip on him was slightly too secure to be pleasurable. Before answering he squirmed and tried to wriggle free, but she tightened her grip even more, lifted her leg over his hip, and rolled against him.

Afraid of what she might do to him in such a position, Emiliano chose his words carefully. "Marriage," he said, "would be best with a woman like you, María. But these are not ordinary circumstances.

God has reached out and plucked me from the hand of Death. Obviously He has guided me home to Torrentino because He wants me to perform my special duty, whatever it might be, surrounded by my family and friends."

"I don't give a damn what God wants," María Castaneda said. Her face was so close to Emiliano's that he could feel her lips move. His own face felt as though he had accidentally put it into a spider's web, and María's moving lips and tongue were the spider's feathery crawl.

But now her entire body seemed to enfold him as she held open her legs and pulled him tight against her. He felt the slick warmth between her legs and the immediate surge of his own desire. Guiding him into her she slid her hands around his back and gripped his buttocks.

"This is what it's like to be mine," she whispered, her hands crawling up his spine, fingernails raking his vertebrae. "No one else can make you feel like this." Leaning heavily into him she rolled him onto his back, she rolling with him and coming up astride his pelvis, one palm pushing hard against his chest while the other reached behind her own buttocks and pulled on his testicles.

Emiliano closed his eyes and allowed his body to ride on the swell of darkness. He cupped her breast in his hand and tried to visualize other women, other lovers, but it was only María's image he could summon forth, only María's breast to fill his palm, the nipple as hard as a pearl button.

Moaning involuntarily beneath her, arching his pelvis toward the ceiling, he felt her hips grind down atop him and heard her voice asking again if he would marry her. He tried not to answer, to hold back all sounds. But just as he began to shudder and convulse, just as he felt his limbs explode, his arms and legs ricocheting off into space, the yes burst from him so much like a scream that María pressed her mouth to his to swallow the sound. Moments later he felt his exploded body gathering together again, hollow and weak, feeling almost tiny beneath the smiling girl and the sweetly purring darkness.

"I wanted you to say you would marry me," María told him later as they lay side by side, Emiliano's head resting sleepily on her arm, "before I told you about the gift I have for you."

Emiliano opened one eye and looked at her.

"It's not a silk shirt," she teased.

"What is it?"

"You try to guess. It's something that only a woman can give to a man."

"Just give it to me," he said, closing his eye. "I'm too sleepy to guess."

"I can't give it to you yet," she told him, and took his hand and laid it upon her lower abdomen, "because it's still in here."

"Oh, sweet Jesus," Emiliano groaned, and turned his face into the pillow.

"Actually, it's far too soon to be certain. But a woman always knows."

"But sweet Jesus, María, I'm only seventeen years old."

"Apparently that's old enough," she answered sarcastically. "I haven't been sleeping with Father Vallarte or any of the other dried-up old men in town, and I haven't yet attempted to seduce any of the little boys, so by all indications seventeen is a sufficient age to become a father."

Emiliano, who in his half-sleep had been considering ways to break his agreement to marry María, now merely groaned again and opened his mouth to bite the pillow.

"It hurts me that you're not as happy about this as I am," María said, though to Emiliano she did not sound especially hurt. "Of course I will allow you a certain amount of freedom; I would expect the same myself if the situation were reversed. And with you being used to having so many women, and the women used to having you, it's the most sensible thing for me to do. I don't want people accusing me of being unreasonable. One night a week to do as you please should be enough to keep everyone satisfied."

Emiliano wished that he were at home asleep in his mother's house.

"But now finally I'll have a little prestige of my own in this stinking little town," María said. "Constancia Volutad might be the only woman in town with a sewing machine, and Alissa Márquez might have the only talking parrot in a huge wrought-iron cage, but before long I'll be the only woman in Torrentino under sixty years old with a husband. And when the baby is born all of the women will gather around me and coo and murmur and be jealous of what I have. If you truly love me, Emiliano, you'd be happy for me. I'm giving you one night a week for which you won't have to make any excuses. It's more than any other woman in my position would do."

Emiliano, who was far too numbed by shock to think effectively, had already resigned himself to his fate. Half-heartedly he mumbled, "Two nights a week would be better."

María gave him her breast to suckle and answered, "It's time you started acting like a husband and a father."

Accustomed to waking before dawn, Emiliano did so once again to creep from María's bed to his own in his mother's house. Just before falling asleep he remembered vaguely his conversation with María and, thinking it a dream, smiled to himself. But when he awoke around noon to find his mother measuring him for his wedding suit, he shuddered involuntarily and groaned. He had the feeling of being measured for his own burial.

Seeing his eyes flutter open, Teresa Fortunato flung herself upon her son and embraced him. "My Emiliano," she cried. "My little soldier. I'm so happy for you! You don't know how I've worried about you since your return, how I've worried about your sleepless nights and the lost, troubled look on your face. You don't know how I've feared that the loss of your arm might turn you into a bitter, brooding man and prevent you from ever marrying and giving me grandchildren. But God has blessed us, hasn't He, my son? Maybe in her youth María Castaneda was a little wild, but who isn't wild in her youth? She'll make a good wife for you, and you will be an excellent husband. Now straighten your legs so that I can measure you for your trousers. I think your father's suit is going to fit you nicely without having to be cut down."

All that day Emiliano lay awake in the shaded dusk of his room, feeling sorry for himself and cursing this cruel twist of fate. Maybe he should run away and take up residence in another village. But where in the world would he find another village comprised almost entirely of amorous women? Maybe it wouldn't be so bad being a father and a husband. What duties did a father and husband in Torrentino have, especially a father with one arm who would be excused from working in the garden, and who certainly could not be expected to do such woman's work as feeding the chickens or gathering grain or hauling wood for cooking? Maybe family life wouldn't be so distasteful after all. He would still have that one night a week María had promised him. And how happy the women would be to see him on that one night! How richly he would be received! It seemed that a few of the women had been growing bored with him lately, saying that he was impatient and selfish, an unsatisfying lover. But they would have to change their tune now or he would strike them off his schedule altogether. To tell the truth, he had of late been growing a little tired of the incessant bedhopping. It was almost a relief to be able to curtail his activities.

Emiliano weighed in his mind the pros and cons of being married to María Castaneda. But throughout the day his thoughts were frequently interrupted by the sound of female voices raised in argument in the front room or outside the house. Young and middle-aged women, upon hearing of Emiliano's impending marriage, came to assault him with their vehement disapproval, came to demand a denial. But Teresa Fortunato, surprised by her son's popularity, turned them all away. The desperate women, however, did not give up so easily. Alone, or sometimes in groups of two or three, they huddled outside Emiliano's bedroom window and cursed him. One of the women even broke the glass in the windowpane and rattled the shade.

"I still have one night a week," he whispered, hoping to placate them. "I promise to visit you first. You won't be forgotten. You know you're my favorite."

"You're the one who will not be forgotten," was the hissed reply.

Emiliano cowered on his bed. Just when he had convinced himself that marriage might not be so bad after all, something like this had to happen. The ferocity of these women, women he had known to be solicitous and gentle, soft-spoken and passionate, surprised and frightened him. He lay on his bed and stared dazedly at the spider web in the corner. The spider, a long-legged, hairy, black-bodied creature with a triangular green marking, had trapped a fly in its web and was in the process of methodically devouring it. Emiliano was horrified and yet intrigued by the silent spectacle. He felt his skin itch and imagined he could hear the spider's jaws crunching up and down on the doomed fly, its wings crinkling like stiff paper.

Later Teresa Fortunato dragged in the spare mattress which Emiliano used to lie on outside in the shade. "Look what somebody did," she said, and pointed to the knife slashings that crisscrossed the thin mattress and caused the stuffing to spill out.

"Who would do such a thing?" she asked him. "And why?"

Emiliano shrugged and sighed deeply. He rolled over and pushed his face into the pillow. Maybe being safely married to María was not such a bad idea after all.

María and Emiliano quickly settled into a comfortable routine. After the marriage they lived together in María's house, where Emiliano was treated by his new wife with much the same deference as he had received from his mother. When María was in a surly mood, troubled with morning sickness or some other temporary ailment, all Emiliano had to do was to walk down the dusty street to his mother's house. Teresa would fuss unsparingly over her son, inquire of his happiness, his state of health. She would fry tortillas and eggs for him, and sometimes even boil a scrawny chicken. Well fed and pampered, Emiliano would a few hours later return to his wife, who by then would remember what a valuable asset her husband was and would welcome him home with open arms.

Every Friday night Emiliano was free to go wherever he wished, to do as he pleased with no excuses or explanations. María had judiciously allotted him this night because on Friday nights Father Vallarte heard confessions in the small adobe church at the end of the street. María suspected, and not without some justification, that given the choice of consorting with a married man or receiving absolution of sins, at least some of the women would choose the latter. For although María wished to be fair to her husband and the women of Torrentino, she did not want Emiliano wearing himself thin. She reasoned that the women would not blame her if they failed to enjoy Emiliano's favors on a Friday night, but would recognize the responsibility in their own choice of absolution over sin. And to a certain degree her reasoning was valid. Father Vallarte, however, began to note late each Friday night that two or three women would appear successively for confession each with the musky scent of the bedroom still smelling on them as fresh as the scent of a newly plucked rose.

At the same time, Emiliano was noticing a different trend. An increasingly larger number of women chose to cross the street whenever he approached rather than pass him face to face. Sometimes it would even be one of the women with whom he had recently lain. Their doors, he discovered, might still be open to him on Friday nights, their pillows fluffed and their sheets still perfumed, but some of these same women, in the light of day, gave him wide berth, or simply turned downcast eyes at his flirtatious wink.

Some he spotted more frequently in the company of Argentina Neruda, who, it was rumored, was now regularly conducting public displays of her rituals in her home. Emiliano heard reports that her campaign to expose him as an evil spirit was now more vigorous than ever.

One morning he walked outside to find Argentina Neruda dragging a dead chicken around his house, the chicken's head digging a shallow furrow in the dust to complete a wide circle. While doing this Argentina Neruda puffed frantically on a fat cigar, keeping a cloud of smoke around her head in order to cleanse the air of evil influences.

Emiliano laughed and called her a demented old bag of bones. Snatching the dead chicken from her he flung it back into her face. He then walked off down the street to visit his mother, leaving the old sorceress huffing and puffing on her cigar.

Despite these diversions, it was not long before Emiliano began to feel that his life was assuming an unpleasant odor of sameness. He had been married for less than three months, and yet already he found his daily routine boring. No longer was it exciting to lie in bed all day and dream of María's ripe young body, a body which recently had begun to hint of the bloated appearance of being overly ripe. Nor did the anticipation of sneaking out for a night of stolen pleasure fill him with nervous arousal anymore. His Friday night schedule was widely known, perhaps by everyone in the village except his mother. And to vary from this schedule was, at least as the women saw it, unconscionable; María was being more than generous with her husband, and the other women in town, no matter how much they secretly wished to, would not dishonor the limits of her generosity.

Even sitting in the late morning hours on the shaded steps of Father Vallarte's church with a handful of old men soon became a tiresome routine for Emiliano. At first he regaled these old men with tales of the battle, of whizzing bullets and clashing sabers. But how many times could you tell the same story to the same assemblage of wrinkled faces and rheumy eyes and manage to retain even your own enthusiasm? He took to entertaining them with ribald descriptions of the attributes of each of the young women in town, remarking how this one's tongue was as long and as active as a lizard's, how that one had an almond-colored birthmark in a certain place which, when you kissed it, had the same effect as touching a lighted match to a string of firecrackers.

Though stories such as these would for a moment bring erect posture back to each of the old men, would perhaps even cause them to shudder once or twice with the expulsion of a melancholic tear, more often than not Father Vallarte joined the men there on the steps, in which case the talk turned to the weather, to unanswered, indifferent speculations of whether or not the distant revolution still lived. All too often the men spoke of nothing at all, but sat and watched a threadbare dog sitting in the dust and licking himself, watched a tarantula being harassed by a chicken, or watched an occasional breeze push an occasional cloud across the sky.

So Emiliano Fortunato was not altogether displeased when once again he heard the clopping of horse's hooves and looked up from his seat on the church steps to see Dr. Sevilla, astride his dusty gelding, come jouncing down the street. In fact the alacrity with which he hurried out to greet Sevilla convinced the old men that the doctor and the boy were friends of long standing.

After exchanging perfunctory greetings with Sevilla, Emiliano took the horse's reins and led the animal, with Sevilla still astride it and grinning like a little boy on a carnival ride, to Teresa Fortunato's house. There the doctor and the boy went into Emiliano's former bedroom—for a brief examination, Sevilla explained to Teresa. After assuring himself and Emiliano that the wound was completely healed, Dr. Sevilla lowered the shades and then sat on the bed very close to the boy.

"So," Sevilla said, unable to conceal his happiness, "by the way you greeted me I would guess that you're finally ready to leave this God-forsaken place and come home with me."

Emiliano shook his head. "I'm a married man now," he explained. "My wife is going to have a baby."

Dr. Sevilla looked as though he had been kicked in the groin. His eyes brimmed with tears and he emitted a soft clicking noise from the back of his throat.

"My poor stupid boy," he said when he recovered enough to speak. He laid his hand on Emiliano's thigh. "Don't say such a thing if it isn't true. If all you want is to drive me away again, please don't tell such an awful lie."

"It's not a lie," Emiliano said. "Though sometimes I wish it were. I married María Castaneda because such a thing is a man's responsibility. She's just beginning her fourth month."

Sevilla slumped forward, his head falling into Emiliano's lap, and wept. "It's my fault," the doctor moaned. "I shouldn't have stayed away so long. I thought it best to give you time to get thoroughly fed up with this place. But you're just a poor stupid boy and I gave you too much time, and now look what's become of you."

Emiliano felt a curious twinge of sympathy for the doctor, and stroked Sevilla's hair.

"Before you go," Emiliano said to Sevilla as they stood outside Teresa Fortunato's home, "would you mind taking a look at my wife? Just to make certain that the baby is healthy and that María is in no danger."

They walked together, Emiliano leading the horse, to María's house. María was very happy to be examined by a bona fide doctor; she had been worried lately of Argentina Neruda's resentment of her, and to be tended by a midwife with such primitive beliefs and prejudices did not instill in María the soundest of confidences.

Dr. Sevilla, his superciliousness lost on María, laid his palm on her rounded belly, put his ear to her abdomen and listened for the fetal heartbeat, palpated her breasts, peered at the pupils of her eyes, inquired of her diet, and finally pronounced her as healthy as a cornfed sow.

Though she did not care for the analogy nor for what she mistook as Sevilla's cold professional manner, María was grateful for the diagnosis. She offered him coffee, and he, smiling snidely at Emiliano, accepted. While María was preparing the coffee Sevilla went outside and removed a package from his saddlebags.

Seated again beside Emiliano in the tiny living room, María still busy with her back to them in the kitchen, Dr. Sevilla handed the package to Emiliano and whispered, "After the way you've behaved, I don't know why I'm even bothering to give this to you. You should be ashamed of what you've done to me."

But Emiliano felt no shame. Upon seeing the two silk shirts inside the package, one bright yellow and the other a deep lavender, he felt a familiar twinge of arousal as he ran his forefinger over a smooth collar, as he crushed a silky sleeve against his cheek and felt the cool, hard pearl buttons upon his skin.

Emiliano looked up to see María standing in front of him. She stared at him quizically, holding Sevilla's cup of coffee in her right hand.

"Well, give him his drink," Emiliano scolded her. "Or do you expect him to come and lap it up out of your hand?"

María handed Sevilla the cup. He accepted it, she thought, with an almost lordly air, as though to convey to her what a great favor he was doing by drinking her coffee.

"Look at the gifts Dr. Sevilla brought," Emiliano said, and held the shirts up by their collars. María grasped the tail of each shirt between a finger and thumb and silently admired their color and texture. Then it occurred to her that Emiliano already had one silk shirt, a pink one whose origins he had never explained.

Now Emiliano saw the way his wife glanced back and forth from himself to the doctor, and became suddenly aware of the implications of Sevilla's gift.

"One of them is for you," Emiliano quickly explained. "They are Dr. Sevilla's wedding gift to us. Take your pick. One is for you and one is for me."

"Both are the same size," María said, thinking out loud. "Either one will be too large for me."

"Wasn't it smart of Dr. Sevilla to bring one that will fit over your new belly?" Emiliano's hands had begun to perspire, and there was a band of beaded moisture forming on his upper lip.

Maria looked at the doctor. "How did you know I was pregnant?"

Sevilla smiled and took a sip of coffee.

He has a smile like an egg-stealing fox, María thought.

Emiliano laughed nervously. "What new wife isn't pregnant within a month or two? And after the child is born you can cut the shirt down to fit you more snugly, or just keep it until you become pregnant again. It's a beautiful gift, isn't it? How many women in Torrentino own a silk shirt? Take whichever one you want, María. Personally, I think you would look best in the purple one, don't you, Dr. Sevilla?"

The doctor merely smiled at María, his piercing hawk eyes unblinking. Taking the yellow shirt from her husband's hand, María threw it over her shoulder, said "Thank you very much for the lovely gift," then turned and went into the bedroom.

"Why didn't you help me?" Emiliano whispered to the doctor.

Now Sevilla turned his smile on the boy. "Did you ask for my help in getting her pregnant? Did you accept my help when I offered you a home? You're just a poor stupid boy, Emiliano, and from now on when you get yourself in a tight spot, I'm just going to sit back and watch you squirm the way you've been making me squirm."

Saying this, the doctor set down his cup and stood to leave. Emiliano walked him to the door. He was trying frantically to think of some way to detain the doctor, to get him to stay for a day or two without leading him to any unwanted conclusions. Having someone besides women and tired old men to talk with for a while had been a treat for Emiliano, and he knew that, given time, he and the doctor might discover many interests in common. The truth was that, in the midst of a crowd, Emiliano had begun to feel quite lonely. It was like having nothing to drink meal after meal except sweet wine. Eventually you would begin to thirst for a sip of water.

But before Emiliano could think of anything to deter the doctor, Sevilla pulled open the door to stride outside. Blocking his progress, however, were five young women.

"We heard there was a doctor here," the first one said. Her name was Rosarita Calderón, a pretty, unmarried girl of sixteen with whom Emiliano had spent many pleasurable hours. Her bedroom was separated from her mother's (another room which Emiliano had occasionally visited) by only a thin wall of plasterboard, and when Emiliano was with Rosarita she would hold her pillow over her face so as not to awaken her mother with the uncontrollable squeals of ecstasy she made.

Also in the group were others whose bedroom windows Emiliano had squeezed through at one time or another. In fact, looking over the faces, he saw with horror that there was not one among them he had not known in an intimate manner.

"If it's not too much to ask," Rosarita continued, "we would be extremely grateful if the doctor would consent to take a look at us. Each of us has been troubled lately with a minor ailment, and it would put our minds to rest if we could each receive a brief examination."

With a questioning arch of his eyebrows Sevilla turned to look at the boy. Emiliano had already begun to sweat profusely, and at the same time to shiver. He stumbled back into the house and, like a timid child, watched from around the doorjamb as Rosarita Calderón led the doctor away, the other women following quietly behind.

Throughout that day Emiliano observed from his doorway as Dr. Sevilla was led at intervals of a half hour or so from one house to the next. Darkness fell and Emiliano tended to the gelding tethered outside. María, as she prepared her husband's dinner, wore her new yellow silk shirt, the long tails flaring out over her skirt, the sleeves rolled up and pinned at the wrist.

Emiliano was too nervous to eat. He only picked at his food. "Aren't you feeling well?" María asked. He stared blankly as though he failed to recognize her. María cleared away the dishes and hummed to herself, making Emiliano wonder what it was that made her so cheerful.

Eventually Emiliano's nervousness got the better of him. He went outside and ran down the street to his mother's house. "I just want to be alone for a while," he told Teresa, and headed for the sanctuary of his former bedroom. "Please don't disturb me or allow any other woman to disturb me tonight."

Lying on his bed Emiliano anxiously massaged the stump of his amputated arm. What did all those women want with Dr. Sevilla? He knew by the way his amputated arm throbbed that he was somehow involved. Maybe he even knew what "minor ailment" troubled the women, but he would not allow the thought to take concrete form in his mind.

It was nearly midnight when Dr. Sevilla finally stumbled in and fell on the bed beside Emiliano. Emiliano, wide awake, lay as still as a corpse.

Finally Sevilla heaved a heavy sigh and sat up. "You've been a busy little rooster, haven't you?" he asked.

Emiliano groaned.

"What a horrible day this has been," Sevilla said. "Nearly every woman in town has tried to seduce me." He patted Emiliano affectionately on the rump. "But don't worry, not one of them succeeded. My virtue remains intact."

Emiliano felt a glimmer of hope. "That's all they wanted of you?"

he asked, rolling over to face the doctor. "To get you into bed?"

"Not quite," Sevilla answered. "It seems that seven women in this village, not counting your wife, of course, will within five to eight months have little Emiliano's clinging to their bosoms."

Emiliano felt a surge of nausea overtake him. He jumped up, ran to the window and pushed it open, hoping to steady himself with deep drafts of fresh air. But when he leaned out over the windowsill he saw a young girl, her slender body barely showing the first buds of womanhood, standing not far away, staring moon-eyed at his window while she hugged herself suggestively and rocked on her heels. He ducked inside again, pulled shut the window and yanked down the shade. Fearing that he might soon pass out from dizziness, he flung himself face down on his bed.

Dr. Sevilla regarded him with a mixture of amusement and disdain. "How could you have been so stupid?" he asked. "Didn't it ever occur to you where all of your whorish rutting might lead? Didn't you ever once stop to think that if it could happen to María it could happen to the other women as well?"

Emiliano was seized by a fit of shivering, and began to sob.

"There, there," Sevilla said, and stroked Emiliano's back. "The damage is done, you might as well face up to it. But you needn't worry, I'm not going to abandon you now. I've decided to be godfather to your children. I'll make certain they all come into this godforsaken world red-faced and healthy."

Emiliano could not bring himself to roll over or even to mumble his thanks to the doctor. Sevilla seemed almost to revel in this latest misfortune. Emiliano lay with one eye pressed to the pillow, the other eye staring dully at the dusty spider web in the corner in which the dried and empty shell of a fly was irrevocably trapped.

"Imagine," Dr. Sevilla said, softly chuckling as he ran his hand up and down the back of Emiliano's leg, "a poor, stupid one-armed boy such as yourself, valiantly assuming the task of repopulating a devastated village. It's too bad you don't have a newspaper in this town, Emiliano. What a wonderful story this would make."

In the morning Emiliano viewed Torrentino through new eyes. He had returned to his own home the previous night to a fitful, agitated sleep, leaving Sevilla snoring comfortably in Teresa Fortunato's house. Shortly after sunup Sevilla came by for his horse and found Emiliano standing a few feet back in his open doorway, peering out with the temerity of a man afraid of the sun.

Sevilla laughed. "How do you like your little garden of Eden this morning?" he asked.

"Shhhh!" Emiliano said. María was still asleep and Emiliano dreaded facing her, dreaded her reaction when the awful news of his profligacy became known. "I thought you promised to stick by me now," he said.

Sevilla looked happier than Emiliano had seen him in a long time. "You really need me now, don't you?" Sevilla said. He tightened up the cinches on his saddle, put his foot in the stirrup and climbed atop the gelding. "I didn't make arrangements for a prolonged visit," he explained, "so first I have to return home for a while. But don't worry, little papa. I'll be back soon to see how your family is coming along."

Leaning over the saddlehorn then, clasping the gelding's sleek neck, Sevilla whispered, "I'm only coming back as a favor to you, Emiliano. When this is all over with I expect the same consideration from you."

Emiliano nodded dully. Standing in the shadow of his doorway his watched Sevilla ride away.

When María awoke she put on her new silk shirt and came padding out to the kitchen in her bare feet. There she found her husband slumped forward with his head on the table. She gathered a few sticks of wood from the kindling box and built a small fire in the stove. After setting on the morning coffee she turned to Emiliano and said, "You were late coming home last night."

He lifted his head, lifting it slowly, as though it were either extremely fragile or extremely heavy. "I was with Dr. Sevilla," he explained.

María nodded. "Just so you weren't somewhere you shouldn't have been." There was a strange quality to her voice, a teasing lightness that puzzled Emiliano. "It isn't Friday night yet, you know."

"There will be no more Friday nights," Emiliano said.

"What are you talking about?" She scooped flour from an earthen crock into a deep bowl and added a half-ladle of water from a covered bucket beside the stove. Working the dough with her strong fingers she shaped it into a ball, pulled off a chunk, and flattened it expertly between her palms. She tossed the tortilla into a skillet in which there was hot lard. The smell of the tortilla frying made Emiliano nauseous.

"I said," María repeated, "what are you talking about? What do you mean there will be no more Fridays?"

"Never mind," Emiliano said. He stood up and went out the door.

Almost reflexively Emiliano headed for his mother's house. But three-quarters of the way there he realized that even that sanctuary would be closed to him now. How could he face such a loving and trusting woman, only to tell her that she would soon be grandmother not only to María's child but to seven squealing bastards as well?

Hurrying past his mother's house Emiliano wished that Sevilla had not ridden off so early. Now that Emiliano had his senses about him, he might be inclined to join the doctor, if only to escape for the time being the unpleasantness about to befall him. Within a matter of hours the entire town would know of his sexual extravagance. For the sake of his own skin, he thought it best that he get away somewhere for a while.

Standing at the end of the unpaved street, at that point where
the narrow street tapered off to little more than a rutted goat
path, with the village of Torrentino behind him and nothing but
the side of the mountain ahead, Emiliano came to a halt. Where
could he run? Where would he be safe for a few hours from the
wrath of his wife, his mother's humiliation, the villagers' scorn?
Dear God, Emiliano prayed, if you truly saved me from the battle,
if you see me standing down here now as confused as a dog that's
been kicked in the head by its master, please forgive the lies I have
told and the wasteful life I have been living. I will right all of these
wrongs, dear God, if you will forgive me and save me one last time
and show me some small sign that all of this senselessness is your
divine will.

On Emiliano's right the door of the Mother of the Holy Infant
church swung open. Father Vallarte shuffled out of the door and,
looking even too feeble to push the straw broom he clung to, began
to sweep the dust from the steps. Soon the other old men of the
village would be gathering there to watch the day pass. Emiliano
turned, raced across the street and bounded up the steps.

"Father," Emiliano said, "I need urgently to talk with you. It is
very important. A matter of life and death."

Father Vallarte looked first at Emiliano, then at the straw broom
in his own gnarled hands. For fifty years now he had been sweeping
the steps of the Mother of the Holy Infant church at precisely this
hour each morning. After sweeping the steps he would go inside
and run a dampened cloth over the pews and the altar table. If he
finished these chores in time he would then return outside to sit
with the other old men for an hour or so. Then he would prepare
for himself a light lunch, and then lie down for his siesta. After the
siesta came a brief period of unscheduled time during which he read
his Bible or played a few hands of solitaire.

But these young Indians, he thought, have no respect for the
value of a daily schedule. Upset one aspect and you upset the entire

schedule. He suggested that Emiliano return in the evening, and then resumed his sweeping of the steps.

Emiliano glanced up the street just in time to see Rosarita Calderón going into his wife's house. Groaning audibly, he pushed his way past Father Vallarte and fled inside the church.

Father Vallarte methodically swept all of the dust off the four church steps. He swept from left to right, from the top step to the bottom. Afterwards, inside the church, he set the broom in a corner, lifted the square of woolen cloth from the nail in the wall on which it hung, dampened the cloth with water from the holy water fount, and began to wipe off the seats and backrests of the single row of pews. He worked from the rear to the front, from the left side of the pew to the right. On the fifth pew from the rear he was forced to pause momentarily while Emiliano, who had been lying curled like a frightened caterpillar on the seat, crawled out of the way.

Emiliano crept to the door and peered out. Already a few old men were lounging on the church steps. They were leaning forward and craning their necks to see up the street. Outside Emiliano's house, several women stood in a group. Emiliano recognized María's face among them. He ducked back inside the church and hid himself in the confessional.

When Father Vallarte finished wiping off the pews he wiped off the rickety scarred desk that served as his altar. Then he shook out and straightened the altar cloth. He rinsed out the soiled cleaning rag in a bucket of water, emptied the bucket in the street, and came back inside to hang the cloth to dry on its nail in the wall. Afterward he returned outside to sit for a while with the old men and to wonder with them about what was happening up the street at Emiliano Fortunato's house.

Emiliano had no idea how long he remained in the cramped confessional. It seemed as though he had been there for an entire day. In his mind he had watched the sun travel across the sky to

sink far below the mountain. So when María came and led him
away by the hand, out of the church and back up the street, he was
more than a little surprised to view the sun nearly directly overhead,
the old men not yet adjourned from their seats on the church steps.

What punishment, Emiliano wondered, did María have in store
for him? When she came and took him by the hand she had said
very little, only "What are you doing in here? Come on, I've been
looking for you." And now, leading him up the street, she actually
smiled, as though whatever punishment she had in mind was going
to bring her great satisfaction.

Emiliano prayed that María would remember that it was she who
had proposed the Friday night schedule. For himself, he would have
been content to act the role of the faithful husband, to do what
every other faithful husband did and sneak away now and then for a
little stolen love in the moonlight. But no; María had coerced him
into a strict routine, a well-supervised schedule of infidelity. When
thought of in that way, there could be no doubt that all of this baby-
making business was María's fault.

"It's all your fault," he told her.

She pulled him along and said nothing. From behind the windows and doors that they passed, women peered out and smiled at
him. Had they conspired on some devious retribution, some sinister
plan of punishment that made each of them giggle with a perverse
glee? He could have broken away and run, could have knocked
María down and barricaded himself in his own house. But he felt
weak and dizzy and was barely able to keep his feet beneath him.
He shuffled along through the dust and felt like a schoolboy being
led away to be spanked.

María pushed open the door to her house and then stood aside
so that Emiliano could enter first. He slouched across the room,
expecting to be berated and assaulted, maybe even to have María
pounce on him from behind and box his ears. Instead he saw the
kitchen table stacked high with gifts. A recently plucked chicken
curled like a fetus in a clay bowl, and in another bowl were a half-

dozen delicate quail eggs. Beside this was a jar of amarinth seeds, and hung over the back of a chair an ochre-colored handwoven vest called a xicholi. There were tiny cakes molded in the shape of animals, a clay pot filled with ripened coffee beans, a large yellow gourd heavy with intoxicating pulque, a pair of men's bedroom slippers, slightly worn, and two complete spools of blue thread.

Emiliano felt María's hand at the back of his neck, her fingers affectionately twirling his hair. He shivered. What did she have up her sleeve?

"From now on we're going to live like a king and queen," María said.

Dizzy with confusion, Emiliano asked, "What is all this?"

"Tokens of respect from the mothers of your children," she said. "And later there are bound to be even more. Constancia Volutad has promised that I can use her sewing machine any time I wish. And look in here in the bedroom; see what I managed to coax from Alissa Márquez."

In the corner of the bedroom, beneath the window, sat a huge black wrought-iron birdcage. It was four feet wide by four feet long, shaped like a Chinese pagoda and with a center height of at least three and a half feet. Perched on a swinging bar near the top of the cage and returning Emiliano's unblinking gaze was a green and white parrot. The bird and its elaborate cage had been Alissa Márquez's wedding gift from her husband eleven years earlier, hauled from Orizaba and up the mountainside on the back of a burro. It had been Alissa's pride and joy ever since, openly coveted not only by María but by many of the other villagers as well, and Emiliano was amazed that his wife had been able to talk Alissa into parting with it.

"Is Alissa . . . ?" he managed to say, nearly choking on his words.

"Not yet. But I had to promise that you will pay special attention to her from now on. She wants a baby so badly. I didn't have the heart to refuse her."

Emiliano wondered if this was some kind of a trick. "You're not angry with me?" he asked.

"Why would I be angry? Because you've made me the richest woman in town? How could something like this *not* happen, with you visiting two or three women every Friday night? Didn't you realize it was inevitable? My only concern was that I should be the first to bear a child, which I shall be, but only by a few weeks judging from the looks of Rosarita Calderón's belly. And I admit that I was a litle worried at first that one of the younger girls might steal you away from me, that you might fall in love with someone else. But that hasn't happened, has it? And just look what we have now! And who knows—in a month or so there might be more mothers-to-be to shower us with gifts. There are at least a half-dozen women who have come to me expressing their desire to have a child. With no husbands, what other hope for a comfortable old age do the women in this village have? I promised them that you will continue with the Friday night schedule. I think it best that we do this on an orderly, limited basis. If we are careful and plan effectively, we can assure ourselves of ten children a year for the next several years."

Emiliano felt his legs go rubbery. He groped for a kitchen chair, pulled it away from the table, and slumped into it.

"And as those children grow older," María continued, speaking more to herself than to her dazed husband, "they will all come to you for advice and guidance. I, of course, will be their godmother, and I too will exert a considerable influence over their lives. We're going to be the king and queen of Torrentino," she said, and hugged Emiliano's head against her swollen breasts.

"God spared you from death on the battlefield and brought you home to me for just this purpose. From Torrentino your seed will spill down over the mountain and into a hundred other villages. In years to come your name will be more famous than those of Moctezuma, Zapata, or even King Solomon!"

The table upon which Emiliano's hands rested began to sway

beneath him. His vision blurred and the room began to spin. Emiliano felt his head rolling back and forth on his neck. He was going to be a national hero, a one-armed Biblical legend? Emiliano Fortunato slumped forward and passed out.

Teresa Fortunato, though initially shocked by the news that her hazel-eyed son had become "papacito grande," soon discovered that, as mother of the village progenitor, she too enjoyed a sudden elevation of social status. Young women whose bellies had not yet even begun to bulge with life came to confer with her about the tailoring of baby clothes, about how a child should be raised so as to grow into a brave and unselfish adult like papacito grande himself. Women who yearned for motherhood begged Teresa's advice on how to prepare her son's favorite food, how best to attract his attention, if only for an hour at a time. Older women beyond the age of childbearing came to sit with her, hoping that by proximity they might also be referred to as grandmother and treated with respect. All listened reverentially to stories about how Emiliano even as an infant displayed signs of greatness. The fact that their recollections of Emiliano as a child were not consistent with Teresa's did not seem to disturb them.

Emiliano himself, after recovering from his dizzy spell, quickly adapted to the role of papacito grande and found it to be not at all a disagreeable role. His wife accorded him a newfound courtesy, his mother an almost obsequious deference. Each day he was courted by young women who wanted nothing more than the honor of laundering his shirts or combing out his hair. From the old men who gathered daily on the steps of the Mother of the Holy Infant church he was awarded the uppermost step. The deteriorating old men huddled at his feet as though he were a Zen master who possessed the secret of eternal youth.

Only two sour notes were sounded during this happiest of times for Emiliano. The first came, of course, from Argentina Neruda, who frightened the young women by announcing that their babies were actually reincarnated souls of their slaughtered husbands and fathers and brothers and boyfriends, returning to Torrentino to seek revenge against the liar and coward Emiliano Fortunato, a man with whom they had each consorted and who was probably an evil spirit himself.

The second disparagement, though not as sour as the first, came at the hands of Father Vallarte. Troubled by the questionable propriety of Emiliano's patriarchal status, the old priest nightly searched his heart and petitioned the Lord for some evidence that this epidemic of pregnancies was God's will and not Satan's. Receiving no such evidence, Father Vallarte would every now and then studiously regard Emiliano as he sat on the church steps, and even on occasion inquire seriously of the boy, "But how can we be certain that this is a good thing?"

Emiliano assumed that the old man had finally lost his senses, and subsequently told everyone, including Father Vallarte himself, exactly that.

In this manner the remote village of Torrentino, perched on the side of a mountain, watched another three months pass. At the end of March Dr. Sevilla came riding into town on his dusty, tired gelding. After examining ten pregnant women, the doctor returned to the house of Emiliano and María Fortunato.

"You should give some thought to moving permanently to Torrentino," Emiliano told the doctor. "What's happening in this village could someday make you nearly as famous as me."

The doctor thought Emiliano's tone of voice more than a little condescending, and promptly told him so.

"You were a great help to me once," Emiliano said. "And I realize that no man attains greatness without the aid of several smaller, less important people. I simply want to do a little favor for you in return. Do you have something against seeing your name inscribed in the annals of history?"

Sitting in Emiliano's living room, a room now lavishly decorated with all manner of gifts — fans and baskets woven of straw, hand-woven tapestries, colorful pictures torn from two-year-old magazines and mounted on boards — Dr. Sevilla found the change that had overcome his former patient hard to believe. Emiliano seemed nearly as bloated as his wife, as arrogant as a retired fighting cock. When María, now fat as a heifer ready for the slaughterhouse, excused herself and went off to bed, Sevilla told Emiliano, "I had planned to stay for a while, though not permanently. You seem to have forgotten the agreement we made. So now I think I'll stay just long enough to watch this illusory world of yours come crashing down atop you."

"The world I have created is no illusion," Emiliano said.

"You poor stupid boy. You've been so gorged on stories of your own importance that you've actually come to believe them, haven't you? Don't you realize that these women don't value *you*, they value the output of your glands. Who in this village really loves you for yourself — or perhaps I should say in spite of yourself? Probably no one but me. You're just a poor stupid boy with one arm and the only ready supply of sperm in town."

Emiliano flushed with anger. The veins in his neck bulged and his eyes flew open. Leaping to his feet he flung open the door. "Cabrón!" Emiliano shouted, clenching his fist. "Choirboy! Get out of my house and don't ever come back!"

Dr. Sevilla emitted a soft click from the back of his throat. Chuckling softly, he stood and went outside. Emiliano slammed the door shut behind him. Sevilla walked down the street and spent a comfortable night at the home of Teresa Fortunato in the childhood bed of her son, the illustrious stud.

Teresa Fortunato became Dr. Sevilla's assistant. When young girls came for an examination, it was Teresa who met them at the door, who counseled the mother-to-be on how best to care for her unborn child, which foods and activities should be avoided and which could be indulged. She exacted payment from each patient, insisting that even the briefest of visits be paid for, if only with a warm brown egg or a handful of coffee beans. She considered it an honor to have the esteemed Dr. Sevilla as her houseguest, even if he rejected the women's advances, and when Emiliano reproached her for boarding Sevilla she defended herself philosophically.

"If you had been slain on the battlefield with all of your brave neighbors," she said, "what would I now have, Emiliano? Would I be looked up to and respected by all the other women, or would I be just another childless mother rotting with grief? Are you going to deny me my one opportunity to hold my head up high? Do you think it was mere chance that first led you to Dr. Sevilla? Do you think it was chance that directed the bullet into your arm and not into your heart? Don't you know, my son, that everything is for a purpose? Even here in Torrentino, in this tiny village made of straw and sun-baked mud, even here we are cradled in the palm of God's hand. If Dr. Sevilla has come to live in my house it is because God has directed him to do so. You have become a great man, Emiliano, but are you so great as to believe that God no longer exerts an influence upon your life?"

Emiliano shook his head in disgust and walked away. If his mother wanted to house that clove-sucking cabrón, then he would not try to stop her. But she must be as crazy as Vallarte to believe that God had deliberately sent Sevilla to them. That God had given them Emiliano to raise Torrentino from the dust there could be no doubt. But a clove-sucking, silk-shirt-wearing girl-faced cabrón of a doctor like Sevilla? Ha! There was about as much chance of that being true as there was of Emiliano losing his kingdom.

As the days passed, Argentina Neruda sat in her darkened hut and brooded. Even the handful of women who a few months earlier had joined in her ritual anathematizing of Emiliano had now abandoned her. Why could no one see that devil of a boy as she saw him?

Seated at her kitchen table Argentina Neruda stared down at the contents of the bowl in front of her. Into the clay bowl she had spilled the viscera of a wild duck. By the undulations and alignment of the viscera she could read the will of Huitzilopochtli, the stern and exacting hummingbird god. Argentina had come upon the wild duck yesterday on her daily trip to gather wood for her stove and herbs for her incantations. The duck, its wing broken as it lay on the bank of a small pond, was nearly dead when she found it. She had carried the duck home, fed it a mash of ground maize and water, and this morning put a sharp knife to its belly and spilled its viscera into the enameled bowl.

She studied the viscera for a long time, employing the same skills of intuition once employed by powerful Aztec priests. Finally she was satisfied that she saw in them confirmation of Emiliano's evil. Afterward she prayed to Huitzilopochtli and thanked him for his message of truth. Then, without bothering to remove the duck's head or webbed feet, she boiled the plucked fowl in a pot of steaming water. The intestines she deep-fried in lard until they puffed up crisp and brown. A side dish of delicate water-fly eggs completed her afternoon meal.

When María Fortunato went into labor, Emiliano forgot for the moment that he had not spoken to Dr. Sevilla for several weeks and went running down the street shouting the doctor's name. It was ten in the morning and Sevilla was just finishing a breakfast of fried eggs topped with a spicy tomato and chili pepper relish, tortillas, and strong black coffee, which Teresa Fortunato had cheerfully prepared and served to him.

Hearing his name being shouted so urgently, and in Emiliano's voice, Sevilla smiled to himself. He wiped his mouth on his handkerchief, rose out of his chair, and met the boy at the door.

"María is having her baby!" Emiliano cried, breathless and redfaced, his hazel eyes wide with worry. Teresa Fortunato sighed happily and hurried out of the house.

"Hurry, please!" Emiliano urged the doctor.

Sevilla smiled calmly. "Why?" he asked.

"Why? Sweet Jesus, I told you; María is having her baby!"

"So?" Sevilla said.

"What do you mean, so? Aren't you coming? She needs you!"

"The midwife can attend to her."

"I don't want that old witch near María! Please, doctor, I know you're angry with me, but can't you forget about it for now? I'm sorry I said what I did. Won't you please come? María needs you!"

"You're sorry?" Sevilla asked.

"Yes, truly, a hundred times!"

Lifting his chin into the air, Sevilla smiled, satisfied. He went into the bedroom for his medical bag, then returned to follow Emiliano out of the house. Emiliano ran ahead of him up the street, shouting over his shoulder for the doctor to please hurry. Sevilla walked casually, humming to himself, enjoying the fullness of his belly and the warmth of the morning sun. From his shirt pocket he took a clove and popped it in his mouth.

After nineteen hours, at five the following morning, María Fortunato was still in labor. The baby was in a breech position and Dr. Sevilla could not get it turned around. The umbilical cord had wrapped itself around the infant and allowed no freedom of movement. Dr. Sevilla, at the end of those nineteen hours, was as distraught as Emiliano. His white silk shirt was splattered with blood, his face splotchy with perspiration.

María was so weak and near death herself that Sevilla had no option but to sever the umbilical and pull the infant out by its feet. He carried only weak anesthetics and lacked the proper instruments to perform a cesarean. With a pair of forceps he pulled the slack out of the umbilical cord and snipped it free. For the next ten minutes he struggled, María now unconscious, to get the infant out. The baby, a boy, was of course stillborn. Emiliano ran from the house screaming, pounding his fist against the side of his head. Teresa Fortunato put her face in her hands, chewed at the calloused flesh of her palms, and wept.

When the news of the stillborn child reached the crowd of women who had been standing vigil through the night outside Emiliano's house, Argentina Neruda burst into the house and hovered over the baby. She unwrapped the umbilical from around its neck and blew air into the baby's face. When this had no effect she seized Emiliano's sombrero off its peg in the wall and fanned the wide-brimmed hat over the infant. She fanned frantically, rocking back and forth, spitting out angry chants while Sevilla, shaking his head, slumped against the wall.

Finally Argentina Neruda too gave up and leaned back. She laid the sombrero aside and pronounced the baby in *miccatzintli*, the state of death. A few minutes later she told the women outside that, had she been permitted to preside at the birthing, she could have saved the child. But without the buffer of her presence, Huitzilopochtli had sought his revenge against the village through María. Emiliano had planted a seed of tragedy and Huitzilopochtli had caused that seed to sprout. The same seed, she predicted, grew inside every pregnant woman in town.

A pall fell over Torrentino. Though the pregnant women reassured themselves of the fallaciousness of Argentina Neruda's prediction, they lost their capacity for gaiety and spent their nights filling the front pews of the Mother of the Holy Infant church. Father Vallarte led them in somber prayers for the health of their unborn children. They each in turn made vows reaffirming their faith, and then lit candle after candle beseeching the souls of the dead to intervene on their behalfs.

Upon Dr. Sevilla they descended daily. Sevilla cautioned them against shamanism and stupidity. The older women and those not yet pregnant, though they sympathized with María's tragic loss, studiously avoided the Fortunato home. Alissa Márquez made it known that she wanted her wrought-iron birdcage and parrot back, and were it not that she would have had to confront Emiliano himself, she would have demanded that it be returned to her. Many of the other women, as they had done earlier, now avoided looking Emiliano in the eye or passing too close to him on the street.

Emiliano did his best to console his wife, but he was little comfort to her. Her complexion remained pallid even two weeks after the tragedy. She had little appetite and slept fitfully. She sometimes walked in her sleep, sometimes screamed so loud in the middle of the night that the entire village sat up in their beds. Emiliano suspected that she was among the growing number of women who once again were surreptitiously seeking advice from Argentina Neruda, women who knelt and prayed with Father Vallarte and then ten minutes later requested that the sorceress rattle her pouch of animal teeth for them.

And each night, after the women had silently filed home from the Mother of the Holy Infant church, Emiliano himself stepped out of the shadows and up to the altar, where he lit a candle for the soul of his never-born son. He sought out Father Vallarte to ease the painful burning of his heart, but the timeworn chestnuts of consolation that the priest had to offer provided little solace.

More and more frequently Emiliano took his dinner at his mother's house with Dr. Sevilla. No longer did the pretty young girls call for Emiliano to tease and arouse him. No longer did he find their doors and windows flung open for him on a Friday night.

As each day passed it became more and more obvious to Emiliano that his wife was losing her senses. For hours at a time she would sit and stare at him, not even bothering to brush away the flies as they crawled across her face. When he could stand her gaze

no longer he would jump up and bolt out of the house. More than
once he awoke in the dead of night to find María leaning over him,
eyes wide open, mouth snarling. She took to wearing a foul-
smelling leather pouch hung on a string around her neck. She
became so slovenly and unkempt that Emiliano could barely tolerate the sight and smell of her. And when she wasn't staring
unblinkingly at Emiliano she was sitting cross-legged on her bedroom floor, watching with a catlike patience the green and white
parrot in its pagoda-shaped cage.

Only Dr. Sevilla and Teresa Fortunato seemed willing to share
Emiliano's company. But after only three weeks Sevilla announced
that he would have to return temporarily to his own village. He
would require additional medicines and equipment, he said, if he
wished to prevent a similar tragedy in the future. Emiliano begged
to be taken along. But Sevilla suffered a great deal of guilt over the
death of María's child and her subsequent deterioration, and he
insisted that Emiliano remain in Torrentino long enough to nurse
his wife back to health.

"No matter what," Sevilla warned him, "don't touch another
woman. I'll be back in a week or so to stay until your last child is
born. And on that day you and I will ride off together and leave this
cursed village behind like the pile of chicken dung it is."

Emiliano, nearly paralyzed with grief, could only nod quiescently.

Four mornings later Rosarita Calderón was spotted walking out
of Torrentino, flanked on her right by María Fortunato, on her left
by Argentina Neruda. Behind this solemn vanguard trailed ten or
twelve other village women, a few of them, like Rosarita, pregnant
young girls, the rest older widows, aunts and mothers and even a
grandmother or two.

Teresa Fortunato watched with horror as this gloomy entourage
filed past her house. It was barely nine in the morning; what could
these women be up to? Argentina Neruda wore a red blouse with

the design of a spider web stitched across its front, and of all the women in the crowd, only her face was void of fear and dread.

Rosarita Calderón, who was expecting her child any day now, walked with downcast eyes, practically dragging her feet through the dust. She walked awkwardly and with obvious discomfort, for as she walked she clutched a squealing piglet to her turgid breasts.

Hurrying back inside the house, Teresa Fortunato rushed to her son's bedroom to shake him awake. He had had a lot of pulque the night before and did not appreciate being disturbed. He cursed under his breath and tried to push her away. Finally Teresa had no choice but to grab him by the hair and yank him into a sitting position, holding him upright as he tried to pry her fingers loose. Undeterred, she described for him the scene she had witnessed and explained its implications. At last Emiliano understood. He rose and, still fully dressed from the night before, stumbled out of the house and ran after the women.

A few yards beyond the Mother of the Holy Infant church the women had turned off the street to ascend a narrow, winding mountain path. On a broad ledge of rock that stuck out of the side of the mountain like a tongue and overlooked the village, Emiliano caught up with them. He was out of breath and nauseous from the effort of running, his head throbbing as though a thunderstorm raged inside. Panting and heaving he made his way over the last hundred feet.

A half-circle of women stood grouped near the inner edge of the overhanging rock, partially obscuring Emiliano's view of Rosarita and María, who stood facing one another ceremoniously, the squealing piglet held by four hands against a flat pedestal of rock. Standing with her back to the outer rim of the ledge, Argentina Neruda faced these two women and, with a broad gleaming knife clutched in her right hand, raised her arms in supplication and loudly invoked the name of Huitzilopochtli.

Emiliano shoved his way through the half-circle of women and grabbed Rosarita by her hair. He yanked her around to face him, María struggling now to hold onto the piglet alone.

"What is this?" Emiliano demanded. "What are you doing here? You should be at home, lying in bed. Do you want to have your baby before Dr. Sevilla returns?"

Rosarita stared at him with a blank look. Her usually sparkling eyes were clouded and dull in a way he had never seen on her before.

"Huitzilopochtli must be appeased," she said. Her voice was peculiar, monotonic, so dreamlike that Emiliano felt certain that the old hag Argentina Neruda had fed her some herbal drug.

"If Huitzilopochtli doesn't have blood," Rosarita said, "my baby will end up like María's." For blood she said an ancient Nahuatl word, a word which in the Aztec language could also be interpreted as flowers. But with Argentina Neruda standing nearby, the morning sun glinting off her knife blade, there was no question as to the proper translation.

Emiliano was furious. Stepping up to María he yanked the piglet from her hands and, tossing it to the ground, set it free. The pig scurried away squealing, darting wildly back and forth until it found an opening through the groping hands of the women. Emiliano spun María around and kicked her rear end. "Get home!" he shouted at her. "Enough of this nonsense. Get home where you belong and start taking care of yourself!"

Both Rosarita and María turned to look back at the shrunken old woman who stood near the rim of the ledge, her back to Torrentino fifty feet below. "You old bag of bones," Emiliano hissed at her. He approached cautiously, keeping an eye on the knife she clutched and mentally calculating the extent of her reach.

Stopping at what he determined to be a safe distance, he said, "Why don't you sacrifice yourself, you pile of filth? You stinking old corpse. You walking excrescence. Why don't you slit your own throat and offer your own stinking blood to your stupid god?"

The wrinkled old woman, though angered by Emiliano's cruel epithets, was also extremely frightened. She did not say a word. She stood with the knife poised in front of her, just in case Emiliano decided to come any closer. Glancing over her shoulder at the buildings far below she had a chilling mental image of a body tumbling end over end to shatter on the hard ground. She clutched her knife with both hands and settled into a defensive crouch.

But Emiliano did not venture any closer. He drew back his head and, like a snake ejecting venom, spit a gob of phlegm in her face. Then he spun around and herded María and Rosarita side by side, shoving or kicking one and then the other as he pushed them past the other women and back down the mountain path.

At María's house he kicked open the door and roughly shoved his wife inside. "You stay put and don't go out!" he ordered, and slammed the door. From her window she watched as her husband escorted Rosarita up the street.

With Rosarita he was gentler. He spoke soothingly and guided her toward her house with his hand against the base of her spine.

"María's crazy," he told her, as though imparting a secret. "Her mind has been all stirred up like a sopa seca. We'll find another place for your mother to live and then I'll move in with you. We'll be the king and queen of Torrentino, guapa. You'll be the first mother and I will be papacito grande."

Rosarita said nothing. Her eyes remained dulled and troubled. Emiliano led her into her house and put her to bed, then lay beside her, knowing that her mother was still among the women gathered on the ledge.

Stretched out beside Rosarita, Emiliano nuzzled her neck and stroked her huge belly. "You don't need to worry about our baby," he told her. "It's going to be a strong and healthy boy. You wait and see. It was only because of María and her stupidity that we lost the first one. But I've been lucky all my life and I can feel in my bones that this baby is going to be fine. He'll grow up to be just as handsome and brave as his father."

Emiliano unbuttoned Rosarita's blouse and kissed her breasts. Suckling her right breast he tasted the sweet rich milk, too sweet at first but then warm and delicious.

"You're more beautiful than María," he told her. "And you're younger too. You have nothing to worry about. Stop letting those stupid women frighten you with their nonsense." He licked her breast and then ran his tongue over her stomach to her protruding navel. She lay unmoving, eyes open, palms flat on the bed.

"Even with your big belly," Emiliano said, kissing her stomach, "you still excite me. Right now I want you more than ever. Just forget about what that crazy old witch told you. Give me your hand and let me show you how much I want you. See how hard you make me by just letting me touch you."

He pressed her hand between his legs and moved against it. But when he released her hand to undo his trousers, her hand fell away from him, lifeless. Pushing himself to his knees he saw that she still regarded him with the same blank, unresisting expression. She looked, he thought, almost like an animal frozen in fear, a wounded deer lying on the ground and waiting fatalistically for the stroke of death.

"Jesus," he muttered, and crawled off the bed. "You women are all alike, you know that? You'd better just lie there and don't move until Sevilla gets back. Jesus, you're all so stupid that I can't believe it."

He went out of the house and slammed the door behind him. As he stalked down the street he saw coming toward him the small pack of women who had been on the mountain. Upon seeing him they all stopped in their tracks, and then, as a flock of birds suddenly wheels around in the sky with no apparent signal, they turned as a group and fled into the nearest house. Emiliano muttered angrily to himself and continued down the street to his mother's house. There he drank the last of the pulque and fell into a drunken, restless sleep.

At four in the afternoon, just when the heat of the day was beginning to relent, Emiliano was once again awakened by his mother's screaming. She shook him violently and, tugging him by the arm, dragged him off the bed. With his head still throbbing, feeling now as though a team of burros were kicking at his skull, he could not understand anything she said. She wailed hysterically and at the same time shouted and pleaded with him.

Emiliano allowed his mother to lead him by the hand outside, then down the street and behind the Volutad house. There the entire village had already gathered. They stood peering upward, necks craned to the overhanging tongue of rock fifty feet above. On the edge of the rock stood Rosarita Calderón. She was dressed in her finest clothes, in an azure blue pleated skirt, black toeless shoes, and the lavender silk shirt Emiliano had given her.

From beneath the ledge a chorus of pleadings rose up to her. "Stay where you are!" some of the villagers shouted. "Don't move!" Others urged her to step back, away from the dangerous edge. But to all these remonstrations Rosarita seemed oblivious. She stared straight ahead, her palms resting flat against her swollen belly.

Argentina Neruda ordered that a pig or a chicken or even a scrawny dog be brought to be sacrificed on the spot, and two small children ran off to find an unlucky animal. María Fortunato, standing beside the old woman, stared silently up at the ledge, her face as expressionless as Rosarita's. Standing next to her, Father Vallarte fingered his rosary beads and mumbled a prayer. Halfway through he lost his place and was forced to begin again.

In the meantime Emiliano was running down the street toward the narrow path that ascended the mountainside. Having grown overweight and out of shape during the past months, he ran

laboriously, out of breath, his lungs burning and his vision blurred
by the throbbing pain inside his head. As he ran he mumbled aloud
and tried to communicate telepathically with Rosarita. "Don't
jump," he muttered. "Don't jump. Stay where you are, guapa, I'm
coming, please stay where you are. Don't jump, don't jump, don't
jump, *don't jump!*"

He struggled up the path, thinking with each stride that he could
not go a step further. Finally he rounded the top and came within
sight of the rock ledge. The ledge was empty, a flat platform
leading to empty sky. Emiliano sank to his knees on the hard
ground. He felt paralyzed, unable to move. He could not make
himself crawl to the rim of the ledge and peer down. From below
came a wailing of voices, a keening that filled his skull with a
ballooning, cutting pain. He fell face forward onto the ground,
determined never to rise again.

Only vaguely was Emiliano aware of the women approaching
him. He knew that a great deal of time had passed since prostrating
himself on the ground, for night had fallen more than an hour ago.
At dusk he had listened to the screech of a white-breasted hawk,
had even felt its shadow pass over him as the bird wheeled and
circled through the sky. And now, more than an hour later, he
heard the approaching footsteps of a dozen or more women. In his
dazed, self-pitying state he imagined the sound to be the thumping
of wings of a huge predatory bird, the women's sibilant whispers the
rustle of wind across a hawk's feathers.

With his cheek to the ground Emiliano felt the women gathering
around him. He smelled the fire from their torches of grease-
soaked rags. He lay absolutely still for several minutes. Then it
occurred to him that these women must be very worried about him,
that to them he must appear dead. He pushed himself up on his
elbow and turned his head to reassure them.

The first blow of a heavy stick caught Emiliano squarely between the shoulders. The sudden pain, flashing like lightning through his body and brain, immediately brought him back to full consciousness. Rolling away he curled like an armadillo, his arm protecting his head. A dozen other sticks came lashing down upon him.

"Diablo!" someone hissed, and kicked at his head. "Muerte!" said another, and rammed a thick club into his anus.

Emiliano tried to struggle to his feet but was struck successively on the head, the face, the groin, the stomach. "It wasn't my fault!" he tried to say. "It was the will of God! I'm not to blame!" But his protests were punctuated by his own involuntary yelps of pain, which rendered his words unintelligible.

Sticks broke across Emiliano's back. Rocks and boots tore at his clothing and bruised his skin. Emiliano rolled back and forth, squealing like a rabbit caught in the talons of an owl. For a moment he thought he was going to lose consciousness and felt a pleasant murky numbness spreading over him. But then a violent kick to his chest brought alertness back with a blinding flare of pain.

"*Aiyeeeeee!*" Emiliano screamed, and without knowing where the strength to do so came from, sprang to his feet. His scream was a wild, inhuman scream, the kind of shriek that could arise only from the festering depths of hell. Astonished and frightened, Emiliano's tormentors fell back. Blindly he plunged forward, arm over his face, and broke free of them. A sharp command from Argentina Neruda brought the women back to their senses, and they chased after him, cursing and bellowing.

Shielded in darkness, Emiliano ran without knowing what lay ahead. Rocks and sticks whizzed by his head. He tucked his neck into his shoulders and sprinted blindly, desperately. Within a matter of seconds he heard a difference in their voices, a rise of anger and a diminishment of power, and he knew that he had outdistanced them.

Settling into a comfortable trot, Emiliano ran for another fifty yards. Warm liquid trickled into his mouth and he tasted his own blood. His hand, broken at the wrist, dangled like the clapper of a bell. His spine felt twisted, cracked, wrenched into an impossible position. And yet, despite his discomfort, Emiliano felt exhilirated; he had beaten Death again. His luck still held.

Smiling through his pain, Emiliano slowed to a walk. The thought that he should stop advancing through the darkness and orient himself had just occurred to him when, with the next step, the earth fell away and he tumbled headfirst into a ravine.

When Emiliano Fortunato regained consciousness, he felt himself to be lying on his side. His arm was tied behind his back to a rope that tightly encircled his waist. His broken wrist had been set and was immobilized by a splint wrapped heavily with cloth. His feet were bound at the ankles, and when he tried to stretch his legs he discovered some obstacle that would not permit full extension. A silky strip of cloth had been pulled between his lips and tied at the back of his head so that he could not speak. Everything was dark. Although he felt nothing covering his eyes, he could only assume, from the profundity of darkness, that his eyes had been masked.

By drawing his legs up beneath him, then leaning heavily on his shoulder and elbow and then jerking himself up, Emiliano worked himself into a sitting position. With his feet and head he determined the approximate perimeter of his cell. If he sat leaning slightly forward with his hips pushed against the rear wall he could stretch his legs out completely, the front wall then a mere two inches from the soles of his feet. His cell seemed to taper toward a point at the top, so that if he leaned too far forward or backward from the waist, he banged his head.

A bat, it seemed, had somehow gotten into his darkened cell. Every now and then Emiliano felt the flutter of its wings against the top of his head. He even felt the animal perch on his shoulder for a moment and take a bite out of his ear. He felt the sliminess of bat shit dripping onto his hand, and by the stench of his cell assumed that a good supply of that commodity had already accumulated on the floor.

Only one name came to mind when Emiliano considered whom his captor might be. Apparently Argentina Neruda had dragged him from the ravine, had salvaged him from certain death for some devious and evil purpose all her own. Maybe she planned to publicly sacrifice him, or maybe to torture him by slow, excrutiating degrees. Only she, that vile bag of bones, would be capable of such a thing.

Hearing noises coming from far away Emiliano sat very still, straining to hear. He recognized, or thought he did, the slow rhythmic cadence of a funeral drum. That, of course, would be for Rosarita Calderón. It meant also that night had passed, that it was probably mid-morning of the following day.

Picturing in his mind the funeral procession, Emiliano envisioned it proceeding solemnly down the street toward the cemetery behind the Mother of the Holy Infant church. Rosarita would not be allowed interment in consecrated ground, so a place would be made for her just outside the low cemetery fence. Father Vallarte would be standing at the graveside, mumbling an apology for Rosarita's wasted life. He would lose his place and leaf haphazardly through the moth-eaten Bible, find his place, begin again, and then become distracted by the movements of a cloud or the spiraling flight of a hawk gliding on updrafts.

Emiliano even imagined that he could recognize his mother's weeping. After a long time he heard the villagers returning back up the street, muttering and sighing.

From not far away came several recognizable voices. The most important was that of Dr. Sevilla, who announced that in a week or two he would return to look in on the remaining mothers-to-be. But something in Sevilla's voice told Emiliano that the doctor would not be returning to Torrentino, that he fully intended now to turn his back on the village forever. What, he wondered, had they told the doctor about Emiliano's disappearance? That he had run off, unable to bear the guilt of Rosarita's sacrificial suicide? Or that Emiliano was a demon, an evil spirit who himself had thrown the hapless girl off the ledge and had then slithered back to his dark master?

Emiliano kicked at his cell. He rattled the walls and groaned through his gag in an attempt to be heard. But all he accomplished was to stir up his cellmate, who squawked and flew frantically from side to side, its wings lashing Emiliano's face and frightening him so thoroughly that he ceased his kicking and fell silent again.

Now the sounds Emiliano heard told him that the crowd was dispersing. He heard a door open and close, the latch click. Footsteps shuffled toward him. He heard the soft scrapings as someone knelt outside his cell. He heard excited breathing.

Emiliano wished the gag were not in his mouth so that he could spit in Argentina Neruda's face when she first showed herself.

After Rosarita's funeral, María Fortunato watched Dr. Sevilla riding away with tears in his eyes. Then she returned alone to her house. Once inside, she locked the front door, then crossed the room to the bedroom and the huge wrought-iron birdcage that set now in the far corner. Lately Alissa Márquez had been asking to have her birdcage returned, but María would never part with it now. No, never. She would fight Alissa tooth and nail if necessary, but she would never give up the birdcage.

Kneeling in front of the enormous cage, María lifted off the heavy cover and smiled warmly at her two birds. The green and white parrot did not look very happy; it perched on a swinging bar near the top of the cage and stubbornly refused to face her. The newer bird, however, stared at her with wide hazel eyes. María laughed to herself: how Alissa Márquez would love to get her hands on this bird! In fact every woman in town would covet it if they learned of its existence. María would have to be very careful and discreet if she wished to keep this bird for herself. It was the kind of bird that would fly away forever if you did not clip its wings.

But what a handsome, valuable bird it was! María would have been content just to sit there in front of the cage, to sit for hours at a time with her demented catlike patience and merely stare at the bird's pretty face. Gingerly she stuck her hand through the wrought-iron bars and with her long ragged claws stroked the huge bird between its legs. The bird seemed to like that. Anyway, it was smart enough not to resist.

Trash Man

T HE TRASH COLLECTOR lay in bed and did not want to get up. Already it was nearly 6:00 A.M.; he should have been out on the road in his truck a half hour ago. His eyes were open wide and sleepless. His body, though thin, felt as heavy as an overloaded trash can, its hull so badly battered that the lid would no longer fit.

"I put your breakfast in a paper bag," his wife told him, coming for the fourth time to stand in the bedroom doorway. "You can eat it in the truck."

He lay very still. How could he move? He was a garbage man, a man made of egg shells, of coffee grounds and condoms.

"You keep this up and you're going to lose the business," his wife said sternly. "And then where will we be? Is this any way for a grown man to behave?"

There are grown men and then there are grown men, he thought to himself. Some who look like grown men are mere babies. Others are made of garbage, of orange rinds and broken chairs.

"I'm giving you five more minutes," his wife said. "And then I'm leaving without you." She turned and stomped back down the stairs.

Warren Schimmel, forty-one years old, trash collector, sanitation engineer, lay in bed and gave the situation some thought. His wife could run the route alone, there was no question about that. He had done it often enough himself during that rash of irresponsible helpers four years ago, before Goony had come along. It was simple: pull up to the curb, stop the truck, climb out, heave the garbage into the truck, set the empty can on the sidewalk, climb into the truck, run the crusher, shut off the crusher, drive ahead to the next house. His wife could do it. It would take her eight hours for a four-hour route, but she could do it. Why shouldn't he let her?

Sure, let her, he said to himself. That's just what a man like you would do, isn't it? That's just what you'd expect from a man made of toenail clippings and snotty Kleenex.

With a groan that came from so deep inside him as to sound almost prehistoric, like a belching of swamp gas from some bubbling primordial bog, he sat up and swung his legs over the edge of the bed. He sat there, wearing only his undershorts and T-shirt, until he heard the garbage truck rumble to a start in the driveway. His wife, in the driver's seat, raced the engine. On legs that felt as sturdy as splintered bamboo canes he stood and went to the window. His wife sat in the truck, peering up at him through a circle she had cleaned on the frost-glazed window. She had the windshield wipers going—*clackclack, clackclack*. And Christ, there was snow on the ground, it was winter. What month was this—November? December? What the hell had happened to his life? He had been throwing it away, that's what. Tossing it in the dumper, can by battered can.

Stepping outside, stiff in too much clothing, Warren Schimmel trudged across the frozen yard to the driveway and the waiting garbage truck. He stepped up onto the little platform behind the driver's door, slipped his arm down through the metal rung mounted at shoulder level and, gripping the rung in his elbow crease, banged on the side of the truck to tell his wife to pull out.

She wound down the window and looked back at him. "Come ride inside until we get to the start of the route."

"I'm fine," he said, not looking at her but at the truck's headlight beams cutting a frosty path through the gray to the house across the street.

"What's the sense of freezing yourself to death?" she asked.

"Just drive," he said.

"You'd better get a hold on yourself."

"Just *drive,*" he said.

"You're acting like a baby."

"For Christ's sake, Sharon," he said, leaning back wearily against the barrel-shaped hull, "can't you just shut up and drive?"

She looked at him for a moment, at his eyes already watering from the cold, the frozen vapor of his breath. "Go ahead, then," she said. "Freeze your silly ass off." She wound up the window, slammed the gearshift into first, and pulled out of the driveway with a jerk.

Warren clung to the cold loop of metal and kept his eyes on the curb racing by. What day is this? he wondered. Thursday? If it's Thursday we do Madison, Tremont, Baker, Fifth, and Monroe. No, wait—we did those streets yesterday. Today must be Friday. Today the route runs north and south. He liked the north-south routes better than the east-west routes because on the latter he spent so much of his morning squinting into the rising sun, that orange ball of light glaring off the windshield and filling the cab with a soporific heat.

But that was when he had been the driver and Goony was his helper. I'm Goony now, Warren thought. He clung to the metal rail and stared through the fading gray of dawn at the rushing curb and the fleeting sewer drains and tried to see the world as Goony must have seen it. But how does a thirty-year-old man with the brain of a nine-year-old view the world? He always smiled, that was one thing. So Warren smiled. Also, Goony hummed to himself. So

Warren started to hum. Goony ogled the landscape, the same landscape he saw day after day, week after week, the way a country boy ogles his first skyscraper. So Warren opened his eyes even wider. He stared at each house flicking by, each telephone pole. His eyes watered in the chilly wind, and the tears, pushed by the wind back along his temples, froze in his sideburns.

And, as the truck slowed to approach the first pair of overflowing trash cans, Warren lept from his platform as Goony would have done, not waiting for the truck to stop, his feet striking the street and his momentum carrying him onto the sidewalk and, losing his balance, into a snowy yard where he lost his footing, rolled and tumbled, giggling, and finally came to rest lying peacefully on his back while staring at the rosy-edged sky overhead.

Sharon rammed on the brakes and stopped the truck with a screech of tires. She flung open the door and jumped out. "Warren!" she screamed.

He sat up, grinning.

"You idiot!" she shouted. "Goddamn you, you could have killed yourself!"

Suddenly the crisp clarity of the world disappeared. Suddenly Warren felt tired again. Pushing himself to his feet he walked back to the sidewalk and picked up the first garbage can.

"What's the *matter* with you?" Sharon said, standing now at the rear of the truck, her teeth chattering. "Do you *want* to end up like him?"

Warren heaved in the first load of garbage, then with a clang set the empty can back on the sidewalk. From deep inside the dumper came a steamy smell of rot, mold, and decay.

"Just get back in the truck and drive," he said. He reached for the second garbage can and swung it up. His arms felt as weak as rolled-up soggy newspapers.

At the end of the pick-up, just a few minutes after eleven, Warren dropped Sharon off at the house and then drove the truck

out of town to the garbage dump. The dump was in fact a huge
bowl carved out of the earth, its sides gently sloping. On the upper
rim of this bowl Warren sat in his truck and watched the two
bulldozers at work far below, crawling like insects to scrape up dirt
and then smooth it out again, covering each successive layer of
garbage with six or eight inches of steaming ground.

Some day, he wondered, far in the future, what would that
garbage be? What would the weight of a million tons of earth
pressing down do to it? Warren chuckled to himself, picturing in
his mind a horde of prospectors ten thousand years hence, digging
up every garbage dump all over the world. Bean cans would have
turned to emeralds, chicken bones to pearls. Was a thing like that
possible? he wondered. Probably not. But, on the other hand, what
did he know? He was no scientist, he was a garbage man. All he
knew was that there was a lot of garbage down there. A lot of lives
in torn scraps and broken pieces. There were dead pets buried
down there — cats run over by cars, parakeets who had tumbled off
their tiny wooden swings, keeled over from loneliness. There were
children's bicycles down there, the frames rusted, handlebars bent
and twisted. I'll be there some day, Warren thought to himself; and
then, a full two minutes later, wondered why in the world he had
thought such a thing.

There were three other trucks in line ahead of his — one belong-
ing to a competing garbage hauler, the other two filled with debris
from a nearby construction site — so Warren knew that he would
have at least a half-hour wait before being signaled down into the
pit to dump his load. He drove his truck up close behind the others
and shut off the engine. The day had become clear and bright, the
cab so warm that he had already removed his jacket and gloves. He
would have liked to roll down the window for a little fresh air, but
the air at the garbage dump wasn't all that fresh. He was better off
with the windows closed.

The breakfast that Sharon had packed for him in a paper bag
still lay on the seat beside him. He opened the bag and looked

inside. There was a fried egg on a hamburger bun, four strips of bacon wrapped in a paper towel. When he unfolded the paper towel, parts of it stuck to the coagulated grease of the bacon. He crumpled the bag up and, feeling sick to his stomach, tossed it onto the muddy floor.

Leaning back against the seat, he closed his eyes. The drone of the bulldozers a hundred yards away was, strangely, very relaxing. Warren felt himself drifting into sleep, but made no attempt to keep himself awake.

In a gray fog of chilly vapors and dream-mists Warren threw a lever to tilt up the hull of his truck hydraulically and let its contents spill down over the sides of the garbage pit. The trash poured like a thick liquid, a lumpy plasma of hairballs and fried egg sandwiches. He watched it from two perspectives: he saw himself sitting in the cab of the truck, hunched over the steering wheel, hands manipulating the levers, and he saw also the flow of garbage from the rear of the truck, spewing out like an anal effusion.

When it seemed that the truck was empty he lowered the dumper again and prepared to drive off. But from out of nowhere came the bulldozer operator, wearing his white hardhat, his face severe and angry. He pounded on the side of the truck with his fist, then yanked open the door. "You're not empty!" he shouted. "You've got something clogged up in the back!"

Warren was very sleepy and could not quite come awake. "I'll get it tomorrow," he said, his tongue feeling greasy and thick. "You'll get it now!" the bulldozer operator growled. Seizing Warren by the front of his jacket he dragged him out of the cab. "Crawl back in there and see what's got you jammed up," he ordered.

On legs that felt as heavy as concrete posts Warren made his way to the rear of the truck. Nearly slipping down the sides of the garbage pit himself, he peered into the smelly black cavity of the truck's dumper. It seemed to stretch into darkness for several hundred yards. Finally he turned back to the bulldozer operator. "I can't see anything," he said. The man in the white hardhat told him, "Crawl up in there and clean it out."

"Don't make me get in there," Warren said. "Can't I scrape it out with a stick or something?"

"We don't have time to go looking for sticks. You're holding everybody up. Just look at the delay you're causing."

Warren turned and looked back at the garbage dump's rim. Garbage trucks waited bumper to bumper for as far as he could see, their horns honking, headlights flashing angrily.

"Don't make me get in there," he begged.

The bulldozer operator grabbed him by the shoulders and thrust him up into the hull. "You get in there and shut up. Just do your job. Get that mess cleaned out of there."

Warren turned and peered down over the edge of the truck at the bottom of the pit miles below. There was a tiny figure down there waving at him to hurry up. That must be Sharon, he thought. She's getting mad at me.

He turned away from her and, moving cautiously, his head lowered so as not to scrape against the curved ceiling, ventured farther back into the black abyss. The floor was slippery and difficult to see; but he could feel beneath his feet wilted lettuce leaves and rotten banana peels. The walls dripped with mucous and grease. The smell was inescapable; though he held his breath he felt the rancid odors seeping into his pores and sealing them up, clogging his nostrils. He turned once and looked back toward the opening, which was now only a tiny circle through which blue sky shone.

"Keep going!" the bulldozer operator yelled, his voice echoing off the gelatinous walls.

Warren walked and then crawled for nearly a quarter of a mile before reaching the back of the hull. Here the crusher bar was jammed; some obstruction, invisible in the darkness, prevented it from swinging out to the mouth of the hull. Squeamishly, sick to his stomach, Warren slipped his naked hands along the length of the slimy bar and felt for its bottom edge. There, he had it, something soft and warm holding the crusher bar in place.

He pulled on it but could not maintain a good hold. His feet kept slipping out from beneath him. As he yanked on it, the invisible mass began to moan. "Worn," it said. "Worn, don't."

"Let's go in there!" the bulldozer operator shouted. "Get moving! You're holding things up!" In the background was a cacophony of honking horns. The noise rushed into the hull in a solid bellowing mass, swirled round and round, amplified and swelled. And then, shrieking like a carrion-eating bird, a vulture, it batted its wings against Warren's face as he swung out blindly to chase it away.

"Worn, don't," the groaning mass beneath him said.

Warren, crying now, swallowing hard to keep himself from throwing up, shouted back at the bulldozer operator, "It won't come loose! I need some help!"

"It's your truck!" the operator screamed. "It's your goddamn fault! Rip it free!"

"Worn, don't," the mass said.

Warren dug his fingernails into the protesting form. Yanking with all his strength, grinding his teeth, he tore loose an arm. The thick fingers, slippery with blood, squirmed against his face like fishing worms. Wailing out loud now, Warren flung the arm toward the opening. It sailed out into blue sky, the fingers twitching, and then fell from view down into the pit.

"Get the rest," the bulldozer operator called. "And hurry the hell up!"

"Worn, please don't," the mass beneath the crusher said. "Don't no more."

Warren was on his knees now, his stomach heaving as his hands slid across the slippery floor in search of something to grasp. He felt a foot, seized it with both hands, braced his own feet against the crusher bar, and, twisting and yanking, finally tore the leg free at the hip. He heard the bone pop from the hip socket, heard the muscle rip. Tumbling backwards from the effort, he heaved the leg over his head and outside.

Warren felt himself covered with slime now, felt his hair matted with it, felt the thick sludge beneath his fingernails. Vomit bubbled up in his throat. He gagged, but kept his mouth locked, and swallowed it again.

"Why Worn?" the voice said to him in the darkness, very weak now, very small. "Worn? Oh shit, Worn. Oh dear Jesus."

"Shut up!" Warren screamed. "For Christ's sake shut up!"

Blindly he grabbed for it, found an arm, broke it free, threw it out. His hands felt in the muck until they discovered the other leg, twisted it loose, threw it away, far out into the blue morning sky. Now the torso, the bloody stump of body. He pulled and yanked at it, but the head, locked on the other side of the crusher bar, held the body in place. Rising to his haunches, Warren picked up the torso and began twisting it, round and round, once, twice, three four five six seven times, seven full revolutions before the neck snapped free of the head with one final "Worn, don't. Wor—"

Warren flung the heavy body with all his strength. It bounced off the inside wall, skidded toward the opening, teetered on the edge, and then tumbled out. Seizing the head now Warren held it by the hair and ran with it toward the opening. He was sobbing uncontrollably, his stomach in spasms. He raced toward the circle of sky, wanting to fling the head away, far far away, out of the garbage dump, into the blaze of sun. But the opening came upon him suddenly, too soon; he tried to stop himself but had no control over his legs, his feet slid and slipped beneath him, and he knew with a hollow stomach-turning feeling that he was going to continue out over the edge.

Warren tumbled down into the trash pit, painlessly, smoothly, clutching Goony's head to his chest. He rolled over and over through the lava flow of garbage, plowing through it, sliding to the bottom. At the bottom Sharon came walking up to him and took the head from his hands. She dropped it into the paper bag in which she had collected all of the other body parts. Closing up the bag, she handed it back to Warren. "Here," she said. "You can eat in the truck. Get moving."

He awoke with a start when the truck behind him, honking its horn, nudged his bumper. Dazed, his mind whirling, he started the engine and drove the garbage truck down into the pit, swallowing hard to choke down his nausea.

In the evening Warren put on his gray suit and drove alone in Sharon's Chevette to the hospital. Before going upstairs to the fourth floor he stopped at the gift shop in the lobby. He looked at the magazine rack, the candy bars, the stuffed animals. Nothing seemed appropriate. After all, what does one buy for a broken bottle? What is a suitable gift for cheering up a crushed eggshell?

His hands empty, Warren rode the elevator to the fourth floor. He walked past the nurses station, down the corridor to his right. His palms were hot and sweaty and he had the feeling that every person he passed—nurse, orderly, candystriper, patient—turned to stare at him. He felt marked with guilt as surely as if he wore a sandwich board proclaiming it. He felt dirty, stained with garbage, even though he had taken a long hot shower and had scrubbed himself hard with Sharon's bath sponge. He wondered if there was a smell to him—some unwashable, ineluctable odor that immediately marked him as a dealer of refuse, a handler of life's debris.

Outside room four-nineteen he paused for a moment. Peering around the doorframe he saw Goony's parents, one seated on each side of the bed, each holding one of Goony's big hands. Across the room from them, mounted on a shelf near the ceiling, a television played, its volume turned low. All three of them, Goony and his parents, stared blankly at the television screen.

Rubbing his palms on his trousers, Warren took a deep breath and stepped into the room. The two older people turned immediately to look at him. Goony's head turned a few moments later and with a great deal more effort.

"Hello, folks," Warren said quietly, coming to stand at the foot of the bed. Goony smiled at him. Mr. and Mrs. Wilson, Goony's parents, made no reply.

Warren was surprised to see how old Goony's parents were. He had never actually considered it before. Now, after a single glance, they appeared terribly old to him, too old to have a son who was only thirty. And yet there they sat, white-haired and fragile-looking, holding onto their broken son's hands.

"How you doing, sport?" Warren said, and squeezed Goony's foot beneath the sheet.

"He can't feel that," Mrs. Wilson said, her voice as flat, Warren thought, as a flattened milk carton.

Warren looked at her own hand still holding her son's. "He can't feel anything," she said. Lifting Goony's lifeless arm she laid it at his side and drew her hand back into her lap.

Warren, clutching the metal rail, stared down at Goony's big feet. He wanted to cry, but, for some reason he could not articulate even in his own thoughts, he restrained himself. He felt silly standing there in his gray suit. He felt stiff and pretentious, and the longer he stared down at the white sheet the less certain he was that he could ever lift his head again.

"Come on, mother," Mr. Wilson said, standing up. "Let's go get some coffee."

Mrs. Wilson stood and kissed her son on the forehead, then followed her husband out of the room.

Warren remained in the same fixed position, head down, as motionless as Goony's oversized feet.

"Worn," Goony finally said. Warren lifted his head and looked up, tears stinging his eyes.

"S'okay," Goony said weakly, smiling, his voice slow and husky with sedatives. "Don't feel bad, Worn. I ain't mad at you."

"Okay, buddy," Warren said, and reached for Goony's foot again. At the last moment he remembered Goony's paralysis and, as though he had done something shameful, pulled his hand away.

Warren sat in the chair vacated by Mr. Wilson and looked up at the television screen. Every now and then he and Goony looked at one another and smiled. After fifteen minutes Mr. Wilson poked his head around the doorjamb. Seeing Warren still there, he turned away again.

Warren stood up and very lightly tossed Goony's thinning hair. "I'll see you later, buddy," he said. "I'll come back tomorrow, okay? You want me to bring you anything?"

"Nope," Goony said. "Nothin'." He tried to grin, showing a white foam of saliva at the corners of his mouth. Warren swallowed hard, nauseous, turned and left the room.

In the lounge he sat on the vinyl-covered chair facing Mr. and Mrs. Wilson. He clasped his hands over his spread knees, looked at the old couple sadly, shook his head, and put his head down. He began to cry. Tears splashed onto the tile floor between his feet.

"You took advantage of him," Mrs. Wilson said. Her voice wasn't loud, but it boomed inside Warren's head.

Warren answered without looking up. "I've already told you a hundred times, but I'll tell you again. I'm sorry. It shouldn't have happened. I'm sick about it."

"You're sick about it and he's got a broken back," she said. "You'll feel better in a couple days, but he'll never walk again."

Now Warren looked up at her. "I told Goon—I mean Raymond, I told Raymond a thousand times to keep clear of that crusher bar. I told him every day for Christ's sake. He knew better than to reach in there after the bar started moving."

"If he knew better, why did he do it?"

"He was always digging stuff out of the garbage," Warren said. "He'd see something in a trash can or in the truck and make a grab for it. He must have brought a ton of junk home with him. You know what he was like."

"I know what he was like," Mrs. Wilson said. "He was a big strong baby that you took advantage of. You never should have had him working for you."

"I didn't take advantage of him," Warren said. "I thought I was helping him. Keeping him out of trouble."

"You did a good job of that, didn't you?" Mrs. Wilson said.

Warren looked away again. How could he defend himself against a grieving mother? How could he defend himself against his own conscience?

"What's done is done," Mr. Wilson said. "Only thing now is, who's going to pay for it?"

Warren wiped his eyes with his fingertips and stared at the shiny splashes on the tile. "I called my insurance company," he said. "And since Raymond wasn't officially on the payroll, he's not covered.

"You see what I mean!" Mrs. Wilson said. "How can you sit there and say you didn't take advantage of him? You paid him in cash just so you wouldn't have to pay the taxes and insurance on him."

Warren looked up at her. "For almost four years I've been paying Goony in cash. Why didn't you complain about it before now?"

Ignoring this, Mr. Wilson said, "We can't handle those hospital bills, that's for sure. All I've got is my pension and social security. We don't want to have to make you pay, Warren, but if . . ."

"Nobody has to make me do anything. I'll make sure that Raymond's taken care of.

"He's only thirty years old. You going to take care of him for the rest of his life?"

"Jesus," Warren said, and stood up. "I said I'll do what I can."

"What you can do ain't going to be enough," Mr. Wilson said.

"Warren, we're going to have to sue you. That way the money will come from your insurance company, and not from your own pocket."

"You sue me and I'm out of business," Warren said. He went to the window and looked out. Without touching the glass he could feel its coldness, the chill of the frozen air outside.

"We can't help that," Mr. Wilson said. "It wasn't us who nearly broke him in half."

Warren flinched. A pain, hot and raw as a fire-baked sawblade, cut through his back. Wincing, he put his hands against the glass and leaned into it for support. His breath came back to him from off the glass; it smelled of fish skins and boiled cabbage.

"It wasn't my fault," Warren said, almost to himself.

Mr. Wilson answered very softly, without emphasis. "If not you, Warren, who?"

Warren had no idea how long he remained leaning against the window. Mr. and Mrs. Wilson said nothing more. After a while he turned and walked away from them, down the corridor and to the elevator. He pushed the elevator button and stood with his back to the nurses station. Could they identify him through his gray suit, see his condom-stained skin, smell the used tampons and ear swabs, the years of dandruff and pus?

When the elevator door opened, Warren, the trash man, stepped inside. He punched the CLOSE DOOR button before anyone else could come along, and rode down to the lobby alone.

Warren drove up in front of his house but did not pull into the driveway. Through the window he saw the ghostly blue flicker of the television set. At the rear of his driveway, pulled up close to the garage, was his garbage truck. Just looking at it, he felt his stomach begin to churn. Why would any sane man ever become a garbage collector? he wondered. There was lots of money in it, that's why. Lots of money in garbage. The world was swimming in garbage, there was no end to the garbage people created. Seven hundred pounds per person per year, that was the figure he had once heard. That was a lot of garbage, a lot of waste. A lot of money.

Never mind that people always looked at you and grinned when you told them your profession. Never mind that if you went into a bar to have a beer, you drank alone. Never mind that people shied away from shaking your hand, from touching you in any way, as though you wore a perpetual scum of stink that might rub off. Never mind that you inevitably came to view life as a lonely, filthy business which, like sardine cans and potato skins, could be crushed into a tight package and conveniently buried out of sight.

Warren quietly slipped the car into gear and pulled away from the curb. It was a nice clear night—round white moon, bright stars, a good evening for a drive. He wound down the window and let the fresh clean chill of the air wash over him. He turned the radio up loud and began to sing along with it. He opened his eyes wide to see clearly each house flicking by, each telephone pole. He saw every object with a clarity he had never experienced before. Wood and concrete, glass and steel. Everything breaks, everything falls apart in the end. Cloth and hair, bones and flesh. Everything rots, everything disappears. He drove with a lightness, an unconcern, on the road that led out of town and toward the garbage dump. Maybe he would stop the car and turn around before he reached the edge of the bowl-like pit, the garbage graveyard. Maybe he would. Maybe he wouldn't.

Prayer and Old Jokes

G UTIÉRREZ was a painter in oils in the third booth from
the end in the fifth row of stalls in what is called the free
district of Tijuana. The free district is an untaxed area
approximately two hundred yards deep, between the city itself and
the Mexican-American border. Here Gutiérrez would stand at the
mouth of his stall, just off the muddy alleyway. With the noise and
traffic of other vendors and tourists all around him, the tourists
often pausing to watch him work or to inquire of his prices,
Gutiérrez would lay the colors on thick with a palette knife, or
smooth out a snowbed on a mountainside with a stroke of his brown
thumb, or he would plant avocado trees down the face of a terraced
cliff with a cotton swab dipped in viridian.

When the pedestrian traffic was heavy, as it is on warm Sunday
afternoons February through May, Gutiérrez might complete three
or sometimes even four paintings in a single day, finishing quickly
and with little concentration the paintings that he knew would most
easily sell, the busts of Elvis in a sequined suit on a black velvet
canvas, the animated figure of a matador coiled in a low-swinging
veronica while the bull, head-lowered and horns glinting, snorted
past him.

When a tourist stopped by to try his command of Spanish out on
Gutiérrez, pointing at a certain picture and shouting unnecessarily

loud, as though speaking to a deaf man, "Cuánto? Cuánto?,"
Gutiérrez would smile and say in his practiced pidgin English,
"How much you pay, meester?"

But Gutiérrez seldom enjoyed such sales, seldom enjoyed playing
the semiliterate native or the necessary accompaniment of haggling
the tourists felt compelled to engage in because their guidebooks
had warned them that the natives would not respect them if they
didn't. After such a sale he would often disappear to the back of his
stall where no one could hear him and mutter, "Jesus. Jesus, what
bullshit. Why do you put up with this bullshit, Gutiérrez?"

In the back of his stall were the paintings he enjoyed having
made, the ones he called paintings and not cartoons like the portraits of Elvis and the matador on black velvet. He kept these true
paintings stacked against one another in the corner, because for
some reason the tourists seemed uninterested in good paintings,
they wanted the caricatures of things they had known since childhood, the bright and gaudy portraits of Speedy Gonzales and the
Roadrunner and Elvis and the matador with the bull. There in the
back leaning against one another were landscapes of human suffer-
ing and natural beauty: the orange groves of Chula Vista, where
scores of migrant workers stretched from ladders to fill their baskets; more mirgrant workers stooping in fields of onions, their
spines bent like taut bows; a shrunken vieja clutching an infant in
one hand and holding out an empty saucer for coins with the other
while squatting in a filthy corner at the mouth of the underground
arcade beneath Avenida Revolución. There were paintings of the
ocean, of surf breaking over the beach and sending out lacy fans of
foam, and in the distance, like a reef of rounded boulders exposed
at low tide, the blue-black humped backs of whales in their balletic
migration past Point Loma. There were the crackerbox buildings of
a Mexican village crowding one another for space on a precipitous
hillside. There was the desert with three dust devils churning the
sand. There was a group of resigned Mexicans spread-eagled

against a cyclone fence while the Border Patrol frisked and then herded them into the police van. There was the Coronado bridge at night, its graceful concrete arch glittering with lights like a golden bracelet suspended above the bay.

These pictures and many others were stacked against one another in the back of Gutiérrez's stall. If by chance one of them caught the eye of a prospective buyer, Gutiérrez would let the painting go for next to nothing, so pleased was he that someone desired the best he was capable of. The simpler paintings, however, the repetitious caricatures on black velvet, these he sold for as high a price as he could get. He believed that anyone not concerned and knowledgeable about quality in art did not deserve a bargain.

Sometimes at noon or at the dinner hour I would walk across the bridge over the Tijuana River and sit on a crate in the shade of Gutiérrez's stall and watch him paint. If it was the dinner hour, when most of the tourists were in restaurants sipping their third margarita or already on their way back across the border, I would bring a bottle of Número Uno from the duty-free liquor store where I worked then as a clerk, and I would sit on the crate and get slowly drunk watching Gutiérrez paint. Sometimes I would fall asleep and not wake up until Gutiérrez laid down his painter's knife and reached for the half-empty bottle of tequila I held between my legs.

"Jesus, Ellie," I said to him one time (his first name was Eligio, but he would not permit anyone but me to call him Ellie), "if you were any good at that you'd have made us both rich a long time ago."

"You and your sister the puta," he said, tilting up the bottle for a long drink.

"My sister the puta resents you calling her that," I said.

He shrugged. "She's a nice girl for a puta."

"That's more like it. I'll tell her you said so."

"Send her over some night and I'll tell her myself."

"I would if I had one," I said.

I watched as he covered his canvas and then set it in the corner, folding the easel and laying it out of the way. Then he closed up the stall and the two of us sat together in the darkened corner, the air smelling of oil paints and perspiration and dust as we passed the bottle back and forth.

"Do you want to go to the jai alai tonight?" I asked.

"I don't know. I don't have much money."

"When did we ever have much money?"

"It's just that I'm tired of going and never being able to bet anything. What's the good of going to jai alai if you can't bet?"

"That never stopped us before."

"Nobody's talking about before."

"Christ, what's wrong with you tonight?" It was unlike Gutiérrez to complain about anything. "You know I wasn't serious when I said you weren't any good."

"Maybe you weren't, but it must be the truth."

"Christ, you're sounding bad, Ellie. Didn't you sell anything today?"

"I sold two Elvises, a Super Chicken, and W. C. Fields. And I got a commission to do a portrait for a hundred dollars."

"Jesus. You're practically a rich man already. What are you complaining about?"

"The commission is for the portrait of a dead cocker spaniel. I'm supposed to work from a snapshot."

"You didn't turn the commission down, did you?"

"I wouldn't be so disgusted with myself if I had."

"Even so, a hundred dollars is a lot of money."

"Not that much," he said.

"It's five Elvises," I told him. He looked at me out of the corners of his eyes, my face exaggeratedly serious until he finally grinned and yanked the bottle out of my hand and after drinking what was left in one long swallow tossed the bottle against the rear wall.

"You pig," I said. "You didn't have to drink it all."

"Oink," he said.

"You do a good smell impersonation too."

"Your sister," he said.

"If I had one," I said.

He laughed and stood up and reached for my hand to pull me to my feet. We went out of the stall trying hard to feel good as we made our way across the plaza and down the Avenida Revolución to the jai alai palace.

We sat in the general admission seats and watched the athletes bounding off the fronton walls, crouching and spinning as they caught the pelota and then ejected it from their cestas, the curved wicker baskets strapped to their wrists, the ball rocketing off the far wall, banking off the side wall, the player who was to catch it squatting slightly, his body tensed and poised and intuitively waiting until just the right instant to leap, catch the pelota with a back-handed stab and then twist and hurl it away from him again all in a single fluid motion. The crowd cheered when a point was well played or missed, depending upon where their money was riding, and the pelota striking and rocketing off the fronton wall echoed with a pleasing, hollow sound.

By the end of the evening we had each won a few dollars and Gutiérrez was feeling a little better. We walked up Madero to the all-night Cactus Licores store and bought another bottle of Número Uno.

"You might as well stay at my house tonight," Gutiérrez said after taking a swallow of tequila and passing the bottle to me. "Mama won't mind."

"How is mama these days?"

"This morning she thought she was back in Kansas," he said. "Maybe by now she thinks she's in Oz."

Gutiérrez's mother suffered from Alzheimer's disease, and though she was sometimes perfectly rational, she was more often

confused and even lost in her own small home. She had come west
from Kansas at the age of twenty-three with an older brother after
their parents had both been killed in a house fire. Half a year later
she met Gutiérrez's father in a cabbage field near San Jose. Her
brother soon tired of picking vegetables and set off alone for
Alaska, and was not heard from again. When Gutiérrez's father
was later picked up as an unregistered alien, Gutiérrez's mother,
then four months pregnant with Eligio, returned to Mexico with
him. They lived in Tijuana because it was easier from there for
Gutiérrez's father to slip across the border to harvest beets and
onions and broccoli and whatever happened to be in season at the
time. He had a criminal record from his early days in Mexico and
was unable to obtain any kind of legal visa. After each foray north
he returned to Tijuana only when the Border Patrol or immigration
authorities brought him back, though he always told Gutiérrez's
mother that he had allowed himself to be caught so as to take
advantage of the free transportation.

When Gutiérrez was thirteen he saw the last of his father, and
two years later was told by a cousin that his father was dead, shot as
he ran from the home of an avocado farmer near Escondido. The
cousin had heard that Gutiérrez's father had been attempting to
steal the farmer's collection of gold coins, but he had also heard
that it was the farmer's golden-haired daughter Gutiérrez's father
was really after. The cousin told Gutiérrez that there was probably
a great deal of truth to both versions of the story. Gutiérrez, in
turn, told his mother and three brothers that Papa had drowned
while trying to cross back over the Tijuana River at night, that his
body was never found and was now peacefully asleep at the bottom
of the Presa Rodríquez.

"Where will you make me sleep tonight?" I asked Gutiérrez
after we had left behind the shops and the music from the cafes and
had come onto the dirt streets that never felt the heelprints of a
tourist.

"You have the same choice as always." Gutiérrez said. "You can sleep in the living room with me and Carlito or you can sleep outside with the chickens."

"Can I sleep with your sister?" I asked.

"You could if I had one," he said.

Of Gutiérrez's three brothers, fifteen-year-old Carlito was the youngest and only one still living at home with Eligio and his mother. Both Leandro and Tomás were living somewhere in Los Angles. Neither had a green card, nor could they prove they were American citizens, for there was no available record of their mother's birth so Gutiérrez knew that he would probably never see his brothers again. Once or twice a year he received greetings from them via other unregistered aliens who had been caught and returned to Tijuana. His brothers were working in the construction business, had wives and were starting families of their own. They had no intentions of ever returning to Tijuana. And as long as they could avoid the immigration authorities, they would never do so.

Gutiérrez's mother was only fifty-two years old but at times looked closer to one hundred. Her face, though not as naturally dark as her sons', was deeply lined. When the Alzheimer's had a good grip on her she sometimes resembled one of the wasted little viejas who sell chewing gum on the Avenida Revolución.

On this night she was still awake when Gutiérrez and I returned from the jai alai games. In the kitchen she threw her arms around Ellie and called him Tito, which had been his father's name.

"They caught you again, didn't they, Tito?" she said. "Were you able to get any work before they caught you? Why can't those bastards let people make an honest living?"

Gutiérrez was drunk and very tired. He looked at me over his mother's shoulder and rolled his eyes. After embracing him his mother turned to me and, hugging me tightly, she said, "Did they catch you in the same place? What were you doing with your father? What happened to your job building houses?"

She thought I was Leandro.

Gutiérrez said, "This isn't Leandro, mama. It's Michael, from the liquor store."

She stood very close and peered up into my face. "Who is he?" she asked.

"The President of the United States," Gutiérrez said.

"Don't tease her," I said.

"It doesn't matter to her. You could be Christ Himself and she wouldn't know the difference."

Gutiérrez was being unnaturally unpleasant that night. Often his mother's confusion saddened and frustrated him, but tonight it seemed to make him angry as well. Nor was it just because of the tequila we had drunk. All day long he had been surly and complaining. It was unusual for Gutiérrez to act this way.

But he was right about his mother; she seemed not even to notice that he had said I was not Leandro.

"I had a feeling you two would be back tonight," she said. "I went to Zola this afternoon and she said to expect you very soon. That's why I have rice and beans warming on the stove. Sit down and I'll get some for you."

Zola was a fortune-teller who had died eight years ago.

Gutiérrez shrugged and sat down at the table. I sat across from him. He turned in his chair, leaned backward, and opened the refrigerator door. He took out two cans of Dos Equis and slid one across the table to me.

"When you're finished eating," Gutiérrez's mother said, "I want you to look in the living room, Tito. There's a little boy sleeping in there and I don't know where he came from."

"That's Carlito, your son," Gutiérrez said, taking the plate of rice and beans from his mother. He used a folded tortilla like a spoon to scoop the rice into his mouth.

Gutiérrez's mother looked at me quizically. "I'm not Carlito," I told her. "The boy in the living room."

She looked at Gutiérrez again. "Go to bed, mama," he told her. "We're all home now. You go to bed and get some rest."

She kissed each of us on the cheek and then turned to walk away. At the threshold she turned toward us and said, speaking in a whisper, "Don't forget about this little boy, Tito. Don't step on him in the dark."

"Sí," he said, very tired. "We'll be careful. Go to bed now, mama."

When she left the room we ate in silence, Gutiérrez not looking up from his plate. After a while I said, "She doesn't seem unhappy, Ellie."

He did not look up but I could see tears shining in his eyes. "At least she's back from Kansas," he said.

Later, in the darkness of the living room, I streched out on the floor with Gutiérrez. Carlito was already asleep in the middle of the small room, rolled like a sausage in his sleeping bag, so instead of moving the boy and maybe waking him we lay down with Carlito between us. The sofa was too short and sagging for anyone, even Carlito, to sleep on comfortably. I had a pillow from the sofa to put under my head. On the pillow were embroidered the first two lines of the child's prayer that begins "Now I lay me down to sleep," and a pair of prayer-folded hands. This was the pillow Gutiérrez always gave me when I spent the night at his house. It had started out as a joke maybe five or six years earlier, the first time Gutiérrez and I got drunk together, and it had been part of our friendship ever since. So much of our friendship had become just that—old jokes repeated so often that we would no more leave them out of our conversation than a priest would forget his litany.

"Are you sober enough to remember your prayers?" Gutiérrez whispered to me through the darkness.

"No," I said, repeating the old joke. "If I die tonight I die a sinner."

"Then make sure you have that pillow under your head, so when God looks down He'll see the pillow with the prayer on it and mistake it for that soft brain of yours."

It was no longer a funny joke; it had been funny only once, and then because we were young and happy-drunk. But I had grown as used to the joke as I had to the pillow itself. With the pillow under my head I felt more comfortable and safe, as though the embroidered prayer in some small way actually did protect me from God.

Gutiérrez's mother could be heard snoring in the next room. There was only a serape hung across the doorway to separate the two rooms, so her breathing reached us undiminished. With every exhalation she emitted a muted groan, an almost musical sigh. It was on the inhalations that her snoring was loudest, as though the taking in of another breath was a chore for her. While listening to her it occurred to me that having Alzheimer's disease must be a little like never waking from a dream. Except that the dream keeps changing on you, and the confusion is seldom pleasant.

Lying between Gutiérrez and me, Carlito snored with his mouth open. He had began to snore only within the past year or so. I knew that I would soon have to start changing the way I thought about Carlito. He was no longer a little boy. Already he had had some trouble with the police. In some ways he was older than either me or his brother.

Also as I lay there with my head on the pillow, trying to fool God, I heard Gutiérrez crying. It was more his effort of trying not to cry than the actual act of crying that I heard. He sniffed back his tears and tried to regulate his breaths.

I lay on my back with my hands behind my head and stared up at the ceiling. "Ellie?" I whispered.

After a few moments he sniffed loudly and then rolled onto his back. "What?" he asked.

"We should have gotten some women tonight."

"We should have done a lot of things."

"Next time let's forget about the tequila and get some women."

"No woman would have you unless *she* had a lot of tequila."

"Your sister would have me."

"My sister's a puta."

"Yes, but where is she when I need her?"

He said nothing for a while and I began to worry again, for I did not want him to go to sleep sad. It was a theory of mine that if you went to sleep sad you would wake up even sadder. So sometimes it was necessary to fool yourself into thinking you were not quite as unhappy as you knew you were.

"What are you going to do with your hundred dollars from the commission?" I asked him, whispering and arching my words into the air so that they rose over Carlito and then fell on the other side of him.

"I'll buy more canvases so that I can paint more dead dogs so that I can buy more canvases," Gutiérrez said.

"You ought to give yourself a little vacation. When was the last time you had a vacation?"

"The only vacation I get is when I sleep," he said. "And you're making me miss it."

"I don't think you should feel too bad about taking that commission. There's nothing wrong with painting a portrait of a dog."

"Not if you're a dog artist," he said.

"Jesus," I said. "Why didn't we get some women tonight?"

Gutiérrez did not answer.

"Don't go to sleep unhappy," I told him.

"Do you want me to stay awake the rest of my life?"

"You should try to see the good side of things."

"What good side?"

"You're going to be a hundred dollars richer soon."

"A hundred dollars is nothing."

"Christ," I said. "I've never heard you talk like this before. What's wrong with you tonight?"

"Look around," he said.

I had to admit that Gutiérrez was right; he did not have much to be happy about. Even in the darkness it would be difficult to fool yourself about that.

In the morning Gutiérrez's mother again thought that I was Leandro. She was awake before any of us, frying eggs and making coffee, and later after I had awakened and washed my face I sat at the kitchen table with Ellie and Carlito and watched her and found it hard to believe that she was as ill as she was. Physically she had more energy than either Gutiérrez or myself. She appeared in perfect health. The only trouble was that her brain was deteriorating, actually shrinking like a raisin inside her skull.

She set a plate of eggs and buttered tortillas in front of me. "I don't want you going back to Los Angeles," she said. She stood behind me and stroked the back of my neck. "I don't like that city. I worry every night that something will happen to you there."

Gutiérrez and Carlito looked up at me, Carlito only briefly and with a peculiar twist to his mouth that meant he was either amused or disgusted with me. He was trying so hard to act like a man. Somewhere he had gotten the idea that being a man meant having no feelings.

Gutiérrez, still looking as tired as when he had gone to bed the night before, told me, "You can explain it to her if you want to. But it will only confuse her more."

"Explain what?" Gutiérrez's mother asked. Her hand was warm on the back of my neck. I did not really mind her thinking of me as her son.

"Nothing," I told her, turning my head to smile up at her. "These eggs are delicious."

Later Gutiérrez and his brother and I walked back down the hillside and toward the Tijuana that the tourists knew. His mother would be watched over throughout the day by neighbors who took turns keeping an eye on her. Occasionally one of the neighbors might come to Gutiérrez at his stall to report that his mother had somehow slipped away. Knowing that she had probably gone out to buy some fruit or coffee at the native market but, once there, had forgotten where she lived, he would have to leave his stall and roam the city in search of her. But this did not happen so often any more. As her condition degenerated the neighbors got better at keeping a close watch on her, and no longer were they hesitant to order her about or to punish her like a child.

As we walked down the dirt streets into the business district the sun was on our right, still huge and red hanging just above the horizon. There was as always a clean light morning mist, but this would soon give way to the odors of sewage and decay. But for now the morning was new and untouched and the only things that kept me from feeling good were Gutiérrez's sadness and the strain of Carlito trying to be a hard unfeeling man.

"Hey, Leandro," Carlito said to me, pulling a small wad of dirty dollar bills out of his pocket. "How about bringing a bottle home with you tonight?"

"Put your money away," I told him. "And don't ask me again until you're old enough."

"Where did you get that money?" Gutiérrez asked.

"None of your business. I get it where I get it."

"If you need money, you ask me for it. You get caught with your hand in some gringo's pocket again and this time you're going to be in serious trouble."

Carlito had already been arrested once for shoplifting and once for picking pockets on the Avenida Revolución. He had been given two years probation on the pickpocket charge and was placed in the custody of his brother. Carlito was one of three reasons why Gutiérrez would not leave Tijuana. The second was his mother, who, no matter where she imagined herself to be, whether in Kansas or San Jose or Tijuana, adamantly refused to leave her home. The third reason was fear.

I could see Carlito stiffening and I knew that if the conversation continued on its present course he and Eligio would quarrel. Eventually Ellie would lose his patience and grab Carlito by the shoulders and shake him. Carlito would swing at his brother's face and soon they would be fighting in earnest. I had seen it happen that way many times before. But Carlito was only an inch or so shorter than Ellie now. The last time they had fought, Ellie had sustained a bloody nose and a broken lip before finally subduing his brother.

To change the subject I asked, "Why do you suppose your mother thinks I'm Leandro? I don't even look like him."

"He was the baby of the family for so many years," Gutiérrez explained. "He's her favorite. You notice she never mentions me or Tomás. She's practically forgotten about us."

"She thinks I'm some fucking stranger," Carlito said.

"Watch your language."

"It's true. Most of the time she doesn't know who I am even after I've reminded her."

"You can't blame it on mama," Gutiérrez said. "She can't help what's happening to her."

Carlito looked as though he was going to cry, but he was fighting hard not to feel anything.

"You're still my favorite," I told him, and nudged him with my shoulder.

But Carlito did not answer. He stepped out ahead of us and started walking down Río Fuerte.

"You get your ass to school," Gutiérrez called after him.

Carlito raised his hand in an obscene gesture and continued walking without looking back.

"Jesus," Gutiérrez said, and shook his head. We walked down Los Héroes past the Hotel Lucerna with its broad flat face and its swimming pool with the walking bridge across it. But Gutiérrez was not looking at the hotel. "I don't know what to do with him anymore," he said. "These days I can't even frighten him into behaving."

"It must be hard to have never had a father."

"He's never said anything, but I think he knows the truth about what our father was like."

"You've been a good father to him."

"Shit," Gutiérrez said. "I haven't been a good anything."

We stopped at the corner of Los Héroes and Madero. Gutiérrez would have to go in one direction to his stall, and I would take the walkway across the Tijuana River to the duty-free liquor store at the border.

"What day is this?" I asked him.

"Friday," he said.

"The hounds will be running tonight. Do you want to go?"

"I don't know," he said. "I guess so. Do you want to meet here or are you going home first?"

"I'll come to your stall around five," I said.

I had a small apartment across the border in Chula Vista, but there was no need for me to return to it. In my car, which was parked in the guarded Mexican Instant Auto Insurance parking lot, I always kept a couple of changes of clothing. I had more clothing in my car than there was back home in my closet. My apartment was just a place to go when everyone else was tired of seeing me. There weren't even any plants there that needed watering.

"Paint good," I told Gutiérrez. He turned left down Madero and raised his hand to wave.

That night at the dog track I hit on the forty-niner handicapper and came away with the equivalent of over four hundred American dollars. Gutiérrez was happy for me even though he had won only a few small bets and barely broke even. We celebrated for a while at the Caliente racetrack, drinking margaritas with other winners and buying drinks for some of the more attractive losers. Afterward we migrated as a group back up Revolución to the bar at El Torito's. I bought a hugh platter of shrimp burritos and more margaritas and tossed coins off the balcony to the mariachis on the street below. People I had never seen before followed me wherever I walked, or seemed content to stand behind my chair as I sat with a margarita in my hand. It was my first experience with the kind of popularity that being a winner brings. Maybe they thought I was someone important because of the way I was spending money. It was a false popularity, but it was certainly better than being ignored.

There was an American girl who seemed very interested in Gutiérrez. She had been in the group that came away from Caliente with us, and at El Torito's I noticed that she could not take her eyes off him. She seemed almost spellbound by his sharply defined Anglo features and his dark Mexican complexion. I sneaked up behind her and whispered in her ear, "Do you know who that man is?"

She turned and looked at me. She was wearing a yellow knit shirt with one of those little polo players stitched over her left breast, her nipples raising tiny points on the shirt front. Her hair was cropped short, she was slender and of medium height, and she looked very good in her tight corduroy jeans.

"Who?" she asked, touching me lightly on the arm when she spoke.

"That's El Gato," I said. "Mexico's matador primero."

"El Gato?" she said. "The Cat?"

"He's famous for his grace and fluidity of movement. He moves just like a cat on the prowl. You must have heard of him or seen his posters."

"Yes," she said, still admiring Gutiérrez. "I think maybe I have."

"He's also famous for his prowess with the women," I whispered.

"Is that right?" she said, already moving away from me. She too moved with a feline quality of grace and stealth, maneuvering between the crowded tables to the other end of the balcony where Gutiérrez stood staring down at the street.

She walked up to him and touched his arm and, nodding back toward me, spoke to him. Gutiérrez stood on his toes to look at me over the heads of the crowd. I winked and mouthed "Ole!" Shaking his head and smiling, he said something to the girl, who then leaned out over the balcony, shook her finger at me, and laughed good-naturedly.

She did not seem to mind that Gutiérrez was not El Gato. For a medium-sized person she did a good job of keeping him cornered at the far end of the balcony. She ran her hand up and down his arm when she spoke to him. Once I saw her lean her body against his and kiss him on the lips. But her obvious interest in him did not make Gutiérrez happy. After an hour or so he came to me and whispered that he was leaving.

"I told her I was going to the bathroom," he said. "I'm going to sneak out while I can."

"You can't leave yet," I told him. "I've already paid the maria-chis to play you two a love song. They're working their way over there now."

"I'm sorry. I'm not staying any longer."

"Then I'll go with you. Besides, I've spent all the money I want to spend tonight."

On the way out people I had never met before stopped me to ask where we were going. I smiled and told them to order themselves a drink and that I would be back in just a minute to pay for it.

Gutiérrez and I got off Revolución quickly and headed up Madero. "What's wrong?" I asked him.

He shook his head. "Are you staying at my place tonight?"

"Of course. You don't want me driving in this condition, do you?"

He slowed a little as we came onto Los Héroes, as though the silence and darkness of that street finally allowed him to relax.

"You should have heard the things she was asking me," he said.

"What kinds of things?"

"At first just questions about me and my family. She wanted to know how it felt to be a Chicano."

"She asked you that?"

"She said, 'Psychologically speaking, how do you view yourself—as a white man or a Mexican?'"

"Jesus."

"Then she wanted to know what kind of women I perferred."

"Christ. What did you tell her?"

"What could I say? I said I liked all women."

"Sorry, Ellie. I wouldn't have sent her over if I had known she was going to psychoanalyze you."

"Wait a minute, you haven't heard the best of it yet. She wanted to know which sexual position I most preferred, and whether when I made love to a white woman I ever felt the urge to get rough and aggressive."

"Oh Jesus," I said, and could not help laughing. "And she looked so normal."

"I'm glad you can laugh about it," he said. "She scared the hell out of me."

"You should have sent her back in my direction."

"Believe me, I tried. But she said that white men make bland lovers."

"Ha. I would have dispelled that myth in a hurry."

"You would have confirmed it," Gutiérrez said.

"You think so? Why don't you ask your sister about that."

"I will next time I see her," Gutiérrez said.

We were walking up the hillside now on the unlighted dirt street toward Gutiérrez's home. Away from the brightness and the music of El Torito's our drunkenness gave way to weariness, and in Gutiérrez's case a sadness that smelled of poverty and open sewers. That commission he had been offered had changed something inside of him. He could not afford to turn the commission down, and yet by accepting it his esteem for himself as a serious artist had dropped considerably. Up until then he had been able to do the Elvis and Roadrunner paintings and tell himself that he was only fooling an unknowledgeable segment of the public with his intent. He and God knew of his seriousness, and eventually God would reward him with a public recognition of his talent. But now he felt, I suppose, that the prostitution of his talent had fooled even God, so that in the future only opportunities befitting a cartoonist would be directed his way. Had I not thought he would resent me for it, I would have offered Gutiérrez twice the amount to resign the commission.

The episode with the American girl had not done his mood much good either. We did not speak again until we were inside the door to his house.

"Thanks for all the money you spent on me tonight," he said.

"No problem," I told him. "I spent just as much on people I've never seen before."

"I know. But you wouldn't have done it if I hadn't been there too."

I had not thought of this before but now that I did I saw that Gutiérrez was right. Had he not been with me I would have taken my four hundred dollars and gone home. But I had tried to make Gutiérrez forget about his sadness for a while. He knew me so well that he had recognized even before I had what I was doing.

"If you're really grateful," I told him, "you'll let me sleep with your sister tonight."

He opened the door and we stepped inside to the kitchen. "If you can find her," he whispered, "you can have her."

In the living room we undressed in silence and lay on the floor with Carlito snoring between us. Leaning over his brother, Gutiérrez handed me the embroidered pillow.

"What's that smell?" he asked.

"It smells as though someone's been sick."

"Carlito's been drinking again," he said. "He probably threw up on himself. If it bothers you too much I'll wake him up and make him take off his clothes."

"Let him sleep," I said. "I'll hold the pillow over my face."

"Don't suffocate."

"If I do you'll have to give me mouth to mouth resuscitation."

"I'll let my sister do it," he said.

That night I had a sexual dream about the ocean, about myself standing waist-deep in the water and actually making love to the waves crashing against me. It was a very erotic, very satisfying dream. I awoke shortly after dawn with what I thought was a good idea clear and fully formed in my head. I got up and washed and then made breakfast. When the eggs were ready I went into the living room and gently shook Gutiérrez awake.

"What time is it?" he asked, pulling his blanket over his head.

"It's almost seven."

He groaned. "I just went to sleep a few hours ago."

"I know. But breakfast is ready, get up. You can sleep on the beach this afternoon."

He pulled the blanket down over his face and, still lying on his back, looked up at me. "What beach?"

I smiled. "I'm taking you and Carlito to Ensenada for the weekend with the money I won last night."

"No you're not," he said.

"Yes I am. It's my money and I can do whatever I want with it. So get up and eat your breakfast."

"I can't leave mama for the whole weekend," he said. "And I can't afford to close up my stall for two days."

"If you don't get away from that place for a while you'll go crazy," I told him. "We'll be home tomorrow night. We'll get Amado to watch over your stall, and I'll be happy to pay one of the neighbors to stay with your mother."

"Amado's a cheat."

"What's a few dollars compared to a two-day vacation?"

"I shouldn't leave mama."

"Think of the good it will do Carlito to get away from here for a weekend." It would do Eligio a lot of good too, but I did not want to have to say this.

"It will cost too much money," he said.

"What do I need money for? If I don't spend it on this, I'll just throw it away on the horses tonight."

"I don't know," Gutiérrez said. I could tell that he wanted badly to go, but he felt guilty about the money and about leaving his mother.

"Just think of the paintings you could do," I told him. "Have you ever painted the beach at Ensenada?"

"No," he said, but I knew that he was thinking about it now, picturing the white expanse of sand in his mind.

Just then Carlito rolled over in his sleeping bag and sat up. "What are you two talking about?" he asked.

I told him, "We're going to Ensenada for the weekend as soon as we eat breakfast. Get up and get ready."

"Really?" he said. He was as excited as a small child and in his grogginess did not attempt to hide his excitement.

"Really," I told him. "I won some money on the dogs last night. The sooner you're ready, the sooner we leave."

Carlito unzipped his sleeping bag and crawled out and hurried to the bathroom.

"Did you see how excited he was?" I asked Gutiérrez. "Do you want to be the one to disappoint him?"

Finally Gutiérrez sat up and threw off his blanket. "You're a devious white devil," he said.

"Coming from El Gato himself, I consider that a compliment."

He grimaced. "Let's not even talk about last night. I've got a headache a mile long."

"Get up and eat your breakfast," I told him. "Do you think you should wake your mother and tell her our plans?"

"No," Gutiérrez said. "Let mama sleep."

So we did not wake Gutiérrez's mother before we left. She never reacted well to her sons leaving the house. There was no telling whom she might believe us to be, or where she might imagine we were going. Gutiérrez arranged with one of the neighbors, Mrs. Ferretis, to stay with his mother until we returned Sunday night. He believed it would be wiser just to let his mother awaken to find Mrs. Ferretis sitting in the living room, thumbing through an old copy of *Life*.

Gutiérrez made a deal with Amado, the leather-worker who owned the stall adjacent to his, and after retrieving my car from the fenced-in Mexican Instant Auto Insurance parking lot we drove down what is called the "old road" through Rosarito Beach and then inland to Ensenada. From the back seat Carlito watched every mile pass by through the open window. It was a bright warm morning and he looked almost like a puppy with the wind in his face and blowing back his hair. He seldom spoke and was very well behaved. Eligio, sitting in the front seat, often turned and looked back at his brother and smiled.

In Ensenada I wanted to rent us a room at the San Nicolás, the best hotel in town, but Gutiérrez refused to get out of the car and insisted that I find a less expensive place.

"Are you going to act like this all weekend?" I asked him. "Counting every dollar I spend?"

"I'm not going to let you waste your money on us, if that's what you mean."

"Maybe you'd rather we slept on the beach?" I said.

Carlito said, "Maybe you'd rather we stayed awake all weekend."

"Don't start being a smartass," Gutiérrez warned his brother. "You've behaved yourself up till now, so don't start acting like him."

"What's wrong with the way I act?" I asked.

"Yeah," Carlito said. "What's wrong with the way he acts?"

We stood outside the car in front of the San Nicolás and looked threateningly at Gutiérrez. "Get out of that car," I said, "so that your brother and I can beat you to a pulp."

Gutiérrez smiled at our parody of anger. "There's a place not far from here that looks like a castle," he said. "It's called the Misión Santa Isabel and it costs half as much as this place."

I opened the door and pushed Gutiérrez toward the driver's seat. "Drive on," I told him. Carlito climbed into the back.

Sitting straight and tall behind the steering wheel, Gutiérrez looked happier than I had seen him in a very long time. At the red-roofed, colonial-style Santa Isabel we hurriedly unpacked our bags in a second-floor room, stripped to our swimming trunks, and rushed out across the Bulevar Costero to the beach of Todos Santos Bay. We went running into the clear azure water, splashing and yelping. None of us could swim more than a few strokes, so after cooling off Gutiérrez and I came back to the beach and spread our towels on the warm white sand.

Diving like a dolphin into the low waves, Carlito rode them back toward the beach with his body held as stiff as a board, then turned and splashed outward again to meet the next wave.

I sat on my beach towel and let the sun dry my skin. "I can't believe how well Carlito is behaving," I said. "In four hours he hasn't cursed or sworn at either of us."

"He's just like a little boy again," Gutiérrez said. He lay stretched out on his back, eyes closed, palms down and fingers spread, his feet covered with clean white sand. "But I know how he feels. This is like being born again."

I lay down beside him. "Feels good, doesn't it?"

Without opening his eyes or moving his head he reached out and momentarily touched my hand. "Gracias," he said. "Amigo buenísimo."

"Speak English, you illiterate half-breed."

He laughed and drew his hand away.

We lay side by side with the sun hot on our faces and chests and legs, the ocean and beach noises sounding further and further away as I slipped into a drowsy, half-conscious state. After a while Carlito came and without speaking spread his beach towel on the sand and lay down beside his brother. He was breathing hard from his swimming and diving and I enjoyed lying there listening to his breathing as it became shallow and regular again.

Just when I thought that Gutiérrez must be asleep he said, softly and dreamily, "I'm going to pretend that I never have to leave this place."

Neither Carlito nor I answered. It would be easier for Gutiérrez to fool himself if we did not acknowledge his self-deception with a reply.

We slept until nearly one in the afternoon. I awoke to find Gutiérrez sitting up beside me, staring out across the bay.

"Jesus," I said, "look at you. You've gotten as black as a Watusi."

"And you're as red as a drunken Irishman."

"I guess I'd better get out of this sun for a while. You want to go somewhere and have a drink?"

"I thought I'd make a few sketches," he said. "I was just about to walk back to the hotel for my sketch pad when you woke up."

"Bring my shirt back with you," I said. "I guess I'll sit here for a while and watch the girls go by. Where's Carlito?"

"I don't know. I woke up and he wasn't here."

"Well, don't worry about him. He's old enough to take care of himself."

"That's what worries me. He takes care of himself too good."

"He's been behaving himself all day."

"I only hope it lasts." Gutiérrez got up and started toward the hotel. While he was gone I leaned back on my elbows and looked at all the girls in their bright bikinis. Some of them knew they were being watched and walked close as though to tease me with their nearness. Others acknowledged my attention with a smile, while still others were shy and walked briskly, their strides becoming suddenly stiff and unnatural as they tried to keep their hips from jiggling.

When after half an hour Gutiérrez had not returned, I stood and walked down the beach to the piers that jut out into the bay. I watched the fisherman and of course the girls and then returned back up the beach to find Gutiérrez sitting on his beach towel with his sketch pad propped up on his knees.

"What took you so long?" I asked him.

"Nothing," he said. "Your shirt's there on your towel, and there's beer in the paper bag. It's probably warm by now."

I pulled on my shirt and then reached into the bag for a can of beer. Then I stood behind Gutiérrez and looked down at his drawing. He was not sketching the beach or any of the bay scenery, but was drawing the portrait of a young Mexican girl.

"Who's she?" I asked.

"Just a girl I saw."

"At the hotel?"

"I saw her when I went to buy the beer." He made crisp, delicate strokes with his charcoal pencil. "She was down on López Mateos in front of an expensive gift shop, staring in at the window display."

"She's beautiful," I said.

"If I can get her right," he said.

I could tell that he did not want to talk, so I sat on my beach towel and drank my warm beer. The beer made me sleepy again and after drinking a second one I lay back on the towel and closed my eyes. I could hear the scratch of Gutiérrez's pencil making lines on the heavy paper. It was a pleasant, fulfilling sound, and soon I fell asleep again feeling good with myself for having brought him here.

When I awoke a second time it was to a headache and a painfully bright sun and to the sound of Gutiérrez and his brother arguing. I sat up and saw them both standing, facing one another, Carlito with an orange boogie board tucked under his left arm. A boogie board is a cut-down version of a surfboard, made of compressed styrofoam and plastic and used to lie on like an air mattress to ride the waves. Usually they cost between thirty and seventy dollars, and I knew that Carlito could not afford to buy even one of the cheaper models. The board he held beneath his arm was three feet long and came equipped with a long rubber safety cord that fastened with a velcro strap around the wrist.

"Even so," Gutiérrez was saying, "people don't just walk away and forget things like that."

"I knew you wouldn't believe me," Carlito said. "But I didn't steal it. I sat there for half an hour waiting for someone to come back and reclaim it. There wasn't anyone within fifty yards of it. It was washed up down on the rocks where the water's too rough for swimming anyway."

"Which only proves that somebody lost it," Gutiérrez said.

"Of course somebody lost it! But I didn't steal it. What do you want me to do, go up and down the beach asking everyone I meet if it belongs to him?"

"You should have left it where it was. It doesn't belong to you, Carlito."

"Stop calling me Carlito. My name is Carlos."

"If you want a man's name you'd better start acting like a man. Take that board back where you found it."

"I didn't steal it," he said. He looked as though he was going to cry, but he was trying very hard not to.

"Not if you take it back," Gutiérrez said. "But you're stealing it if you keep it."

"If I take it back someone else will come along and pick it up."

"Then let someone else be a thief. I don't like having a thief for a brother."

Carlito looked at him a moment longer, almost losing the struggle not to cry, then turned away angrily and started back down the beach.

After watching him for a few seconds Gutiérrez shouted, "Carlos! Wait a minute!" He grabbed a can of beer from the paper bag and trotted down the beach to hand it to his brother.

Gutiérrez came back up the beach and sat beside me and took the last beer out of the paper bag.

"It's not going to be easy remembering to call him Carlos," he said.

"Maybe that's all he needed. For someone to treat him like a man."

"Maybe. But it wasn't easy not to just grab and shake him."

"I don't think you'll have to do that anymore."

"I hope not," he said. He took a sip of beer and then passed the can to me. The beer was hot and bitter but it still felt good going down. The skin across my forehead and beneath my eyes felt so tightly stretched that it hurt just to raise my eyebrows.

"I've got to get out of this sun for a while," I said.

"We'd better go back to the hotel. You're as red as a langostina."

"I feel like one," I said.

We picked up our beach towels and shook the sand off them. Gutiérrez picked up his brother's.

"I was thinking of buying one of those boogie boards," I said.

"No you don't," Gutiérrez said.

"It would be for all of us. As poorly as we all swim, we could use something to hang onto."

"There's no sense buying one just for tomorrow."

"We could use it back home too. We'd get plenty of use out of it."

Gutiérrez slung his towel and his brother's around his neck. "If you buy one," he said, "I could pay you back a little at a time."

"It would be for all of us."

"Then I should help pay for it."

"We'll see," I said.

Gutiérrez bent to pick up his charcoal pencil and sketch pad. He blew the sand off the picture of the Mexican girl, then with his fingertip brushed away the last grains of sand. He was very gentle when he did this, almost reverent. It was then I realized that Gutiérrez was in love, either with the Mexican girl or his portrait of her. I did not yet know which.

In the evening the three of us shared an inexpensive dinner at a small restaurant called Chico's on Avendia Alvarado. We ate huge portions of spareribs and rice and finished with coffee and coconut pie. Sitting between Eligio and Carlos, who were already blackened by the sun, I must have looked very odd with my sand-colored hair and sunburned skin. With the darkening of their faces they seemed to have lost their Americanness, and behaved more and more like natives, with that somber and dignified manner Mexicans often display.

They were so unlike the Mexicans closer to the border who had to humiliate themselves daily that I began to feel bad for them, knowing that tomorrow night they would have to return to that kind of life. At the same time I felt bad for myself, because they were the closest thing to a family I had and yet they were so unlike me. Carlos and Eligio seemed nearly copies of one another, their short black hair and brown faces and broad-shouldered, long straight backs. I saw us in the mirror against the wall and saw myself as a duck in a chickenhouse.

Gutiérrez put his foot against the rung of my chair and gave it a shove. "What's wrong with you?" he asked. "You're sitting there with your face nearly drooping in your pie."

"Too much sun," I said.

We paid the bill and then went outside and stood on the side-walk. "Where does everyone want to go?" I asked.

"I don't care," Carlos said. "Just so we don't have to go back to the hotel already."

"I heard about a bar where they make all different kinds of coffee drinks," Gutiérrez said.

"I don't think I want anymore coffee," I said.

"They make other drinks too. It's only five or six blocks down López Mateos."

"There must be something closer," I said. "I think we passed a place just around the corner."

"Well let's go somewhere," Carlos said, "and not stand here all night trying to make up our minds."

"This place down on López Mateos is supposed to be the place where clamatos were invented," Gutiérrez said.

I asked him, "Where did you hear about this place?"

"Some people told me about it," he said.

"What people?"

He smiled. "Some people I met when I bought the beer this afternoon."

I knew then why he was so eager for us to go there. "Then we'd better go have a clamato," I said. "It wouldn't be a vacation if we didn't have a clamato."

"What's a clamato?" Carlos asked. We came off Alvarado and turned to the right down López Mateos.

"It's a combination of ingredients you wouldn't dream of drinking by themselves," I said.

"Like what?"

"Like clam and abalone piss."

"You're not serious," Carlos said.

"Yes I am. Ask your brother. Aren't we all going to get drunk on clam and abalone piss, Ellie?"

But Gutiérrez did not answer. He was walking briskly and thinking of what lay five blocks ahead.

The name of the bar was La Manzana Verde. It was crowded and the music was loud and we had to stand against the back wall

for nearly twenty minutes before a table became available. Gutiérrez had worked his way to the bar and brought us each back a
clamato, an iced drink made of clam and abalone and tomato juices
and vodka in a tall slender glass, and we stood sipping these and
watching the people and hoping that no one would notice that
Carlos was underage.

"I think this is a couples' bar, " I said to Gutiérrez, having to
speak loudly into his ear over the blare of music. "There don't
seem to be any single girls here."

He nodded but did not answer. He stood looking from one
corner of the room to the other, searching intently. Just before a
table became available near the front of the bar, he saw her.
Apparently she had noticed him as well, for she soon motioned for
us to come forward and turned other people away from the empty
table until we got there. She was even prettier than in Gutiérrez's
drawing, though he had done a good job of capturing her likeness.

"What's her name?" I asked him as we made our way through
the crowd.

"Rosario," Gutiérrez said. He pronounced it with a strong Spanish inflection, prolonging the second syllable and trilling the
final "r."

She smiled at him as we sat down. "Gracias," he said. She was
very shy and lowered her head and turned away quickly. He
watched as she returned to the bar to pick up an order of drinks
and deliver them to a nearby table. Gutiérrez could not take his
eyes off her.

I leaned close to him and said, "She's beautiful, Ellie."

He nodded. He watched her wherever she went. Now and
then she would look back at him and smile shyly. She had black
shoulder-length hair, brown eyes, and a delicately shaped nose and
mouth. She was perhaps five feet three inches tall, had a slender,
well-formed body, and lovely small breasts. It was easy to see why
Gutiérrez had fallen so quickly in love with her.

"I'm going to get another drink," Carlos said.

"You can't go to the bar. They'll see that you're underage."

"I look old enough," he said.

"Don't take any chances," I told him. "I'll go."

"I'll get them," Gutiérrez said, and before anyone could reply he had stood and was on his way to the waitress station at the end of the bar where Rosario stood.

She too was in love but much shyer about it than was Gutiérrez. He spoke to her and she laughed and looked away and then looked up at him again and smiled.

"Who is she?" Carlos asked me.

"Someone your brother met earlier today. Don't you think she's pretty?"

"Sure," he said. "But what good is it doing us? If he ever comes back down to earth he'll probably forget to order the drinks."

"You should be happy for him."

"I'd be happier if I had another one of those drinks in my hand."

Gutiérrez waited at the end of the bar, and each time Rosario returned from delivering an order of drinks she returned to him. He whispered to her and touched her arm and she nodded and laughed softly.

"He's forgotten all about us," Carlos said. "I'm going to get us another drink."

"I'll get them," I said. "You just sit here and try to look older."

We should probably not have been buying drinks for Carlos, but we thought that as long as he was with us he couldn't get into any trouble. He wanted so badly to be thought of as a man. At the time we saw nothing wrong in treating him like one.

I brought back the drinks and handed one to Carlos. He had grown restless from just sitting quietly against the wall, and in less than five minutes he had finished his clamato. He kept tapping his fingertips against the table and glancing nervously about the room.

"How long is he going to stand there talking to her?" he asked.

"How long would you talk to a beautiful girl you had fallen in love with?"

"What does he expect us to do—just sit here and wait for him?"

"Where else do we have to go, Carlos? Why don't you try to relax and drink your drink and listen to the music."

"I finished my drink. Anyway, I don't want anymore of this clam piss. I'm going to get some tequila."

"Sit down. You'll only call attention to yourself."

"I look old enough to drink," he said. "Do you want any tequila?"

"If you want tequila sit down and I'll get it for you."

But he turned and pushed his way through the crowd and up to the bar. He stood at the opposite end of the bar from his brother, so Ellie did not see what was happening. Carlos, already slightly drunk, ordered his drink. The bartender leaned toward him over the bar and asked him something. Carlos looked up at him and shouted in his face. The bartender motioned with his thumb for Carlos to get outside. Over the loud music I could not hear Carlos's reply, but I had no doubts that it would be obscene and challenging.

The bartender came toward him around the end of the bar. Carlos stood waiting, refusing to retreat even a single step, and when the barman was close enough Carlos swung with a wide right hook at his head.

The barman, of course, had been expecting it; leaning back from the waist he reached up and seized Carlos's wrist and twisted him around, cranking his arm up behind his back. With his left hand he held Carlos by the shirt collar, his right hand pinning Carlos's arm painfully behind his back, putting so much pressure on the arm that Carlos, as he was pushed toward the door, was forced to rise on his toes to keep his arm from breaking.

Gutiérrez did not see any of this until Carlos and the barman were at the door. Then he must have become aware of the catcalls and laughter. He looked up to see the barman kick open the door and roughly push Carlos outside. The barman returned wiping his hands in an exaggerated manner, in parody of similar scenes from old cowboy movies. The crowd cheered and applauded.

Gutiérrez spun quickly and looked across the room at me. I signaled for him to stay where he was. Hurrying outside I found Carlos standing on the sidewalk, facing the door, his fists clenched.

"Are you all right?" I asked him.

"That sonofabitch nearly broke my arm." There were tears in his eyes but he was shaking with anger, his jaw muscles clenched.

"You should have stayed in your seat. I would have gotten your drinks for you."

"Where's Eligio?" he demanded.

"He's still inside."

"Tell him to come out here, I want to leave."

"Carlos," I said, "you can't expect him to give up his night just because you've gotten yourself into trouble."

"Did you see what that bastard did to me?"

"He had every right to throw you out. You were underage and causing trouble."

"I just wanted a goddamn drink."

"You should have stayed in your seat."

"Are you going to get Eligio or not?"

"Just try to understand how it is for him."

He spit toward the door and then turned away angrily and started up López Mateos. "Why don't you go back to the hotel," I called. "We'll be there in a little while."

He did not acknowledge me in any way.

As I was coming back inside the bar, Gutiérrez met me at the door. "Where is he?" he asked.

"On his way up the street."

Gutiérrez came out on the sidewalk and with his hands cupped around his mouth called his brother's name. But Carlos did not respond.

"What happened?" Gutiérrez asked.

"He went up to the bar to order tequila, and the barman saw that he was underage and threw him out."

"What was he doing drinking tequila?"

"He hadn't been drinking any, but he wanted some. I tried to make him stay at the table but he wouldn't listen to me. I guess he got tired of waiting for you to come back to the table."

"I wasn't gone all that long," Gutiérrez said.

"You were gone nearly an hour."

He looked at me, surprised. "I hadn't realized it was that long."

"I think he's a little jealous of Rosario. He mentioned something about you forgetting that we were sitting there waiting for you."

"Jesus, Mike, I'm sorry. I didn't realize . . ."

"Never mind, you don't have to explain anything to me. You're not responsible for what love makes you do."

"Being in love changes everything," Gutiérrez said. He turned now to look back toward the bar.

"I know. But try not to let it make you forget about your little brother."

"I've never been in love before, Mike."

He seemed almost sad when he said this. He was still in a kind of daze. He stood looking at the door as though trying to see through it to Rosario inside.

"I'm happy for you," I told him, and put my hand on his shoulder. "Do you think I should go after Carlito?"

"Was he hurt?"

"He had a big hole in his pride. Other than that he seemed all right."

"Good. At least it didn't develop into anything serious."

"With him, everything is serious."

Gutiérrez nodded. "Where did he say he was going?"

"He didn't say. I told him to go back to the hotel, but I doubt that he'll take my advice."

"I shouldn't have let it happen."

"Neither should I. But he wants to be treated like a man, doesn't he? We can't force him to do anything anymore."

"The problem is that he's still just a boy."

"I know, I worry about him too. I'll go after him if you think I should."

"I'm the one who should go after him."

"You go back inside with Rosario. I'll go look for Carlito."

Gutiérrez said, "Why don't you come back inside too? He isn't Carlito anymore, remember? Besides, you couldn't find him now anyway. I think we'd better just let him go off by himself and let his pride heal a little."

"You think so?"

"He'd only get angry at us for chasing him. As long as he wasn't physically hurt I think we should leave him alone."

"He wasn't hurt."

"Then come on. Let's go back inside."

Rosario had kept our table free for us until we returned. Gutiérrez sat with me for half an hour, then asked if I would mind if he went to talk with Rosario for a while. He had reached that stage where it was painful for him not to be close enough to touch her. Having never been in love before he must have believed that if he could not touch her she might slip irretrievably away. I sat by myself and drank clamatos and watched all of the other couples in various stages and degrees of love.

After a while three American girls came in and stood uncertainly by the door. Their faces were all as sunburned as mine; and each girl carried a large straw purse which she had probably bought just that afternoon at Bazaar Moctezuma or the Government Sponsored Store. One of them wore a camera with its long black carrying strap slung over her shoulder.

They seemed unsure of whether or not to come further inside. They huddled by the door, whispering and giggling to one another. I stood and waved to them and signaled that there was room for three at my table. After more whispering and giggling they finally made their way over to me and sat down.

"Buenas noches, señoritas," I told them. "Estoy aquí. Atáscate ahora que hay lodo."

"You're not Mexican," one of them said. She was a tall, big-boned girl, though not overweight, and she had a lovely freckled face and sun-bleached hair.

"I most certainly am," I said. "In fact I'm the hijo bastardo of El Presidente himself."

The big-boned one asked, "You're the what?"

The girl sitting next to her, a pretty dark-haired girl with a large voluptuous mouth, answered, "He said he's a bastard." She did not seem very pleased to be sitting with me.

The big-boned one looked at me and smiled. "I can believe it," she said.

The third girl, who was a few pounds overweight but who might have been pretty had she not been sitting between the other two, asked, "Can I take your picture?"

"It won't come out," I said. "There's not enough light."

"It has a built-in flash," she said, and removed the camera from the carrying case.

I put my arm around the big-boned blonde and pulled her toward me and tried to do the same with her dark-haired friend, but the brunette slid her chair away from me and said, "Leave me out of it."

The girl with the camera snapped the picture and giggled. I took my arm from around the blonde girl's shoulders, but she did not slide her chair away from me.

"What's that you're drinking?" she asked.

"You don't want to know."

"Yes I do. That's why I asked."

I handed her the clamato and she tasted it. "Mmmm," she said. "It's good. What's in it?"

"You don't want to know. It tastes better than it sounds."

"Tell me what's in it. I like it."

"You won't like it if I tell you what's in it."

"Yes I will," she said, laughing. She was sitting very close to me and stretched her leg out against mine.

"Just tell her what's in it, for God's sake," the dark-haired girl said.

I leaned toward the blonde and whispered, "Is it just me or does she hate all men?"

She laughed and whispered back, "All men. But she loves horses and dogs."

"Both at the same time?" I whispered.

She laughed loudly and slid her hand under the table and squeezed my leg. The girl with the camera giggled and asked, "What are you two whispering about?"

The dark-haired girl said, "They're just being childish, that's all."

I stood up. "I think I'll get us all some of those unmentionable drinks."

"I don't want any," the dark-haired girl said.

The one with the camera said, "Come on, Beth, try one. I'm going to."

"I said I don't want any. Can't you tell they're making fun of us?"

I stood behind the dark-haired girl and made a face at the top of her head. The blonde girl smiled at me and winked, and the one with the camera covered her mouth with her hand and giggled. The dark-haired girl twisted in her chair to look up at me, but I turned away quickly and headed for the bar.

Gutiérrez remained close to Rosario near the waitress station. Whenever he could he reached out to hold her hand. He was trying hard not to be conspicuous but he could not stop himself from wanting to touch her. He was so much in love that whenever she left the bar to deliver drinks he followed her with his eyes and looked as though he would rather die then even momentarily be separated from her.

When I returned to my table with the drinks, only the tall blonde was still there. "Where is everyone?" I asked.

"Beth convinced Charlene that they weren't wanted here."

I sat beside her and handed her a clamato. "Where in the world would she get an idea like that?"

She laughed and stretched her leg out against mine and sipped her drink. "Mmmm," she said, her voice as throaty as a cat's purr. "Now then, tell me what it's like to be a bastard."

It was nearly midnight when I went up to Gutiérrez at the bar and told him that I was leaving.

"I've acquired a new friend."

"I noticed," he said.

"We're going to take a walk along the beach."

He smiled and patted my shoulder. "I'm glad you found someone to have some fun with. I know it doesn't seem like it, but I feel bad about abandoning you and Carlos tonight."

"You just take care of yourself and Rosario. She's a beautiful girl. I'm happy for you."

"She's finished here in an hour or so," he said. "I'm going to walk her home and then I'll see you back at the hotel."

The blonde, whose name was Diane and who was a history major

at UC San Diego, walked with me to the beach and took off her
shoes to wade in the warm water of Todos Santos Bay. We stopped
for a while to lie in the sand beneath the piers and listen to the
waves crashing against the pilings. Afterward I walked her back to
her hotel, the San Nicolás, and then walked alone back to the
Misión Santa Isabel. I felt hollow and sad and almost wished that
the blonde-haired girl had not come along that evening to sit at my
table. I remembered the almost pretty girl with the camera and
hoped that her feelings had not been hurt.

When I turned on the light and went into our hotel room at the
Misión Santa Isabel I saw that Carlos was already in the bed near
the window. Anyway I assumed it was Carlos, for he lay with the
covers pulled completely over his head and was curled into a tight
ball like a wounded animal. I undressed quickly and turned out the
light and slipped naked beneath the covers of the other bed.

Although physically tired I was not really sleepy and knew that I
would be awake for a while. The smell of Diane was still on me,
especially rich beneath the light cotton blanket. I wondered if
perhaps I should get up and take a shower after having been with
her. But I did not want to wake Carlos, and anyway it occurred to
me that Diane was probably lying in bed too wondering if she
should get up and wash after having been with me. Although I
smiled to myself this thought made me feel bad again. If you
couldn't have Gutiérrez's kind of love you shouldn't have to feel sad
and worried afterwards with the other kind. It shouldn't make any
difference what kind of love you experienced: any love should make
you feel the way Gutiérrez and Rosario felt. But I suppose it isn't
real love if you worry that you should have washed afterward.

I heard Carlos in the bed next to me, crying softly. At first I was
not sure what it was I heard, or even if it came from the same room.
But I lay on my back and listened carefully and soon realized that
Carlos was crying into his pillow, trying to muffle his sobs.

"Carlos," I whispered, "are you all right?"

He did not answer, but held his breath and tried not to make another sound.

"Don't feel bad about what happened tonight," I said.

Still he did not answer. I decided to be quiet and leave him alone.

Five minutes later he rolled over and spoke to me. "Mike," he said, "are you still awake?

"I'm awake."

"Is Eligio here?"

"He hasn't come in yet."

Now he sat up in bed. "Will you come take a look at my eye?"

As I was getting out of bed I asked him, "What's wrong with your eye?"

"I can't see out of it," he said.

I switched on the light and went to him. His left eye was swollen shut, the eyebrow cut and the surrounding skin puffy and ugly. There was a little blood still in his nostrils, but he had already cleaned most of it away.

"How did this happen?" I asked, gently probing the swollen discolored skin around his eye.

"I can't open my eye," he said. "Am I going to be able to see again?"

"You'd better get some ice on that to bring the swelling down. I'll see if I can find some."

I pulled on my pants and went downstairs and brought back a bucket of ice from the ice machine in the lower corridor. I wrapped some of the ice in a washcloth and held it to Carlos's eye.

"You should have gotten ice on this right after it happened," I told him. "It wouldn't look so bad now."

"Is it going to be all right?"

"I don't see anything wrong with the eye itself," I said, though really I didn't know. "But maybe we should go find a doctor just in case."

"No," Carlos said. "I'm not going to any fucking doctor."

I held the ice to his eye as he sat there with his arms crossed over his stomach. "It's a good thing your skin is dark," I told him. "This won't look so bad in a day or two."

"I've had black eyes before, but they never felt as bad as this."

"You took a good one. What did you get hit with—a shovel?"

"It felt like one."

"Who were you fighting with?"

"I don't know who he was. Some gringo cabrón at a bar down on Macheros."

"What were you doing down there?"

"It wasn't my fault, Mike. This guy beat me up for no reason."

"You must have done something to provoke him. Were you trying to buy drinks again?"

"I *was* buying drinks. I was standing right up at the bar and drinking with everyone else. I told you I look old enough."

"Then how did you get yourself beat up?"

"I told you, it wasn't my fault. There was this guy standing next to me at the bar. He and his buddy were telling stories about how many fish they had caught down by the piers that day. I was just standing there listening to his stupid stories like everyone else. Then he reached for his wallet to pay for some drinks, but he couldn't find his wallet until he turned around and saw it lying on the floor behind him. And then the bastard accused me of trying to steal it!"

I had been sitting on the edge of Carlos's bed, holding the ice to his eye. Now I sat back and handed the washcloth and ice to Carlos.

"Keep that on as long as you can," I told him, standing up. "You can wring the washcloth out every now and then in the ice bucket."

I turned my back to him and took off my pants.

"I wasn't stealing the bastard's wallet, Mike," he said. "If I had wanted to steal it, he wouldn't have found it lying on the floor."

I switched off the light and got into bed again. Maybe he was telling the truth. With Carlos it was never easy to tell.

"I believe you," I said.

"The bastard wouldn't have been so brave if he hadn't had his friends there with him."

"Did they gang up on you?" I asked.

"No, but he had them there in case he needed them. He wasn't alone the way I was."

"You should have never gone in that bar in the first place." I was feeling tired and a little bit disgusted with him. "Stop trying to be a goddamn grown-up all the time. You're only fifteen years old. Besides, being grown up isn't all that terrific."

He started crying again. "You should have seen what he did to me," he said. "He held me up by the collar and kicked me all around the room."

Now I wanted to sleep. I wanted to forget all about Carlos or Carlito, forget about feeling hollow and sad and just remember the warm sand beneath the pier and the crash of the waves breaking against the pilings. I was even willing to sacrifice Diane and just think of myself there alone, or maybe put beside me the slightly overweight, almost pretty girl with the camera, who would be very shy and a little bit frightened in the darkness, and who when I kissed her would tremble and cling to me as though if she did not hold tight I might slip irretrievably away.

"That bastard won't be so brave when I get him alone," Carlos said.

"You just go to sleep and forget about everything else."

"I didn't take his goddamn wallet. He didn't have any right to do that to me."

"A lot of things happen that don't have any right to. Just forget about it. In the morning you and Ellie and I will go back to that place and find out what happened."

"I already told you what happened. Anyway I don't want Eligio to know about it."

"He'll know as soon as he takes a look at that eye."

"Maybe the swelling will be down by then."

"Just make sure you keep that ice on it. Now go to sleep and let me do the same. And just forget about what happened tonight."

"You wouldn't forget it if it happened to you."

He had barely finished saying this when we heard Gutiérrez at the door. Carlos whispered, "Don't tell him," slid the ice bucket beneath the bed, and pulled the covers over his head.

Gutiérrez came in and softly closed the door and undressed in the darkness. With his hand he patted the foot of the bed, felt where I was lying, then went around to the other side of the bed and climbed in.

I could smell the scent of Rosario's perfume on his skin. It was mixed with the odor of cigarette smoke from the bar, but I was able to separate the clean spicy aroma of the perfume and enjoy it alone.

"Did you have a nice time?" I whispered.

He turned his head toward me. "Is that you, Mike?"

"It's not Doris Day."

"Sorry. I thought this was mine and Carlito's bed."

"He was asleep in the other one when I came in, so I took this one."

"I'll move over to the other bed," Gutiérrez said.

"Don't bother. Let your brother sleep."

"How is he?"

"He must be all right. He's been sleeping ever since I came in."

"I was worried that he might hang around outside and pick a fight with the bartender."

"I think he's outgrown that kind of thing," I said, hoping Carlos would hear.

"I hope to God he has."

"How was your night?" I asked him.

"Good. Beautiful," he said. "Did you have a good time with your new friend?"

"For a while," I said.

"You smell like you had a good time."

"You smell pretty happy yourself."

"Not like that," he said.

We did not speak then for a while. We both lay on our backs, very close but careful not to touch one another. After several minutes Gutiérrez said, "Be sure to say your prayers, Mike. You didn't bring your pillow, so you can't fool God tonight."

"You say them twice," I said. "And He'll think one of them is from me."

"I wish it were possible to fool God," Gutiérrez said.

"Too tired to say your prayers?"

"It's not that. I'm afraid that if God finds out how much I love Rosario, He'll take her away from me somehow."

"Don't you believe that God wants you to be in love?"

"I don't know. Feeling this good makes me worry a lot. Nothing this good has ever happened to me before."

"Maybe your luck is changing," I said.

He was silent for a moment. "I'd like to bring mama down here," he said.

"We can drive down here any time she's willing."

"I mean I want her to move down her. I know she'd like it if only she wasn't so afraid of moving. She thinks Tito and Leandro will come home some day and won't be able to find her."

"Maybe you can talk her into it," I said.

"I'm going to try."

After that he was silent again, and then rolled onto his side, his back to me. And then, as though he had remembered something he wanted to say, he rolled over again and whispered, "Mike. I have a favor to ask you."

"Go ahead," I told him.

"I want to buy Rosario a present from that store where I first saw her looking in at the window display."

"You can have as much as you need," I said.

"I hate to ask because it's such an expensive store."

"She deserves the best, doesn't she?"

"I'll give you the commission from that dog portrait when I get it."

"Don't worry about paying me back. Get Rosario something pretty. And don't worry about how much it costs."

He lay there for a moment, not answering. Then he rolled toward me and kissed the side of my head. "Mi hermano," he whispered.

"I'd rather have your sister," I said.

He laughed softly and rolled over once more. I lay on my back, feeling tired, wishing I could sleep. I heard the melting ice in the cardboard bucket beneath Carlos's bed shift position and fall. The air conditioner by the window hummed softly. Within a matter of minutes Gutiérrez was sleeping. In my mind I said the Lord's Prayer, first in English and then in Spanish. After that I said Hail Marys and Glorias, repeating the novena to St. Jude over and over again until finally I fell asleep.

It was just after ten the next morning when I awoke. I dressed and washed quickly, not wanting to wake Gutiérrez. Carlos was not in his bed. I assumed that he had gotten up early to go to the beach to get more sun on his face. By the time Gutiérrez finally saw him Carlos would have a good excuse for the condition of his eye; he could say that he had injured it body surfing, or that he had slipped and fallen while climbing over the rocks.

Outside the hotel I walked down López Mateos to a department store on Avendia Gastelum, only a block from the bar where I had drunk so many clamatos the night before. In the department store I

bought Carlos a boogie board just like the one he had found on the
beach and had been made to return. From there I crossed the
Bulevar Costero, and then to the beach. I took off my shoes and
socks and, carrying them in my right hand, the boogie board tucked
under my left arm, walked back up the beach toward the hotel.

On the beach just above the piers an ambulance had made deep
tracks in the sand and was parked near the high-tide line. A crowd
had gathered around the rear of the ambulance to watch a man
who, strapped into a gurney, was being loaded inside. Someone
picked up the man's fishing tackle and shoved it in beside him. The
doors were slammed shut and the ambulance pulled away, its spinning tires throwing sand. It bounced over the curb and sped down
Costero, its siren wailing.

Three local policemen were talking to an American who had
apparently witnessed the incident. They stood over a spot on the
beach where the white sand had been kicked up and stained with
blood.

"No more than eighteen," the American was telling the
policemen, one of whom was writing down the remarks in a small
black notebook. "Probably closer to sixteen. Mexican. About five
feet eight or nine inches tall. He must have just sneaked up on Dick
while he was fishing and attacked him."

"You didn't witness the attack yourself?" the policeman with the
notebook asked.

"Not the start of it, no. I was maybe twenty-five or thirty yards
down the beach. I was on my hands and knees, filleting a corgina I
had just caught. I heard Dick yell and I looked up to see this kid
swinging at him with that knife."

The man speaking nodded toward the policeman's feet. I looked
down and saw two plastic bags, each containing a knife. One knife
was a long, pearl-handled switchblade, the kind commonly displayed in shops along Avenida Revolución in Tijuana. The other

was a knife for the filleting and scaling of fish. Both knife blades were coated with blood and sand and stuck to the insides of the bags.

"That's when you came running up and stabbed the boy?" the policeman asked.

The man telling the story looked out at the ocean and began to cry. "I didn't have any choice, did I? He had Dickie down and I couldn't get him to stop."

I did not wait to hear the rest of the story but went back to Costero and pulled on my shoes and ran to the hotel. In the lobby Rosario was sitting on one of the leather sofas, an open magazine in her lap. She looked up at me and smiled.

"Where's Ellie?" I asked.

"He hasn't come down yet. What's wrong?"

"Wait here," I told her, and hurried upstairs.

Gutiérrez stood in front of the bathroom mirror in our room, combing his hair. I burst into the room, saw him and said, "Carlito's in trouble."

"What kind of trouble?"

I tossed the boogie board across the room onto Carlos's bed. "He stabbed a man."

"Oh sweet Jesus." Gutiérrez stood there holding the black comb at his side. "Do the police have him?"

"No," I said. "But it would be better if they did. I think he must be cut pretty badly himself."

Gutiérrez pushed past me and went running out of the room and down the hall. I caught up with him on the steps. "Where did it happen?" he asked.

"On the beach near the fishing piers. Down below Alvarado."

"Why would he do such a thing?"

"I don't know," I said. There was no use telling him now what had happened to his brother the night before. The only practical thing was to try to find Carlito; or, if he was very badly cut, to pray that the police would soon find him.

Rosario stood and met us as we came into the lobby. "We've got to find Carlito," Gutiérrez told her, whispering so that the desk clerk would not hear. "He's hiding from the police. Where are some places where he might be hiding?"

"I don't know," Rosario said, looking confused. "I suppose there are many places."

"Jesus," Gutiérrez said. "Sweet Jesus, help me. If we were in Tijuana I'd know where to look for him."

"We'd better start going up and down the streets," I said. "There's no place along the beach to hide, so he won't be there."

"What's he done?" Rosario asked.

Gutiérrez said, "I should have been paying more attention to him. It was my responsibility to keep an eye on him."

To Rosario I said, "You'd better go back home. We'll let you know later how things have turned out."

"If I had been spending more time with him," Ellie said, "this wouldn't have happened."

I took him by the arm. "You go left down López Mateos," I said as I led him outside. "And work your way back along the side streets. I'll go up the other end and come back along Reforma and Juárez. Meet me back here in thirty minutes."

"I'm going to wait for you out by the swimming pool," Rosario said.

Gutiérrez, feeling quilty and responsible, ran through the front courtyard and out onto López Mateos. I went in the opposite direction. Neither of us had any specific ideas about where we should look. We simply hoped to come upon Carlito by accident, or to make ourselves visible enough that he might see us and call to us.

I had gotten nearly to the end of López Mateos, at the junction with Avenida Reforma, when I remembered my car parked in the lot at the rear of the Misión Santa Isabel. It was possible that

Carlito might try to break into the locked car, hot-wire it, and drive back to Tijuana. The more I thought of this the more plausible it seemed. In Tijuana Carlito would feel safe, in the dirty narrow streets and dark alleyways. He would know people there who could bandage his cuts and hide him for as long as he wanted to hide.

I ran up Reforma and then turned left down Juárez, turned left on Castillo and crossed over López Mateos to come off Castillo at the rear of our hotel. There was blood on the left front door handle of my car, plus several drops of blood on the pavement. Carlito had been there, but he had not tried to break into the car.

I was standing there beside my car, trying to think of where Carlito might have gone, when I heard Rosario's voice. "Carlos!" she was screaming. "Carlos, por favor! Please come back!"

I hurried to the front of the building. Carlos had crossed over Costero and was headed down the beach toward the water. He was fully dressed and running awkwardly and he ran dragging the new orange boogie board behind him.

Rosario, when I went running past her, shouted, "He came running out past me! He must have sneaked inside from the back!"

I was fifty yards behind Carlito, Rosario following me, both of us calling his name. He splashed into the water up to his waist, fell forward onto the board and, kicking and splashing, paddled out into the bay. I followed him into the ocean until the water came up around my neck. A wave broke against my face, drove me under, and I felt the undertow pulling me further out. Fighting to get back to the shore I went under several times, then finally I found the bottom with my feet and pushed myself back to where I could stand and walk.

At the water's edge Rosario came up beside me. "Can't you go after him?" she said.

"I can't swim."

We watched Carlito getting smaller as he paddled out into the bay. Did he think he was going to float the whole way across Todos

Santos Bay, or did he simply wish to get away from the noise and
confusion so that he could comfortably bleed to death? Maybe he
thought that dying alone was the manly thing to do. With Carlito,
neither boy nor man, there was no telling what his intentions might
have been.

"Aren't there any lifeguards around here?" I asked Rosario.

"There's a rescue station on top of the fishing piers," she said.

"You stay right here. Don't move. I'm going to bring the
lifeguards back and they'll need to know where he went in."

Turning, I saw a crowd had formed behind me. "What's going
on?" a man asked. I pushed past him and started running down the
beach. I had gone perhaps two hundred feet when I heard Gutiérrez
call Rosario's name. He stood just off the Bulevar Costero, looking
down at her. She waved for him to come down and as he ran toward
her she pointed out into the bay. Gutiérrez stopped long enough to
pull off his shoes, and then, tugging at his shirt, ran toward Rosario
at the water's edge.

Now I did not know which way to run. Gutiérrez was no better
swimmer than I. But he was already into the water, running and
falling, then lunging forward, his arms flailing awkwardly as he tried
to keep his head out of the water. I saw him go down once and then
come up again and try to keep on swimming. Running toward the
lifeguard station I prayed out loud as I ran, "Our Father, who art in
Heaven, hallowed be Thy name . . ."

When I returned ten minutes later with the lifeguards, helping
them to drag their rubber raft, Rosario was already sitting on the
beach, waves breaking over her feet and legs, her face in her hands.

At about ten o'clock on Sunday night I returned alone to
Tijuana. When I paid Mrs. Ferretis she asked where Eligio and
Carlito were and I told her that I would explain in the morning.
Gutiérrez's mother was already asleep, so I sat at the kitchen table
in the darkness and tried to think of what I would say to her. I made

coffee and drank a cup and eventually fell asleep with my head on the table.

I awoke to the soft touch of Gutiérrez's mother stroking the back of my head. When I looked up at her she leaned down and kissed my cheek.

"I knew you would be home tonight," she said. "I went to Zola today and she told me you'd be home any time now."

I swallowed hard and tried to think of how to tell her.

"My Leandro," she said, leaning forward with her arms around my head as she embraced me. "I'm so happy you've come home again. And this time I want you to stay."

I turned in my chair and held out my arms to her.

"Sí, mama," I said. "Now I'm home."

One Night with a Girl
by the Seine

THE MAJOR'S WIFE was nearly blind, and so made a great deal of noise as she searched the kitchen for a teabag. She unscrewed lids from tins and glass jars and, after squinting at and sniffing the contents, dropped the lids ringing on the table. She banged shut cupboards and drawers, and finally, muttering to herself, shuffled through the front room and out the door to beg a teabag from her neighbor.

Major Zoya lay in bed and looked down at the white hairs of his chest. To himself he said, "I'll bet she doesn't get a teabag for me."

Tired and dry-mouthed, more weakened by sleep than refreshed by it, Zoya lay there on his back until his wife returned. Then he rolled onto his side and watched Nana muttering and shuffling in the room they called their kitchen, but which was actually little more than a crowded alcove furnished with a small round table, a hotplate, a stack of pots and cracked dishware. The major noticed with detachment how broad through the hips his wife was becoming, and realized how small by comparison he must now look to others whenever he stood next to her.

Nana fumbled through the stack of pots until she found a saucepan. Next she shuffled into the bathroom and filled the pan with water, then returned to set the pan on the hotplate. She waited placidly until she heard the gurgle of boiling water, filled her cup,

131

extracted the borrowed teabag from her housecoat pocket, and counting out loud, dunked the teabag fifty times. She spilled a third of the tea as she carried her cup into the room in which the major lay. She sat in the Morris chair and stared out the window.

"What time is it?" the major asked, still supine on his bed.

Nana said, "Why ask me? How would I know? I couldn't read a clock if you held it to my face."

"Then why," the major asked, tiredly sitting up, "do you waste your time sitting there and staring out the window?"

Nana sipped her tea but did not reply.

"Even if you had the eyes of a hawk," he told her, "there isn't much of a view from that window."

Still she said nothing.

"Are you deaf and dumb as well as blind?" Zoya asked.

Nana sipped her tea noisily.

The major sighed and pushed his legs over the edge of the bed. He stared down at his feet. His toenails were thick and rough, ridged like old bark, the toes themselves yellowed and wrinkled and fat. They did not look to him like his toes. For the past forty years he had been looking every morning at that same pair of feet, and not once had they looked to him as he expected his feet to look. They had changed on him back in Russia, when he was just a boy and serving in the army. And as a result of that experience he now had, here in America, more than forty years later, what appeared to be somebody else's feet.

To his wife the major said, "You're not missing anything by being blind." He stood and, shuffling nearly as clumsily as his wife, went into the bathroom.

Major Zoya stood for a long time at the toilet, and when he came away from it he felt that he had not accomplished anything. Maybe, he thought, when I inherited some stranger's feet I inherited his prostate gland as well. He wondered if perhaps Nana was meant to be somebody else's wife.

After dressing, the major went into the kitchen and poured the water remaining in the saucepan into another cup. There was, as he expected, no second teabag, so he fished the one Nana had used out of the trash and dipped it in his cup. He waited for three full minutes before removing it, but even with repeated dunking and squeezing of the teabag the water in his cup did little more than turn to a very weak tea, the color of chicken broth. Nor was there anything to add to it. He collected the various wine and liquor bottles that lay scattered about the house, but was unable to coax more than a few drops out of all of them combined.

Afterward he stood beside his wife's chair and, like her, stared silently out the window while sipping his tea. When he finished he rinsed the cup in the bathroom sink, set the cup on the kitchen table, and started for the door.

"There's nothing in the house to eat," his wife told him.

"Now you talk," he said. "When there's something you want."

"There's nothing in the house to eat."

"How would you know? Have you learned now how to examine the cupboards by smell?"

"We can't even afford to buy food," she complained. "The welfare doesn't give us enough to live on."

"Why should they? We're not their responsibility."

"I can't borrow anything more from the neighbors. They lock their doors when they see me coming."

"You'll just have to sneak up on them."

"Of course," she said. "It doesn't matter to you if I have to go begging door to door."

"I thought we had a son in this town," Major Zoya said. "Or am I mistaken?"

"You know he's no better off than we are."

"He's young and strong, isn't he?"

"Thirty-eight isn't all that young," she said.

"I was still young and strong when I was thirty-eight."

"But you are Major Zoya," she said sarcastically. "Major Zoya will always be young and strong."

He did not like it when his wife called him Major Zoya. She did so only in an attempt to embarrass him. It was sometimes pleasant when others called him major, as though he actually deserved the title, but it never sounded like praise when it came from his wife. Even long ago when he had first told her of his adventures in France, of how he had been a captured soldier of the lowest rank conscripted to Germany and later to France to help build Fritz Todt's Atlantic Wall, even then she had smiled disdainfully. He recounted for her how he, along with hundreds of other soldiers and townspeople and released prisoners had broken into the streets while church bells tolled LeClerc's liberation of Paris, how every window and balcony was festooned with flags, how everyone had been nearly hysterical with joy. He described for her, perhaps a bit overdramatically, the steady popping of sniper fire near the Arc de Triomphe being answered by French rifleman, the sight of a German tank burning in the Tuileries gardens, an artillery shell exploding at the end of the Champs Élysées. He told her how that day he had discovered the discarded jacket of a German major, how he, Zoya, had ripped off the insignia and wore it pinned upside down on his shirt, and then, playing the clown, had performed an hilarious burlesque of a frightened, fleeing German.

Those joining in the revelry began referring to him as the upside-down major, and years later the story grew to the point where Zoya himself had killed the Kraut and was awarded the insignia as his prize.

But none of this tale, not even with its embellishments calculated to impress Nana, had ever elicited as much as a nod of approval from her. To this day she still called him major only mockingly.

But perhaps, Zoya told himself, he should not have expected an American girl to understand the significance such a day held for a twenty-two-year-old Russian boy. After all, she never came out to watch him when he marched, wearing the inverted German brass, in the local Veterans Day parades. Not that she with her near-blindness would be able to distinguish him from the other gray-haired soldiers, each with his own repertoire of lies and personal distortions of history. Even so, it would be a nice gesture.

Probably he never should have married her. She was only the second woman he had known in an intimate manner, the first and only in America. Maybe in his innocence back then he had believed that two lovers was already wearing himself thin. Had he stayed in Kharkov and not been seduced by a dream of riches, he might have a few acres by now, a strong uncomplaining wife, and three husky sons. He would not be rich but he would have as much as his neighbors, and even if the land was not truly his it would be his to toil and grumble over. Here all he had was a blind woman who stared out the window all day and who each night loudly lamented the smell of his feet, feet ruined by army boots and wet European winters.

Again Zoya sighed. "Maybe we should just forget about eating and let ourselves starve to death."

"You do it first," Nana said. "And then I'll decide whether or not I want to follow your example."

The major turned away from her and went outside.

Out of his house Zoya began to feel a little better. The house always had a faint odor of mildew about it, even in late summer when he threw open all the windows. It was only June now, but the morning sun was hot on the major's face, and as he walked he could feel his pores responding to the increased warmth, could feel some of the stiffness of his joints easing away like slowly melting butter.

He walked in the soft dirt along the highway, close to the guardrail beneath whose stretched wires wild grasses grew. He walked leisurely, in no hurry. He was going nowhere special. The goldenrod and alfalfa and purple-flowered vetch all smelled very good to him. If he had a bottle of vodka now he could walk off the highway to where the grass was high and untrampled and lie there with his chest bared to the sun and drink his vodka and eventually fall asleep dreaming of a girl he had once known in Paris. Every soldier he had ever met had a story about a girl in some foreign country, but his, Zoya thought, was different. His was exceptional somehow. He wished he could get quietly drunk and remember her.

But the major had no money to buy vodka. He hadn't a cent in his pocket. Yesterday he had earned some money by selling a few pieces of old copper plumbing scavenged from a garbage dump, but he had used that money to buy a large can of spaghetti and a box of crackers which he had taken home to his wife. Nana had eaten her share and then complained that it was not enough to live on. Zoya had not failed to notice, however, even though he kept silent about it, the odor of boiled cabbage and potatoes that she had worn like a perfume all night. He knew by this and other signs that she was fed nearly every day by one of the neighbors. So Major Zoya did not worry about Nana. She grew fat and complained that she was starving while he wasted away in silence.

For himself, one good meal every two or three days was sufficient. And since he had eaten just last night, Zoya was not thinking about food now. What he thought about was a bottle of vodka and that girl in Paris. He thought about them as he walked toward town, now and then stepping over the guardrail to retrieve an empty soft-drink bottle from the grass.

The major could sometimes redeem soft-drink bottles for a nickel each, and though it was not reasonable to hope that he would gather enough to buy a full pint of vodka, it was conceivable that he might be able to purchase a shotglassful. And with that exquisite portion warming his belly he might even find some chores to do in town, so that perhaps by early afternoon, while another two hours of sunlight still brightened the sky, he would have earned sufficient money to buy a small bottle.

As he kept an eye out for soft-drink bottles and walked toward town, Zoya tried not to think in too much detail of the girl of Paris. He wanted to save the best of her for when he was lying face up to the sun in the wild alfalfa. But the harder he tried not to remember her, the more the details of their night together came back to him.

Her name was Charlotta and she could not have been more than fifteen years old. He remembered how, later on the day of his release from the prisoner-of-war camp, after the German surrender to LeClerc at the Gare Montparnasse and the victory parade toward Notre Dame, he had moved with the flowing mass of people like a chunk of driftwood caught in the tide until he found himself inside a crowded cafe, where so much fruit and food and champagne was pressed upon him that finally he piled it all atop a table as a kind of open buffet.

Charlotta had been one of the many girls who kept the retired combatants continuously supplied with food and drink. And Zoya remembered how, when he was very drunk, he had finally given in to his desire and seized her by the wrist and pulled her close to him and kissed her. Nor did she protest or push herself away. Until that night he had never been kissed in such a manner. And when an opportunity came, he and the girl had slipped away and found a quiet spot for themselves along the banks of the Seine.

Zoya never would have believed that a girl so young could know so much. Did the French teach their children the art of love in public schools? Her legs were long and thin, their fine blond hairs as soft as down. Her breasts were no bigger than walnuts, and just as firm. The hair in her unshaven armpits was softer and sweeter smelling than the most fragrant, tender grass. She spoke no Russian and he no French, but every now and then throughout that night she had looked at him and smiled sleepily and said words which he first mistook for words of endearment, but which he found out later, when he repeated them for a friend, were "God bless the United States."

It had not mattered to Zoya that, dressed as he was in nondescript green trousers and a bright orange shirt given to him by a stranger, the German major's insignia dangling brashly upside down from his breast pocket, Charlotta assumed he was an American. In fact it was those misinterpreted words, heard a half-dozen times that night, which had helped him to make his decision to come to this country.

Knowing what fate might be his for earlier "allowing" himself to be captured by the Germans, Zoya managed to escape forced repatriation and eventually sailed for America. He had believed that, if the words "God bless the United States" could be accompanied by such passion in a beautiful young girl, then America must truly be a wonderful place.

That had been just over forty years ago. And now here he was in the God-blessed United States, where he had Nana and rotting feet and where he searched for discarded bottles along the roadside. That was what one night with a girl by the Seine had done to him.

By the time he reached the edge of town, Zoya had gathered eight soft-drink bottles into his arms. It was not quite enough for a full shotglass of vodka, but Capello, the tavern owner who redeemed Zoya's bottles, was a generous man. If his wife was not around, Capello might even be counted on to extend a little credit. With this in mind Zoya quickened his pace and allowed himself to grow more optimistic as he headed for the tavern.

Along the way Zoya decided to make a short side excursion so as to pass behind the McNaughton house. Mr. and Mrs. McNaughton were devout Catholics who, with the aid of natural birth control methods, had raised eight roomsful of children. And eight roomsful of children consumed a lot of soft drinks. Many times Zoya had discovered a bottle or two half-hidden in the grass along the periphery of the McNaughton yard. After all, why ask Capello for credit if asking for credit could be avoided? There would be enough times in the future when credit would be needed.

His arms full, the bottles clanking softly as he walked, Zoya worked his way along the perimeter of the McNaughton yard, pushing over the unmown grass with his foot. His efforts turned up only one additional bottle, and a broken one at that. Not wanting one of the little McNaughtons to slice open a bare foot while chasing a ball through the yard, Zoya deposited his burden beside the sidewalk and carried the broken bottle to the row of three overflowing garbage cans lined up against the McNaughton garage.

Major Zoya spotted the case of empty soft-drink bottles even before he had thrown away the broken one. There was a full case of them, twenty-four in all, the wooden box jammed tight against a garbage can. Obviously the box was marked for disposal, though Zoya could not understand why anyone would be throwing away an entire case of redeemable bottles. Twenty-four bottles at five cents apiece, he thought. Five times four is twenty, carry the two . . . why, that's a dollar and twenty cents! With the additional eight bottles lying out beside the sidewalk he had enough to buy a *pint* of vodka. By 10:00 A.M. he could be lying in a field of knee-high grass, his chest bared to the sun, the scent of purple-flowered vetch wafting over him as he dreamed of his night with Charlotta by the Seine!

Major Zoya could not believe his good fortune. Why would anyone be throwing away such a valuable item? Maybe they had only wanted to get it out of the way until they could redeem it themselves. But no; it was obviously meant to be picked up with the rest of the garbage. And today, Zoya thought, unless I am mistaken, is collection day. If I don't claim these bottles for myself, then the garbage collector surely will. And certainly I need them more than the garbage collector does. After all, he gets his pick of the town's cast-offs. It's only fair that I should have these.

The major looked up at the McNaughton house. The windows were as blank as closed eyelids, most of the curtains drawn. No doubt the children were already off somewhere at play; the father at work. Mrs. McNaughton had probably dragged herself back to bed, exhausted by the effort of making waffles and sausage breakfasts, the remainder of which the major identified in one of the garbage cans, for so many children and a husband. It would be cruel to wake her just to inquire about a case of empty bottles. Obviously Mr. McNaughton did not consider a dollar and twenty cents worth bothering about. He would probably be glad to have them taken off his hands. To Major Zoya the bottles were worth a great deal of bother. He picked up the case and quickly turned away from the house, the bottles rattling as the wooden box banged against his thighs.

On the sidewalk Zoya set down the heavy case and laid each of the additional eight bottles across the tops of the others. These extra bottles rode precariously, two of them toppling off into the grass when Zoya first lifted the box again. But the bottles had not broken, and after a few more tries Major Zoya was finally on his way, one dollar and sixty cents clanking and rattling with every step.

The major kept to the back streets as he made his way to Capello's tavern. He saw no reason to make himself an object of curiosity by walking bowlegged down Main Street, stoop-shouldered from the weight of his precious load.

Panting and wheezing, his heart thudding protestingly, Zoya approached the rear of the tavern. Here in the back was an open patio where Capello was known to escape for a few minutes on summer nights, leaving the smoke and noise of the bar behind while he relaxed on the patio swing that hung by chains from the ceiling. On this swing, because his knees felt too stiff to permit him to lower the case all the way to the floor, Zoya deposited his cargo, first having to shoo away two huge cats that had been asleep on the swing.

The swing chains and Zoya's knees creaked as he settled the wooden case onto the seat. He steadied the swing so that its swaying motion did not topple the bottles onto the concrete floor, then went up to the back door, peered into the kitchen, saw no one, and went inside.

Circumspectly Zoya walked through the kitchen and into the barroom. Capello's wife, a short, thickset woman with a carefully layered nest of artificial yellow hair, was presiding behind the bar. Zoya stood at the end of the bar and waited for her to notice him.

Capello's wife was aware of Zoya patiently waiting, but she did not bother to acknowledge him until she had finished washing a half-dozen glasses and had set them on the shelf beneath the bar to dry. Then, as though Zoya's presence irritated her, she turned and looked at him, but did not speak.

He smiled apologetically. "I was hoping to talk with Capello for a moment."

"Keep hoping," she said.

"He isn't here?"

"He went to get a haircut."

"How long do you think it will take?"

"How do I know? Do I look like a barber?"

For a moment Zoya considered redeeming his bottles with Capello's wife, but almost immediately he decided against it. Besides giving him an extra quarter or so for the bottles, Capello would probably treat Major Zoya to a jigger of vodka before sending him on his way. And that little taste would feel good in Zoya's belly and throat, warm as a glowing cinder, and it would help the memories to come even easier when finally he could lie back in the tall grass with his own bottle in his hand.

"Do you mind if I wait for him?" Zoya asked.

Capello's wife regarded him dully and shrugged. "Do you want anything to drink?"

"A glass of water, if you don't mind." Zoya eased himself onto a bar stool.

While sipping the cool water Zoya watched the two men who were seated opposite him at the other end of the horseshoe-shaped bar. They were, Zoya knew, men in the same general economic situation as was the major, and yet there they sat drinking double shots of whiskey with cold beer chasers. Zoya watched them and felt his mouth tingling. He drank his water in noisy gulps. Finally he left his empty glass on the bar and walked across the room to sit with the two men.

"How are you, George?" he said to the one nearest him, then leaned forward over the bar to smile at the second man. "And Curtis," he said, "how are you?"

George smiled drunkenly. "Major Zoya," he said. "How's everything with you?"

"Everything's fine. It's a beautiful day outside, isn't it?"

"It certainly is," Curtis said. He stared down at his beer glass and seemed to be in danger of falling asleep.

"What brings you here so early?" George asked.

"I have some business to discuss with Capello."

"He went to get a haircut," Curtis said.

"A business deal?" George asked.

"Just a small matter to discuss."

"You always land on your feet, don't you, Major?" George said. "Just like a Russian cat." George laughed at this and nudged Curtis with his elbow. "Did you hear what I said?"

"I heard you. A Russian cat. What's so funny about that?"

But George continued to smile at his own joke, smiling until he felt the corners of his mouth turning down as if by some inexorable force of barroom gravity.

Staring into his glass, he said, "Curtis and me can't seem to get nothing going for ourselves."

Major Zoya did not reply. He watched Curtis drink half a glass of beer in a single gulp.

"But you always manage to land on your feet," George repeated. "Just like a goddamn Russian cat."

Perhaps, Zoya thought, he should return to his original seat to wait for Capello. He was about to do so when Curtis roused himself sufficiently to call for another drink. "Bring two more double Velvets," he told Capello's wife. "And two more beers."

All three men watched reverently as Capello's wife poured the whiskey and then drew the foaming beer from the tap. As Curtis was counting out the payment to her from a pile of change on the bar, George turned to Major Zoya and said, "Don't think we're going to let you sit here with us and not drink anything."

The major smiled shyly.

"Bring the major another glass of water," George said.

He and Capello's wife laughed out loud.

Afterward all three men sat in silence, each when not drinking staring down at the glass in his hand. Zoya heard snoring and looked up to see Curtis fast asleep, slouched back on his bar stool. George, when he had finished his own drinks, quietly exchanged his empty glasses for Curtis's nearly full ones. He did this quite casually, as though it were expected of him. He sipped from the whiskey and chased it with beer and then stared down at the lace of foam on the inside rim of the glass.

Every now and then Zoya looked up at Capello's wife. When she met his gaze there was an unsettling contempt for him in her eyes. She had never liked the major, though Zoya could not understand why. Maybe it was simply because her husband *did* like Zoya, liked him genuinely; for it was widely known that Capello and his wife on their best of days could barely tolerate one another. Whatever the reason for the woman's dislike, Major Zoya felt the morning wasting away. He wished that Capello would soon return from his haircut.

After twenty minutes or so Capello's wife left the bar and went out into the kitchen to prepare herself a sandwich. While she was gone Zoya availed himself of the opportunity to lift his head and appraise the bottles of liquor on the shelf behind the bar. Capello stocked two brands of vodka: Smirnoff's and Jacquin's. Zoya preferred the Smirnoff's, though he usually drank the other brand because it was a few cents cheaper per glass.

Looking at the bottle of Smirnoff's as though it were a crystal ball into the past, Zoya remembered that wonderful night in Paris: the clear, clean-tasting vodka, the deep purple and green-tinted wines in tall water tumblers; machine-rolled cigarettes; loud music and singing of "Marche Lorraine" and "La Marseillaise," young Zoya grinning stupidly and attempting to sing along; shrill laughter coming from darkened corners; now and then the distant report of an exploding artillery shell; now and then the crash of a wineglass tossed in exuberance against a wall.

The sound of breaking glass, in fact, was so real, so loud and near, that for a confusing moment Zoya did not know where he was, did not recognize his own lined face in the mirror behind the bar. George, awakened out of his own revery, jerked upright and turned on his stool to face the major.

"What the hell was that?" George asked.

Coming to his senses, Zoya knew immediately what the sound had been. His stomach seemed to turn inside out with fear. Stiffly he spun away from the bar to climb off the stool. Before he could round the end of the bar, however, Capello's wife stepped into the room from the kitchen.

"Who left a case of empty bottles on my patio swing?" she demanded, looking only at Major Zoya.

"Are they all broken?" he asked.

George laughed and said, "So much for your business deal."

"You should have known better than to leave them on the edge of the swing," Capello's wife said.

"But I didn't leave them on the edge. I set them well to the back."

"Then I suppose the wind blew them over." She almost smiled as he stumbled toward her.

Out on the patio Major Zoya regarded his shattered expectations. The wooden case lay upturned on the concrete floor, all but a few of the bottles broken.

"I don't see how they could have fallen off," he said, shaking his head.

"Maybe the cats did it," Capello's wife said. She kicked at one of the cats to keep it from licking the broken glass. "You should have known better than to leave a case of empty bottles there."

Major Zoya stood with his left hand gripping the swing chain as he stared down at the broken bottles. On his fingertips he felt the rust of the chain. He felt weak inside and wished that Capello's wife were not watching him so that he could sit down and bury his face in his hands.

Capello's wife said, "I hope you don't think that I'm going to clean up that mess."

Zoya looked at her. "Could I borrow a broom and a dustpan, please?"

He carefully swept up the broken glass, setting aside the four unbroken bottles until he was finished. Then, certain that not a speck of glass remained on the concrete, he picked up these four bottles and stood beside the rear door. Not wanting to go inside the tavern again, he knocked on the door and waited politely for Capello's wife to appear.

"Everything is cleaned up," he told her. She peered critically over his shoulder.

"I was wondering if I could redeem these four bottles with you. By some miracle they survived being broken."

"How do you know they're not cracked?" she said. "I can't use them if there's so much as a nick out of them."

"They're in perfect condition," he told her. "I've checked them over top to bottom myself."

Eyeing him suspiciously, she reached out and took one of the bottles from him. "These bottles are no good to me," she said. "Look at the name of the bottler. Our distributor doesn't use this brand."

Major Zoya looked at her in disbelief. Capello had never said anything about different bottlers or distributors.

"Read it for yourself," she told him. "These are Spring Valley bottles from eastern Pennsylvania. No one in this town uses Spring Valley. Our distributor only sells Nehi."

She shoved the bottle back at Zoya, who seemed unsure of what to do with it. Helplessly, he asked, "Do you think Capello will be back soon?"

"It wouldn't matter to me if he never came back."

Major Zoya looked at the bottles in his hands.

"Don't leave those lying around where someone can trip over them," Capello's wife said. She gave him a moment to reply, but he said nothing. She stepped inside and closed the door.

Going to the garbage cans lined up behind the building, Zoya pulled off a lid and dropped the four bottles in among the broken glass. He replaced the lid securely, turned and walked away toward Main Street. Capello's wife reminded Zoya more than a little of Nana. He wondered if Capello had ever had a girl in a place like Paris, and if, like the major, he had ever gotten drunk on vodka and wine and been made love to because someone had mistaken him for an American.

There was a second tavern in town, one known for its disreputable clientele, and it was here that Major Zoya went when he left Capello's. He stood just inside the door, looking over the patrons and the barman. Although he knew them all by name he did not feel that he could ask any of them for so much as a quarter. But seeing that the floors were dirty and that a straw broom stood in the corner, Zoya walked up to the uncrowded end of the bar and waited for the barman.

"What will you have, Major?" the bartender asked, coming toward him behind the bar.

"I notice you haven't had time yet this morning to sweep your floor," Zoya said. "I'd be happy to sweep it for you."

The bartender smiled. "That's Donnie McClaine's job," he said. "You know Donnie, don't you? He usually comes in about this time and cleans the place up."

"He must not be coming in today," the major said.

"He'll probably be in. I've never known Donnie to pass up his free beer."

"I'd be happy to sweep for you," Zoya said. "So that your customers can have a clean floor to walk on."

The bartender laughed. "Suit yourself, Major. But I doubt that any of my customers will even notice the difference."

Zoya hurried across the room and took the broom into his hands. His feet had recently begun to ache, to itch and tingle with a warm inflammation, but he found that if he concentrated on the stroke of the broom, the sweep of the straw bristles across the floor, he did not think about his feet so much. He tried as well not to think too much about the drink the bartender would be sure to offer him, but he found this topic more difficult to avoid.

The major swept all of the dirt into a neat pile in the center of the room and was searching for a dustpan when Donnie McClaine came into the tavern. He was perhaps ten years younger than Zoya, stouter through the middle but the same short stature. When he attempted to snatch the broom from Major Zoya's hands all of the patrons stopped drinking and turned at the bar to watch the struggle.

"That's my goddamn broom," Donnie said, straining hard but unable to wrench the broom free from Zoya's grip. "What the hell do you think you're doing?"

"It's not your broom," Zoya protested. "You weren't here on time so the job goes to me."

The patrons and the bartender laughed and shouted encouragement as the two men, each firmly gripping the broom handle, pushed one another back and forth. Some of the patrons cheered for Donnie and a few for Major Zoya. When Donnie stuck his foot between Zoya's legs, twisted the broom handle and pushed the major backward, Zoya lost his balance, stumbled and fell, his bony flanks meeting the hard floor with a thud.

Donnie raised the broom above his head in victory. One of the patrons applauded; another laughed half-heartedly. Then they all turned on their stools to face their drinks again.

"Give Donnie a beer," one of the patrons said.

The bartender drew it from the tap and set the glass on the bar. Still clutching the broom, Donnie came forward and picked up the glass. The major rose slowly, first to his knees and then to his feet, and brushed the dirt from his trousers.

"How about Major Zoya?" the bartender asked, "He put up a good fight. Isn't somebody going to buy a drink for the major?"

"I'll buy him one," a customer said. "I've been a loser all my life, I know what it feels like."

Hearing this, the major looked up at the men at the bar. Donnie stood there smiling at him, red-faced, a glass of beer in one hand and the broom in the other. The major turned and stepped over the pile of dirt he had made and went out the door.

At noon Zoya sat beside the river, dangling his feet in the cool roily water. He sat on his shoes because the shoreline was strewn with sharp-edged rocks, and wriggled and stretched his toes as the brown water flowed over them.

Twenty yards away sat a young boy fishing, and in the time Zoya had been sitting there the boy had pulled out two fair-sized bass. Zoya had never been much of a fisherman himself, but he was intrigued by the way the boy would deftly work the hook free from the squirming fish, then with his thumb in the fish's mouth push upward and snap the fish's neck, killing it instantly. He saw this done twice and he was fascinated by the skill and insouciance toward death that the boy displayed.

When Zoya saw the boy reeling in his empty line and preparing to leave, he hurriedly pulled on his shoes and socks, stood up and awkwardly made his way up the rocky shoreline.

"Are you leaving already?" Major Zoya asked.

The boy, squinting in the sunlight, turned to look at him.

"You're having such a good day, it's a shame to quit so soon."

"I have to go home to lunch," the boy said. He was only eleven or twelve years old but he spoke to the major as a grown man might speak to an equal, with neither deference nor condescension. "I'll be coming back in half an hour."

"Why don't you leave your fishing pole with me?" Zoya suggested. "So that you won't have to carry it back and forth with you."

The boy regarded the major for a moment, then looked down at his rod and reel and tackle box.

"I'm just going to sit here by the river," Zoya told him. "I'll make sure nobody steals your equipment."

Finally the boy smiled and, proving that he was just a boy after all, said "All right. I'll be back as soon as I can." Laying his fishing pole on the ground he picked up the plastic bucket in which were the two fish he had caught, turned away from the river and began to jog up the road, swinging the bucket as he ran.

When the boy was out of sight, Zoya took the fishing pole into his hands and examined it closely. It was a Shakespeare fiberglass rod with a Garcia reel. The major did not know much about fishing equipment but he knew that this outfit must be worth a few dollars. Not that he entertained seriously any thoughts of stealing it from the boy. If he would not accept a drink from a man who called him a loser, especially when he wanted a drink so badly, then he certainly was not going to steal from a trusting boy. Even so, it was a nice-looking rod and reel.

At the end of the fishing line the lure was still attached, a shiny piece of metal curved like the bowl of a spoon, with a hook concealed in a red and yellow feather. Holding this, the major pulled out a few yards of line, then tossed the lure into the water. He watched it sinking down, undulating like a pendulum, its size and shape distorted by the water, the spoonlike metal glinting and spinning as he slowly reeled it back in.

With practice the major was soon casting the line fifteen yards out into the river. The whir of the line gathering on the spool as he reeled it in was a very pleasant sound to hear, monotonous and relaxing. The sing of the fishing line as it spun out in a cast was equally enjoyable. The major was having so much fun, in fact, with the casting out and gathering in of the line, watching the shining artificial bait jerking and skipping just under the surface of the water, that he was caught by surprise by the sudden tug that bent his rod tip toward the river.

For a moment Zoya did not know what to do and so kept jerking the rod tip into the air. Then he remembered the reel and began to reclaim the drawn-out line. The weight of the fish tugging on the line filled the major with excitement, and he had to restrain himself from shouting out loud. He reeled the fish in slowly, afraid that any sudden movement would cause him to lose it, until it lay flopping in the shallow water at his feet, its round marble eye staring up at him, its mottled flesh glinting like silver in the sunlight.

Wrapping the line around the first two fingers of his right hand, Zoya hauled the fish onto the rocks. It was a bass, as big as those the boy had caught, though to the major it could as well have been a whale. The major's heart thudded rapidly as he reached down and tried to pick up the flopping fish, only to jerk his hand away each time he felt its cold flesh moving against his.

Zoya knew that he should kill the fish quickly as the boy had done, but each time he reached for it it flopped against his hand and frightened him. Finally he decided to return the fish to the water. But when he picked up the line and lifted the fish off the rocks, the hook came free and the fish fell to the ground once more.

Major Zoya took this as a sign that he should keep the fish. He lay the fishing pole behind himself, out of the way. He sat and watched the fish as its movements gradually became less frenetic, as it finally lay quietly against the rocks, its gills opening and closing futilely, its marble eye unblinking. Zoya felt a great deal of sympathy for the fish. He knew what it felt like to be a fish out of water. On the other hand, he could not help wondering what a fish like this might be worth to somebody. And anyway, this fish seemed well resigned to its fate already; it had struggled only briefly and now lay there with every indication of being more or less receptive to death.

After the fish had died Major Zoya wrapped it in grass and hid it in a bush beside the road. He hid it not because he believed that he had stolen the fish from the boy, but because the boy might not like the idea of the major using his equipment. Then Zoya returned to the river bank to await the boy's return.

When the boy had come and picked up his fishing pole, the major asked him nonchalantly, "Did you have a nice lunch?"

"Soup," the boy said, and made a wry face.

"You shouldn't have to eat soup on a warm day like this," the major told him. "Unless of course it's borscht."

The boy, in the process of readying his line for a cast, wrinkled his nose.

"What do you do with all the fish you catch every day?" Zoya inquired.

"I don't fish every day," the boy said.

"But when you do, what do you do with the fish you catch?"

The boy shrugged. "Nothing," he said.

"Do you eat them yourself or do you sell them to someone?"

"Usually I give them to my cats," the boy said.

The major thought about this for a moment. Then he said, "There are probably some people who would pay good money for a fresh fish."

The boy looked up at the major and wrinkled his nose again, but offered no reply.

Zoya, placing his hands behind his back, pushed himself to his feet. His knees creaked. He said good-bye to the boy and walked away from the river and up to the road. When certain that the boy was not watching him, Major Zoya retrieved his fish from the bush. Holding it in his right hand against his thigh, he started back toward town.

Major Zoya knocked on nine doors in a row but could find no one interested in buying his fish. He was nearly ready to toss the fish down a sewer grating when the minister's wife, who had been standing in her flower garden and watching him as he made his way up the street, called out to him.

"Major Zoya?" she said. "What do you have there?"

"A fish," he said, holding it up by the tail. He walked over to where she stood. "I caught it myself just a few minutes ago. I thought perhaps someone might like to have it."

"Don't you want it yourself?" she asked.

"I'd love to keep it but I didn't bring a knife to clean it with. Besides, by the time I get it home it might be spoiled."

"Let me see it," the minister's wife said, and reached out to take it in her soiled hands. "It's a nice-sized bass, isn't it?"

The major smiled and accepted her comment as a compliment to his fishing ability.

"Maybe no one wants it because you're asking too much for it," she suggested.

Major Zoya said, "I wouldn't dream of asking anything for it. It's such a beautiful fish that I'd keep it myself, but I didn't bring a knife to clean it with and I don't want it to go bad. But I wouldn't think of asking any money for it. I even caught it with a borrowed fishing pole."

The minister's wife laughed, though Zoya had not intended his explanation as a joke. "Well," she said, "I'll take it off your hands for you. And if you're not in a hurry to get home, why don't you wait around for another twenty minutes or so. My husband will be back then and he can drive you home."

The major nodded and smiled shyly. "I have an errand or two to run," he said. "But I'll be back in exactly twenty minutes."

Major Zoya, who had no errands to run, went down the street to sit in the little park behind the public library. He sat on the grass beneath a thick poplar and stretched out his legs. His feet hurt, but even so the major smiled to himself happily. Surely the minister would insist upon giving him something for his beautiful fish, probably even two or three times what the fish was actually worth. In America you could always count on the salaried representatives of God to be generous. And afterward Zoya could make some excuse and decline the ride home, claiming that he had just then remembered his promise to call on a friend. And with the money the minister would give him he would call on his friend the liquor store clerk, who would make it possible for Zoya to be with an even better and older friend, a pint of Smirnoff's vodka.

The day, which had started out so promising and had progressed so badly, now looked to the major as though it might turn out all right afterall. By three o'clock Zoya could be stretched out in the vetch with the white hairs of his chest curling warmly in the sun, enough vodka inside him to transport him back to the banks of the Seine for a few hours, back into the arms of his first sweetheart, who would whisper her words of national endearment in his ear.

Major Zoya grinned enthusiastically, thinking it ironic that a minister was going to make all of this hedonistic pleasure possible for him. Maybe God was not such a Puritan after all. Zoya closed his eyes and leaned back against the tree. Even his feet had begun to feel a little better.

Zoya knocked at the back door of the minister's house. The minister, a middle-aged man with thinning hair and drooping jowls, opened the door and then stood aside as he waved the major into the kitchen.

"Come in, Zoya," the minister said. "I'll be with you as soon as I change my shirt." He turned, unbuttoning his shirt as he walked away.

"Don't change it on my account," the major called after him, and immediately realized what a foolish thing it was to say.

The minister's wife, standing beside the stove, laughed softly. "Come see what I've done with your beautiful fish," she said.

Zoya walked across the room to her. She stood at the stove, holding a lid above a skillet. In the skillet was Zoya's bass, two thick fillets lightly sprinkled with bread crumbs and fried in butter. Sharing the skillet with the fish was a mound of fried potatoes and onions, their edges crispy brown, speckled with black pepper. The entire kitchen gave off a pleasant fish-and-onion odor.

The major smiled approvingly. "The aroma alone is enough to fill me up."

"This should make a good meal for two hungry people, don't you think?"

Zoya nodded. "I can't believe it's the same fish I caught."

Though a common enough dish, had the major's thoughts been of food his mouth would have watered at the sight of it. But all the major could think of now was how much this simple meal would please the minister. That was the important thing.

"Why don't you have a seat," the minister's wife said. She nodded toward a kitchen chair, then left the stove to plunge her hands in the sudsy water in the sink. "He'll only be a minute or two."

"In that case I'd better stand," the major said. "It would take me that long to get to my feet again."

The minister's wife laughed softly and scrubbed a plate. Zoya wondered what he had said that was funny. For a minister's wife she laughed a little too easily.

Too shy to turn and face the minister's wife directly, Zoya stood close to the stove and stared down at the pan-fried fish. Fortunately, the minister's wife had removed the fish's head, so there wasn't that unblinking marble eye to contend with. The major busied himself with calculating how many soft-drink bottles he would have to gather in order to purchase his own rod and reel, so that he could become a professional fisherman. Maybe it wasn't too late in life to set himself up in business.

He had calculated enough to buy a secondhand fishing pole when the minister returned to the room.

"Well," the minister said loudly, clapping his hands and startling the major. "Are we ready to go?"

Zoya smiled tentatively, wondering if he would have to ride the whole way home with the minster in order to get the money for the fish.

"Just a minute," the minister's wife said. Coming away from the sink she wiped her hands on a dish towel. After returning the lid to the skillet of pan-fried fish she picked up the skillet and held it out to the major.

"Here you go," she said. "The pan's still hot, so put this towel across your lap so that you won't burn your legs."

The major looked at her uncomprehendingly.

"Here," she said, and pushed it toward him so that he finally raised his hands to accept it. "This will make a nice dinner for you and Nana."

"How is your Nana?" the minister asked.

Major Zoya looked at him, then turned to face the wife again. Then he looked down at the skillet in his hands. "I can't take your dinner from you," he said.

She laughed. "It's not our dinner, I made it for you. You didn't think I was taking your fish for myself, did you?"

Zoya smiled weakly. Holding the skillet with both hands, he turned and looked up at the minister, who was grinning at him.

"I'm ready if you are," the minister said.

"You needn't drive me home. It isn't that far."

"Nonsense. It's a good four miles."

"But I'm used to it. I walk it every day."

"Then you'll be glad to not have to today. Besides, that skillet is heavy. Let's go so that we can get that fish home to Nana while it's still warm."

Major Zoya looked at the minister's wife and smiled helplessly. Then he followed the minister outside. The minister's wife went back to the sink and laughed softly.

"Do you believe that Jesus died for your sins?" the minister asked after they had been riding for a few minutes.

"What?" Zoya said, and turned to look at him. The major had been staring out the window at a hillside speckled with the purple flowers of calf-high vetch, the sun still bright and warm but sinking steadily toward the top of the hill.

"Do you believe that Jesus died for your sins?" the minister repeated.

"Which sins?" Zoya asked. He looked down at the covered pan of fish and potatoes and fried onions resting on his lap.

"All of them," the minister said. "Christ died for all our sins." He said it as casually and naturally as if he had said, "It looks like we're going to have good weather for a day or two."

Zoya did not know what to say. He felt that he should say something. Finally he answered, "That was awfully nice of him."

The car had turned off the road and up the dirt lane leading to Zoya's house. With ambivalent feelings Zoya noticed that his son's pickup truck was parked near the front steps.

"We would all enjoy seeing you and Nana in church this Sunday," the minister said.

Zoya said nothing. Maybe his son had a dollar or two and would drive him back into town.

"Some of our parishioners live near here," the minister said. "I'm sure they'd be happy to give you and Nana a ride."

He stopped the car beside the pickup truck, then turned and looked at the major with a broad, hopeful smile.

"Would you like to come in for a minute?" the major asked, wishing it were not the polite thing to say.

"What I would like," the minister said, "is that we might say a prayer together."

Zoya looked away shyly. "I think my son is here for a visit," he said.

The minister laid his hand on Zoya's left thigh. He bowed his head slightly and closed his eyes, his face screwed up as if, it seemed to Zoya, in pain. "Oh Lord," the minister said, speaking toward the pan of fried fish, potatoes and onions, "we ask your blessing on this man and his family. We ask that you fill his heart with your precious Light, that you guide him into our Fellowship. We ask that you lead him to the One True Way, and that you create in him a living testament to your Mercy and Love. In the name of Christ our Lord, we pray. Amen."

The minister looked up at him and smiled. Major Zoya felt a little dizzy.

Leaning across the major, the minister lifted the door handle and pushed open the door. "Don't worry about returning the skillet," he said. "Maybe you could bring it with you when you come to church next Sunday."

The major crawled out of the car, knees creaking, his feet aching the moment he stood up. Turning and stooping he looked back at the minister. "Thank you for the ride," he said. "I'm sure the fish will be delicious."

He stepped back and closed the door with his hip. The minister continued to smile at him through the glass. Zoya turned and went up the short path to his house.

Inside the house Zoya's son lay sprawled out on the bed, one arm hanging over the side, one foot dangling over the bottom corner. He was thirty-eight years old, balding and unemployed, and at the moment he appeared to be fast asleep. He lay with his head in his mother's lap, she half-sitting up in bed, a pillow wedged behind her back and another beneath her knees. Nana, however, when Zoya came in and dropped the heavy skillet on the table, opened her eyes.

"Is that you?" she asked, squinting toward him.

"No," he answered. "It's someone else."

"Nicky's here."

"So I see."

"He brought a bottle of wine," she said. "If you had been here you could have shared it with us."

"Didn't you save any for me?"

"There might be a little left. You'll have to look."

"Where is it?"

"It's around here somewhere. I don't want to move or I'll wake up Nicky."

Zoya searched the room for the wine bottle. He finally found it, lying on its side with the metal cap removed, beneath the bed. He picked the bottle up and held it to the light.

"There's not enough here to wet my lips," he said.

"You should have come home earlier."

"This is a gallon bottle. You could at least have saved me a glass."

"Nicky drank most of it," she said. "Besides, I'm sure you had more than your share while you were in town all day."

Major Zoya regarded his sleeping son. "Did he find a job yet?" he asked.

"He said something about going to Alaska to work on the pipeline."

"He's been saying that for ten years. Wake him up and see if he has any money in his pockets."

"He said he spent everything he had on the wine."

"Can't you at least reach into his pockets and see if he has anything?"

"If you're going to steal from your own son," she said, "don't ask my hands to do it for you."

With her right hand she stroked Nicky's hair, her left hand resting on his shoulder.

Zoya looked down at his son and sighed. Maybe Nicky was somebody else's son.

The major went into the kitchen alcove, found a fork in the coffee tin in which the silverware was kept, and carrying the pan of fried fish went to sit in the Morris chair by the window. He unlaced his shoes and pried them off, wriggling his toes in an attempt to ease their aching. He looked over his shoulder at his wife and grown son lying like drunken lovers on the narrow bed, one of them snoring and the other barely clinging to wakefulness. Zoya wondered if it were possible that, by some mistake or perversity of fate, he had for the last forty years been living someone else's life.

Holding the pan of fried fish and potatoes and onions in his lap, Zoya lifted off the lid and set it aside. Out the window there was nothing to see but his neighbor's house, little more than a shack like his own, the dirt lane, and barely visible through the trees, a grassy hillside growing dark against the sky.

He thought of his night with the girl by the Seine and wondered, for the first time, if perhaps that was someone else's memory.

Nana lifted her head for a moment and asked drowsily, "What's that smell?"

"I took my shoes off," the major said.

"It's not that. It smells like fish."

"I farted," he told her. "Go back to sleep."

With his fork he broke off a piece of the breaded fish and put it in his mouth. The house stank of wine. The fish had gone cold.

A Walk in the Moonlight

T HE CHARGE against Eddie Bailey was open lewdness and indecent exposure. On the sixth of July at shortly after midnight he had stood in the middle of Main Street and urinated on the center yellow stripe in full view of Sheriff Rankin, who at that time was sitting in his patrol car in the A & P parking lot. When the judge later questioned Eddie as to what he had had in mind when he did such a thing, the young man could not offer a convincing explanation and was subsequently fined two hundred dollars, which he was unable to pay. In lieu of this fine he was sentenced to ten days in the county jail. Approximately two hours after his release from the county jail on the afternoon of July seventeenth, Eddie Bailey was observed leaning on a parking meter across the street from the A & P parking lot while eating a popsicle.

"Why in the world would you do such a thing?"

"I had had a lot to drink, your honor. Twelve beers, if I remember right. Though I tend to lose count after the first nine or ten."

"But didn't you see Sheriff Rankin watching you from his car just a block away?"

"Yes sir, I did. As I recall, I think I even waved to him. He didn't wave back."

"What was your purpose in waving—to attract attention to yourself?"

"No sir. Just wanted to say hi."

"And did you realize you were standing under a streetlight?"

"Yes sir, I did. It was too bright to be the moon."

"But it didn't occur to you to go back an alley or somewhere a little more private?"

"Oh, it occurred to me, your honor. I guess it just didn't occur soon enough."

"Um hmm. How old are you, Eddie?"

"I'll be thirty-three in September. On the tenth, in case you want to send me a card."

"Thirty-three years old. Then you're certainly old enough to know better."

"Oh, I knew better a long time ago."

"Were you deliberately trying to antagonize Sheriff Rankin?"

"No sir, I've got nothing against the sheriff. I think he might have at least returned my wave, though. Or at least tooted his horn at me."

"It seems to me that you're taking this whole thing pretty lightly, Eddie."

"No sir, not at all. This is serious business and I know it. I guess I just joke around like that when I get nervous. Some people sweat when they get nervous, but I joke around."

"But you don't deny the charge against you?"

"I'd like to, sir, but I don't see how I can. I was caught red-handed, you might say."

"Then let me ask you this. You see, Eddie, I'm just trying to understand why you would do such a thing. You said you weren't trying to antagonize Sheriff Rankin, and you were fully aware that your actions were illuminated by a streetlight. So was it just because you were drunk?"

"No sir, your honor. I have never been so drunk that I didn't know what I was doing, where I was doing it or who I was doing it to."

"Then what could you possibly have had in mind, urinating in public like that in full view of the sheriff?"

"Relief, your honor. Nothing else. Just relief."

"And you didn't see anything wrong in relieving yourself in public?"

"The only public around to see me, your honor, was the sheriff. And I just assumed that he had seen that kind of thing before. I guess, though, that he must close his eyes whenever he takes a pee."

"That's enough of that, Eddie."

"Though it seems to me it would be a sloppy way of . . ."

"I said that's enough, Eddie."

"Yes, your honor. I apologize."

"Um hmm. All right, Eddie. I don't suppose a few days in jail would do you any good?"

"No sir, I don't honestly see how they could."

"Your fine is two hundred dollars. Can you pay it?"

"Will you take a check?"

"Do you have any money in the bank?"

"Is that important?"

"You can't write a check without money in the bank to cover it."

"In that case, your honor, maybe you'd better just go and send me the bill."

"Ten days in the county jail."

Father McDonald was not a happy man. The girl who had just now left the confessional, leaving the strong scent of her perfume behind like a dropped handkerchief, a teasing reminder, was so young, no more than seventeen. And yet what sins she had confessed to! Though in the back of his mind Father McDonald questioned the authenticity of her sins. She had seemed almost proud of them, as though she were reciting not abominations of God's law but accomplishments. And then she had tried to justify the wrongs with philosophical abstractions. Her arguments left Father McDonald feeling weak, exhausted. He was only forty-two years old, but when she left him he felt twice that age.

Hers was the last confession he heard after Mass that night, the evening of July seventeenth—it seemed she always waited to be last—and afterward he returned to his small, disorderly office and had a glass of concord wine and tried to put the girl out of his thoughts. Her name was Lori; a tall blonde girl with a full, ample, but not overlarge body. She wore all of her clothes just a little too snug, so that the fullness of her hips and breasts were accentuated. Each time Father McDonald raised the glass of wine to his lips he could smell her perfume on his fingers. He hadn't touched her, had he? Why was her scent so strong on his hands, mingling with his own odors, as though he had stroked her hair or tenderly cupped her face between his open palms?

He finished the glass of wine and then went to the bathroom to wash his hands. Afterward he went outside to cleanse himself in the darkness, to walk the street to the top of the hill where he could look down upon the black river, the yellow lights from cars crossing the bridge reflected like fallen golden leaves drifting across the thick surface of the water.

"Everyone feels desires, Father. I don't think I'm strange or bad just because I feel them a little more often than most people do."

"But you've done wrong by giving in to the desires. When you yield to temptation, that's when the sin occurs. Even Jesus was sorely tempted, but he did not yield and subsequently put Satan behind him."

"I guess I don't know how to not yield."

"You have to call on the strength of God. It's there, for all of us. You only need to call on it to receive it."

"Don't you ever give in to desires, Father? I know you must feel them sometimes. All men do."

"I . . . I'm a man of God, child. That makes a difference."

"What I don't understand is why it's wrong. God made us this way, didn't He? He gave us these desires. So why is it so wrong for us to enjoy them?"

"There is a right and a wrong time to fulfill sexual desire. Desire between a man and his wife is a glorification of God. All other desire is promiscuous, and glorifies not God but Satan. Only when desire is sanctified through the bonds of marriage is it free of sin."

"Then why doesn't God wait until we get married to make us feel desires?"

"It's . . . free will. God wants us . . . He wants us to exercise free will."

"So that when we do we can be punished for it?"

"So that we have the opportunity to choose a righteous way of life."

"What if the only reason a man and a woman get married is so they can have sex?"

"What? Then . . . you mean there is no love between them?"

"No, they don't love each other. They got married just so they could have sex together."

"Then . . . sex without love is a sin."

"What if two people really love each other but aren't married?"

"If it isn't sanctified through the bonds of marriage . . ."

"Like the two people who were married but didn't love each other?"

"Marriage implies love. A spiritually pure marriage is one in which love exists between the partners."

"So all those people out there who are married but don't truly love each other, but who have sex together now and then anyway, all those people are sinning?"

"If not for purposes of procreation, or as an expression of love between partners in marriage, then yes, it's a sin. Love is what elevates sex from a mere physical act to a spiritual bonding."

"And all those people who aren't married but who are having sex anyway, they're sinning too?"

"Yes. Of course."

"Then is there anybody left who isn't a sinner, Father? Besides you, I mean."

"We are all sinners. That's why it's necessary that we cleanse ourselves through confession. I've already given you your penance, Lori. I think you had better go now, it's getting late."

"But I enjoy talking with you, Father."

" 'Confession is good for the spirit.' "

"I feel good when I'm with you."

"You'd better go now. It's late."

In the mid-afternoon of July seventeenth, Eddie Bailey was observed by the sheriff's deputy, Dennis Howard, leaning against a parking meter across the street from the A & P parking lot, eating a popsicle. Deputy Howard drove slowly past Eddie Bailey several times. On the second and subsequent such passes, Eddie waved to the deputy, but made no other gestures. The deputy did not return the greetings.

On the fourth pass Eddie Bailey was observed talking with Lori Martin, teenage daughter of Bud Martin, owner of the Zenith Insurance Agency. At this time Deputy Howard parked his vehicle facing west on Market Street, a half-block above where Eddie Bailey still leaned against the parking meter. After observing Bailey and Martin for several minutes, Deputy Howard summoned the girl to his vehicle. He then cautioned her that Bailey had a history of committing acts of open lewdness. Miss Martin explained that she had only spoken to Bailey in passing and that she was even then on her way home from her father's office.

"What are you eating, Eddie?"

"What's it look like? It's a frozen rat on a stick."

"Let me taste it."

"Just suck it. Don't bite."

"Mmmm, chocolate. You just got out of jail today, didn't you?"

"Not more than two hours ago. I'm free at last."

"Did you miss me?"

"Why do you think I've been standing here, baby face? Just waiting for you to come wiggling down the street."

"There goes Dennis. Boy, is he giving you the evil eye."

"Wave to him. He likes it when I wave. I think he has a crush on me."

"What's he stopping for?"

"He'll just sit there for a while and watch us. That's how macho deputies get their rocks off."

"As compared to some people who like to take their pants down in public?"

"I didn't hear you complaining."

"No, but I was laughing so hard that I thought Rankin was going to see me."

"Did you hear what I told him when he asked me where the hell I thought I was?"

"You said something about the planet earth."

"'Planet Earth, third planet from the sun, outhouse of the universe.'"

"But Rankin didn't seem to think it was very funny, did he?"

"The man has no sense of humor. Too much animal fat in his diet; got his arteries all clogged up."

"What was it like in jail, Eddie?"

"It wasn't a day at the beach, if that's what you mean."

"Geez, locked up for ten days. Did you miss me very much?"

"Look close, sweet thing. This isn't a mouse in my pocket."

"Don't be crude, Eddie."

"I thought you liked me crude. I'm normally very sophisticated."

"Sure you are. Can I have another lick of your popsicle?"

"Here, finish it."

"Oh jesus. What does Dennis want now?"

"Wave to him. He enjoys that."

"I'd better go see what he wants or he'll report me to my father."

"We know what he wants, lover. The question is, will he get it?"

"I'd better go. I'll see you later."

"How about tonight? You and me and my mouse?"

"I'll have to go to Mass and confession first."

"What's a sweet thing like you have to confess?"

"You'd be surprised, Eddie."

"Not after tonight, I hope."

"Okay. But I can't meet you until late."

"I don't care how late it is, just as long as we have more than teasing tonight."

"Will you bring something to drink?"

"Never fear. Midnight by the river?"

"If I'm late you can start without me."

"Not tonight, sugar. After ten days in jail, tonight is Rosie's night off."

"Don't be crude."

"*Excusez-moi.*"

Father McDonald stood on the hill overlooking the river. He could not get the girl out of his mind. It seemed that even the lightest breeze drifting down from the top of the ridge carried her scent. He had instructed her to say one hundred Hail Marys, one hundred Our Fathers, to meditate daily on the grace of God. He had told her that she must learn to focus her thoughts on her heart and mind rather than on her body and the gratification of her physical senses. And yet even as he gave her these instructions he had been inhaling her scent, feeling it fill him like a warmth-producing balm, the sweat trickling down the inside of his shirt. He had watched her lips move when she spoke, he had even imagined that he could taste her breath: it had a warm, cinnamon taste, lingering in his mouth as though he had run his tongue over her teeth. He had felt her legs move beneath the table, and felt her feet scrape the floor; the slightest vibration produced a rippling effect inside of him, an effect which even now, as he reluctantly remembered her, spread out and tingled like a mild electric shock through his limbs.

"How many times?"

"I don't know exactly, Father. I didn't keep track."

"More than ten?"

"Maybe ten. Give or take one or two."

"And each time with a different man?"

"Does that make a difference?"

"Yes! Yes. Yes, in the eyes of God, it does."

"You mean it's more sinful to do it once each with two different men than it is to do it twice with the same man? Father? Did you hear me?"

"Yes . . . it's . . ."

"It's more sinful with two men?"

"In the eyes of God. Yes."

"But why? That's like saying it's a bigger crime to rob two different banks than to rob the same bank twice."

"It's . . . God's law is not the same as man's law. It's a question of involvement. By involving another human being in a sinful act you have compounded the evil."

"Sometimes we just touch each other. You know, with our hands or our mouths."

"Stop. Don't . . ."

"Father? Are you all right?"

"Yes. You must . . ."

"I just don't understand why it's wrong to touch someone. Everyone enjoys being touched. Don't you, Father? Don't you feel pleasure from being touched?"

After cautioning Miss Martin about further contact with Eddie Bailey, Deputy Howard, on the afternoon of July seventeenth, then offered her a ride home. She accepted. She indicated to Deputy Howard that she intended to spend the evening at home with her parents, after first attending Mass and confession. After leaving Miss Martin at her place of residence, Deputy Howard then continued his usual practice of patrolling the borough. At eight o'clock that evening, Sheriff Rankin came on duty, relieving Deputy Howard. Deputy Howard reported to him his observation of Eddie Bailey earlier in the day, but he failed to mention that Bailey had been seen in the company of Miss Martin. Deputy Howard then returned to his own place of residence. He showered, ate dinner alone, and watched television. As to why he later appeared in the small park beside the river, Deputy Howard explained that he frequently had trouble sleeping, and that on such occasions he sometimes went for a long drive in his car, a practice which he found peaceful and relaxing.

"What were you doing talking to him?"

"I *told* you, Dennis. Just talking. What did it look like we were doing?"

"You know why he was in jail, don't you, Lori?"

"Of course I do. Everybody knows why Eddie was in jail."

"I want you to stay away from him. He's a deviant."

"He took a piss on Main Street. Don't make it into such a big deal."

"I suppose you think it's all just a big joke."

"As a matter of fact, I do. So if you're going to take me home, Dennis, take me home. I'm not in the mood for a lecture."

"What are you in the mood for?"

"Right now? How about this?"

"For chrissakes, Lori, not while I'm driving. At least wait until we get out of town."

"Don't pretend you don't like it."

"Jesus, wait a minute, can you? I'll pull over somewhere."

"No, don't stop. I don't have time now."

"You never have time."

"That's not true, Dennis. It's just that I've got to get home before my father does."

"Can you get out for a while tonight?"

"I don't know. Maybe. If it's worth getting out for."

"Listen, you're the one who never wants to go through with it. You just get out. I'll make it worth your while."

"First I have to go to Mass and then confession. And then I'll have to stay at home for a while until my parents are asleep."

"What time can you get out?"

"Meet me in the park by the river at two o'clock."

"Jesus, why so late?"

"I told you, I have to make sure they're asleep before I can sneak out. But if it's past your bedtime, Dennis, forget it."

"You'd better not keep me waiting half the night."

"Just don't get there before two."

"And no games tonight, okay? No excuses?"

"I'm ready if you are."

"Oh yeah? Then how about a little something to tide me over until then?"

"Sorry, Dennis. Daddy'll be home any minute now. Thanks for the ride."

Father McDonald stood on the hill overlooking the river. With every inhalation he filled himself with the scent of the girl's skin and hair and breath. He had been outside for a long time now, trying to concentrate his thoughts on the depth of the star-filled sky, the vastness of God. Instead he could think only of the girl. Her scent was everywhere. It was a warm night but Father McDonald trembled inside his black suit. At the same time he felt sweat trickling from his armpits. He turned his gaze from the sky to the black river far below. The river in the darkness was like another sky, its stars the headlights of automobiles crossing the bridge, the yellow lights of campfires and cottages in a linear constellation along the length of the river. Thinking of the river, of its ever-changing, always-moving sameness, brought a semblance of peace back to the priest. Maybe if he walked down to the river and stood on the bridge with the water churning by invisible beneath his feet he could meditate fully on the eternal mystery again and force the girl from his mind. Maybe he would even go to the small park by the river and sit on the boat launching pad with his feet dangling in the water, as he had enjoyed in his youth. One thing was certain: he was not going to sleep tonight; not unless he found some way of exorcising that girl from his mind.

At ten minutes to midnight, Lori Martin crept silently out of her parents' house, rolled her bicycle off the back porch and pushed it across the yard and to the road. Then, mounting her bicycle, she pedaled casually, in no hurry, the mile and a quarter to the river. She had no fear of the darkness and rode without a bicycle light, the moon illuminating the white stripe along the edge of the highway, the yellow stripes down the center. As she rode she felt the warm wind in her face, felt it clawing back her hair like a lover's wild hands. She unbuttoned her blouse and allowed the wind to pour over her breasts, her nipples hard and erect, her skin stippled with goosebumps. She passed a man who was walking along the side of the road with his eyes raised to the moon, but she did not cover herself or acknowledge his presence in any way. Like a specter, a Godiva, she glided by proudly, her prominent breasts glinting like alabaster in the moonlight. Her eyes were watering from the wind of her movement so that she could not distinguish the man's face, but her body felt his body tremble and quicken, felt the rage of desire the glimpse of her naked breasts stirred within him.

At a few minutes before midnight on the night of July seventeenth, Eddie Bailey swam langourously through the black river, his strokes slow and graceful, arm arching out and then slashing through the water, palms cupped as though to hold a woman's breast. He swam naked, the sudden chill of a cold current tightening his testicles and making him increase his pace until, in the warmer, slower current again, he rolled onto his back and drifted luxuriously downstream, the moon overhead three-quarters full and shining upon him with a smiling Bacchus face.

Father McDonald saw the moon as a broken communion wafer, flat and thin. As he walked he stared at the moon intently and tried to will it to grow in the sky, to become so vast that its immensity would swell and smother him, choking out his troubling thoughts. But just as the wafer began to enlarge, to move out of its flat dimension and toward him, he was distracted suddenly by a low humming noise growing louder behind him. He turned and saw her, her blouse fluttering open and her breasts free, her chin arched like that of a ship's proud figurehead. The breeze of her movement past him brought her scent with a renewed freshness, flooded and filled him with it. He turned once more and followed her, hypnotized, down the road to the river, across the bridge, his body humming in echo to the hum of her bicycle wheels gliding across the bridge's gridwork.

Deputy Howard glanced at the mantel clock again. It seemed an eternity until two o'clock. He got out of his chair and switched off the television. He paced back and forth in the darkened room, going to the window to peer out, then turning from the window, then going to it again. Finally he went outside to sit on his front porch steps. It was not yet even midnight; he rubbed his hand over his groin and questioned his ability to wait another two hours. The night was warm and smelled of mown grass. The moon was large and white and looked to the deputy like a huge unblinking eye, cold and accusative. To escape its penetrating gaze he got in his car and began to drive. He drove fifteen miles out of town; anxious, impatient. Finally, telling himself that he might as well wait for her beside the river, that he might as well be there ready and waiting when she arrived, Deputy Howard made a wide U-turn across the empty highway and drove at an erratic, nervous pace back through the town.

At the river Lori Martin climbed off her bicycle and crept stealthily toward the boat launching pad at the river's edge. There she saw Eddie Bailey's small pile of clothing and heard the murmuring splashes as he swam through the water. She heard him singing softly to himself, heard the water lapping against the rocky shore. Giggling, she scooped up his clothes and hid them behind a tree. Fifteen yards from the river's edge she removed her own clothing, her blouse, shorts, panties, and shoes, and left them in a pile atop a picnic table. Then, advancing lightly, she approached the river. To Eddie Bailey's soft singing she swayed from side to side, dancing, feeling the moon like a spotlight irradiating her body.

Father McDonald could no longer bring himself to look up at the broken wafer of the moon. He followed the girl's scent as surely as if it were a visible, well-marked trail. Veering off the highway, he completed the last hundred yards to the small park beside the river by following now the barely perceptible sounds of someone singing, of splashing in the water. He came into the park and saw her, the vague outline of her dancing body, the gray silhouette of her breasts against a darker background. He felt his legs growing weak, numbing, and knew that he must either sit or fall. Glancing to his left he saw the picnic table and, not wanting to be heard, to interrupt her dance, he walked quickly to it. As he sat he discovered her clothing, and gathered the three pieces into his hands. He pressed the clothing to his face. Her scent, dizzying and sweet, engulfed and overwhelmed him. He swayed from side to side, inhaling her, breathing her in. He felt himself swell huge and diffuse, his body dissipating to become one with her odor. Clutching her clothing to his face, he looked up at her dancing body fifteen yards away, moaned inaudibly and, as her scent overtook him, slumped forward and passed out.

From the river Eddie Bailey saw her there on the shoreline. He swam up to her, not yet emerging, floating at her feet while she danced lightly back and forth. When he rose up from the river to reach her, the moon-limned water dripping from his taut body like mercury, molten silver, she backed away, smiling. He fell back into the water and she came forward again, teasing, dancing, just out of reach. As long as he lay still she hovered over him, stroking her hips, scooping up handfuls of water to pour trickling over her breasts. When he turned as though to rise, she moved away. They did this several times, never touching, she waiting until the last possible moment and then stepping away adroitly. Finally Eddie Bailey, shivering now in the water, could stand the teasing no longer. *Goddamn you!* he screamed, his cry a detonation of sudden noise that startled the girl and brought Father McDonald, still clutching the girl's clothing, back to a dazed and trembling consciousness.

Deputy Howard's car came wheeling around the turn off the highway and made a sharp right into the small park beside the river. He had his finger on the light switch and was just about to extinguish the headlights when their beam caught the two naked figures running like sprites from the river. Eddie Bailey had, just as the headlight beam caught him, seized the girl's wrist and pulled her hard against him. Now, however, after squinting for a moment into the blinding light, he pushed her away and ran for his clothing. She ran toward the picnic table in the opposite direction, where she found Father McDonald sitting rigidly, her clothes clutched in a tight ball and pressed to his chest. Deputy Howard lept from his car and, not knowing whom to pursue, shouted hysterically at Bailey and the girl. In the meantime Eddie Bailey darted back and forth, searching for his clothes, screaming obscenities. The girl, after recovering from the initial shock of finding the priest in possession of her clothing, tried to wrestle them free from his grasp. But he, feeling her hands gripping his, her naked breasts pressed against him, her legs straddling his, understood nothing she said, and held tightly. The touch of her skin upon his black suit burned him like a cinder; scorched him, he thought, like a branding iron. Lori Martin crawled wildly over the priest, her breasts in his face, the brush of her pubic hair scraping back and forth over his leg as she straddled him, tugging and screaming at him to release her clothing. Meanwhile, Eddie Bailey, unable to recover his own clothing, ran laughing to the nearest tree, grabbed a low-hanging branch and swung his legs up over it, then hung by his knees and, scratching his armpits, affected the shrill, cackling howl of a chimpanzee. Deputy Howard stood beside his car, confused, not knowing in which direction he should run, unsure of whom to apprehend. Finally he grabbed his pistol from the glove compartment and fired it into the air. The explosion of gunshots, six thunderous detonations as the deputy unloaded his pistol toward the moon, froze everyone as they stood. It was in this position that Sheriff Rankin, as he sped into the park with his blue and red lights flashing, found them.

"Now let me see if I've got this right. You, Reverend McDonald, had simply gone out for a walk in the moonlight?"

"That's right, your honor. I had some things on my mind that I needed to clear up."

"Anything I should know about?"

"No, your honor. It was a spiritual matter. I thought perhaps a walk to the river would be helpful."

"Do you often take such walks at midnight, Father?"

"On occasion, your honor. Probably two or three times a week, I'd say."

"You have trouble sleeping, I presume?"

"Yes sir. Sometimes a great deal of trouble."

"So your participation in this, uh . . . incident . . . was purely coincidental?"

"Yes, your honor. When I found Miss Martin's clothing there on the picnic table, I assumed that someone had been swimming during the day and had accidentally left her clothes behind. So I had no idea that I wasn't in fact alone. Then all of a sudden Lori appeared, shouting and upset. She startled me. I suppose that's why I reacted the way I did."

"Um hmm. All right, Father; I see no reason to doubt your word. And I can certainly understand how the sudden appearance of an unclothed girl would be a startling sight, especially to a . . . to a man in a meditative state of mind."

"Thank you, your honor."

"Which brings us to you, Deputy Howard. You still claim that you, too, were there purely by accident? That you were out for a drive in the moonlight and . . ."

"And I just pulled into the park to turn around again to go back home, your honor."

"Do you do this kind of thing often?"

"Turning in the park, your honor?"

"Driving around at night."

"Oh, yes sir. You see, me and Sheriff Rankin alternate on night shift. So I'm used to being awake at that time of night."

"You also have trouble sleeping?"

"That's right, your honor. Sometimes I can't get to sleep until three or four in the morning."

"Seems as though we have something of an epidemic here. Now let's see—Sheriff Rankin says he followed you to the park, Deputy, because you, and I quote, 'came roaring through town like a bat out of hell.' What was the reason for your haste, Mr. Howard?"

"None, your honor."

"No reason or no explanation?"

"No reason, your honor. Just carelessness, I guess."

"In that case, I'll leave it to your discretion, Sheriff, as to whether or not you wish to cite your deputy for speeding and reckless driving. I would certainly recommend that you do. I might also recommend that he be issued a reprimand for discharging his pistol willy-nilly. In fact, some additional punitive measures would not be uncalled for, but that's entirely up to you, Sheriff. Other than that, I'm through with you, Mr. Howard."

"Thank you, your honor."

"And the next in line is Miss Martin. Don't look so worried, child; I'm not going to bite you. You went for a swim in the moonlight, is that correct?"

"Yes, your honor. I know it was wrong for me to sneak out of the house like that, but it was so hot last night and . . ."

"And you couldn't sleep."

"That's right, your honor."

"Somehow I knew you were going to say that. And do you often go skinny-dipping alone at night?"

"No sir, I never have before. I don't know why I did it but I'm sorry, I know it was wrong, and I promise that I won't ever do anything like that again."

"There, there, child, you needn't cry. I might, however, suggest to you, Mr. Martin, that in the future you keep yourself better informed as to your daughter's whereabouts each night."

"Yes, your honor. I plan to do that from now on."

"Then I won't be seeing you here again, Miss Martin?"

"No sir, your honor. Never. I promise."

"All right, then. Let's see, where were we? I guess that brings us back to you, Eddie."

"Nice to see you again, Judge."

"Well, we'll see about that. I suppose you couldn't sleep last night either?"

"No sir, as a matter of fact I couldn't. So when I heard that there was an insomniacs' convention down by the river . . ."

"For the moment, Eddie, I'd prefer the truth to your wit. You went to the river for a swim to cool off. But you had no idea that Miss Martin was there?"

"No sir, no idea at all. I mean, what would a sweet young thing like her be doing by the river at midnight? You see, I was already in the water before she ever got there. And when I saw her coming I naturally climbed right out."

"Naturally, Eddie?"

"For the sake of decency, your honor. So that she wouldn't have to share the river with me and all my criminal nudity."

"So instead you just walked right out in front of her, stark naked?"

"Now that was the tricky part. You see, I had to get to my clothes, but she was between me and them."

"Why didn't you just call out to her and warn her that you were there?"

"I guess I didn't want to startle her. I thought maybe I could just sneak out without being seen."

"So you tried to sneak out past her to get your clothes."

"Yes sir. But my clothes weren't there where I left them."

"And just how do you suppose they got moved, Eddie?"

"That's a good question, your honor. I've given it a lot of thought, and I think possibly it was a raccoon."

"A raccoon."

"Well, I think my shoes would be too big for a squirrel to handle. Unless of course there were two or three squirrels working together. But personally, I'm pretty much convinced it was a raccoon. You find a coon with size ten feet and we'll get to the bottom of this mystery in no time."

"You know, Eddie, it's begun to occur to me that you have something of a problem when it comes to dealing with figures of authority."

"You know, your honor, that same thing has occurred to me time and time again. Do you think maybe I had poor potty training?"

"What puzzles me is why, if your only objective was, as you claim, a moonlight swim, you were seen holding Miss Martin by the arm and were also heard swearing at her rather vigorously."

"That is a little puzzling, isn't it, your honor?"

"Do you have an explanation, Eddie?"

"Actually, I wasn't swearing at her at all, but at that damn raccoon."

"Um hmm. So you weren't in fact exposing yourself to Miss Martin?"

"I might have been *exposed*, your honor, but on the other hand, so was she. Not that I'm complaining about it."

"She, however, was observed by Deputy Howard trying to escape you."

"I think maybe Deputy Howard was too busy playing with his gun to have observed anything, your honor."

"Miss Martin has already testified that you did not attempt to molest her. So the only thing I'm concerned with now, Eddie, is Sheriff Rankin's charge against you for a second episode of open lewdness and indecent exposure. Maybe you'd care to explain that business of hanging from the tree and screaming like a monkey."

"Well, your honor, the whole situation struck me as kind of ridiculous. I guess my primeval instincts just got the better of me."

"You did expose yourself to four people for a period of ten minutes or more, did you not?"

"Only until I found my clothes, your honor. Besides, I wasn't the only one running around naked."

"Miss Martin, however, made an obvious attempt to recover her clothing. Nor does she share your illustrious history, Eddie."

"History never was one of my best subjects, your honor."

"Is that all you have to say in your defense?"

"Yes sir, I guess that's about it. But if you'll give me twenty-four hours I'll bet I could find that thieving raccoon."

"I think maybe you've said and done enough already."

"You know, it's kind of funny, but I've been thinking that very same thing myself. Maybe you and me are psychic twins, your honor."

"I doubt it, Eddie."

"You never know. You don't eat animal fat, do you?"

The Fatalist

O N A MORNING in Holy Week, near the end of March, the handyman Augusto Rivera overheard Leona Carneiro de Assíz plotting with her maid to kill the banker, Simón de las Gracias. When Rivera heard this he realized that while the bank manager was being murdered would be the perfect time to rob him.

Rivera had always wanted to rob his friend Simón, ever since they had been boys together playing in the almond grove. This was not because Rivera disliked Simón; on the contrary, he held him in great esteem. And this esteem, along with Rivera's almost instinctual complacency, was why the handyman had never robbed the boy who grew up to be manager of the First National Bank of Popayán, Colombia, even though that boy had always seemed to have a pocketful of money while Augusto Rivera, first as a child and now as a man, seemed always to have none.

Because he liked Simón and even these days played an occasional game of billiards or shared an occasional pitcher of beer with him, Augusto Rivera had been reluctant to engage in a crime which might, if it did not go off just right—and how many crimes do go exactly as planned?—result in some physical harm for his boyhood friend. In other words, if caught in the act of burglarizing Simón de las Gracias' home, Rivera might be compelled by the whims of fate to knock down or strike or even shoot the banker in order to make

183

good his own escape. And this Rivera was never willing to chance. Besides, he was basically a lazy man. In the end, coping with his poverty had always seemed a less onerous chore than making a complicated effort to increase his wealth. If fate wanted him to be wealthy, Augusto Rivera reasoned, wealth would come to him.

So when he overheard the plot to murder Simón de las Gracias, it seemed to Rivera that wealth was being laid at his doorstep. All he had to do was to open the door and pull the wealth inside.

He tried to consider the situation philosophically. If Leona Carneiro de Assíz was intent upon murdering the banker, then perhaps Simón's number was truly up, and Leona was simply the unwitting instrument of fate. It was wisest, Rivera knew, not to attempt to interfere with fate. Let fate take its course. At the last moment you could always rush in and try to gain some advantage from fate's sudden twists. Lucky for him he had overheard fate in the making. Too bad for the banker, of course. On the other hand, Rivera consoled himself, his friend had had a pleasant life, albeit a brief one. Besides, if everything went as Leona Carneiro de Assíz and her maid intended, the banker would have only a minute or so of pain during which to contemplate what had happened to him.

Leona Carneiro de Assíz had sent word to Rivera the night before that she would require his services in the morning. "Be here at eight o'clock sharp," she had told him, "so that you will have time to get the car ready. We expect to do a full day of shopping, so don't plan on getting home until at least six in the evening."

Rivera, of course, had had to obtain permission from his land-lady, Señora Albujar, before he could go off for a full day as chauffeur on a shopping spree. But Doña Carmela would never stand in his way if he had the opportunity to pick up a little spending money. She realized that the three-room guest house she rented to Rivera in exchange for his occasional duties as gardener, chauffeur, handyman, and companion was not sufficient to sustain a handsome young man of thirty-four. She even promised to postpone dinner until his return so that he could tell her of the adventures of his day. Actually she wanted only to hear of the extravagant purchases made by Leona Carneiro de Assíz so that the Doña, an old woman of limited income and experience, could be the first to entertain her ancient friends with a fresh bit of exaggerated gossip.

So on the following morning Augusto Rivera rose with the sun, washed and shaved and dabbed on a little cologne from the bottle Doña Carmela had given him the Christmas before. Then he walked the two miles across town to the villa owned by García de Assíz, the mining engineer who flew around all day in his helicopter, overseeing the operation of various platinum mines up north in the Chocó Department. Rivera could have taken the bus or even a taxi to de Assíz's estate, but to him the early morning, still pink with new sunlight and clean with the smell of dew, was the most salubrious time of day. As he walked he entertained himself with speculations concerning the interrelatedness of all things. He kicked a round stone down the street and wondered if the tumbling motions of that stone somehow altered the equilibrium of the universe. He plucked a flower from a windowbox and, holding the dripping stem to his ear, listened for a tiny complaint. Hearing nothing, he determined finally that the universe existed in such perfect balance that almost no event, large or small, could upset its harmony.

At de Assíz's estate he obtained the key to the garage from the gardener, a small middle-aged Indian who had already worked up a sweat by digging a shallow trench from the back door to the rear of the high stone wall that enclosed the villa. Wiping his head with a handkerchief, the gardener followed Rivera to the garage and complained in a whisper, "Today she wants a brick path that leads nowhere but straight into a stone wall. Next week she'll have me tear up the path and put in a trout stream."

Rivera laughed. "At least she keeps you busy. It's better than being out of work."

"And I suppose that working a man to death is better than letting him enjoy his few moments on this earth? No wonder her husband stays away for weeks at a time."

Rivera swung open the garage door and stepped inside the cool earthy-smelling darkness. "Each man lives the life Fate allocates to him," he said.

The gardener grunted disparagingly. "Thoughts like that are easy to swallow when your life has been dipped in sugar."

Rivera switched on the overhead light, took a chamois that was hanging from a nail in the wall, and snapped the cloth over the car's hood, chasing away invisible specks of dust. "You forget who you're talking to, friend," Rivera said without a hint of enmity. "Look at me: I have nothing. I own no home, no car, I have no money in the bank and only one good suit to my name. My parents died twelve years ago, and my only sister, whom I will probably never see again, ran off with a musician to Buenos Aires. I don't even have a family. You, on the other hand, have four healthy children, a plump little wife, your own house, your own pickup truck, a couple of dogs, a valuable skill, and a steady income. You have everything and I have nothing. Even so, do you hear me complaining about how unfairly I've been treated?"

Again the gardener grunted, then turned and stalked away, mumbling to himself. Rivera climbed into the car, a huge black 1967 Buick brought by boat from New Orleans, and drove it out into the sunlight. While listening to music on the radio he brushed lint from the car's seats with a little whisk broom. Then he cleaned the windows and the dashboard. Afterward he got a can of pine-scented air freshener from the garage and sprayed it throughout the car. He locked up the garage and drove the car around to the front of the house, where he then climbed out and leaned against the side of the car with his face lifted to catch the sun.

Rivera felt content, as he did nearly every morning. Because he was a fatalist it was easier for him to accept his station in life. And because he was also a lazy man, his ambitions were small. And the smaller one's ambitions, he often reminded himself, the greater are one's chances of obtaining happiness.

Twenty minutes later Leona Carneiro de Assíz and her maid Alecia came hurrying out of the house. "Good morning, ladies," Rivera said cheerily, and held open the rear door for them. "Isn't this a glorious looking morning?"

"Let's get going," Leona growled. "We want to have breakfast in the city."

Leona Carneiro de Assíz had once been the prettiest girl in Popayán. She was still quite attractive, at dusk and in candlelight even beautiful. But now, at forty years old, her cynical nature seemed to have risen up from the depths of her heart to spread out in a thin veneer across the surface of her face. Fifteen years ago the flesh of her face had been as smooth and mouth-watering as the meat of the sweetest papaya, but for every wrinkle now creasing her forehead, for every filamenting toe on each of her crow's feet, there was a bitter story of envy and betrayal.

Perhaps if she had had any children her heart might not have hardened like a raisin. But very early in her marriage Leona had realized that her husband did not love her. He loved his helicopter, and flying at a crazy tilt over the sprawling bowls of the platinum mines. He loved playing poker and getting drunk and sleeping with teenage whores who could scarcely spread their legs wide enough to accommodate him. He had married Leona Carneiro for only one reason, because she had been the prettiest girl in Popayán. Someone was needed to manage the villa he had purchased, to play hostess at the lavish dinner parties he then gave twice a month. But the days of the dinner parties were past; these days García de Assíz seldom even came home twice a month. When he did, Leona simply gritted her teeth, clenched her jaw, squeezed shut her eyes, and spread her legs until he went away again. After twenty-one years of gritting and clenching, it was no wonder that her face had assumed the qualities of a maguey bloom—beautiful, yes, but sitting deceptively atop a prickly body of danger and threat.

Her maid Alecia was the closest thing to a child of her own that Leona would ever have. But what an uninspiring child Alecia was. Barely sixteen, a mulatto, Alecia was inarticulate nearly to the point of dumbness. She had been chosen by Leona precisely for the attributes which might have caused other employers to turn her away. For in the past Leona had discovered too many of her shapely, giggly maids earning their wages in her own bed, riding her laughing husband as though he were a hobby horse. Two years ago she had made up her mind to stop acting as her husband's procurer and had deliberately set out to hire as her personal attendant a girl so ugly that not even for spite would her husband be tempted to coax the girl to bed.

Alecia had fit the bill to a T. Pale and shapeless as a slug, she had a mouth that was too wide and crammed full with crooked teeth, a broad nose that seemed always to have a ripe pimple or two peeking out from a nostril, a fuzzy black moustache that make-up could not hide, and several thick black hairs sprouting like mycelia from her chin. So self-conscious was she that she would seldom raise her eyes to you, but if she did you would not know into which eye to return her gaze, for they seemed to be peering off in opposite directions like those of a steer that has been hit in the head with a mallet.

Only when alone with her mistress did Alecia become a human being and not just a mindless blob fit for nothing but ridicule and abuse. Leona protected her servant; she coldly stared down anyone who felt the urge to more than glance at Alecia. Any boy foolish enough to call out one of the cruel epithets to which Alecia had become accustomed soon found himself backed against a wall while

Leona jabbed him with a sharp finger and gave him such a tongue-lashing that he would not show his face in public for a week. A few such individuals even ended up in jail, charged with harassment and verbal assault.

In return Alecia was devoted to her mistress. She constantly praised Leona's beauty and poise, she combed her mistress's hair and ironed her dresses and would allow no one else the honor of polishing Leona's shoes. So when Leona revealed her plan to murder Simón de las Gracias, it was only natural that Alecia should swallow her own misgivings and readily agree to help.

In Popayán Leona and Alecia had their breakfast in the rear booth of a crowded coffeeshop. After returning from parking the car, Augusto Rivera waited near the counter until another booth became available. He was seated and had already ordered a large breakfast, the price of which was to be added to Señora de Assíz's bill, before he realized that the booth adjacent to his, separated by a high, thin partition, was in fact occupied by Leona and her homely maid. Rivera thought nothing of this until he overheard Leona saying "shoot the sonofabitch." Naturally he assumed that she was referring to her husband and speaking only figuratively. He took a sip of coffee, then laid his head against the partition so as to hear better.

". . . get away with it any longer," Leona was saying, her whispered voice husky with suppressed anger. "He's a shit just like every other man I've ever known. When they get tired of screwing you and turning your breasts into shapeless globs with their pawing and sucking, they think they can just toss you aside and get somebody else."

Rivera covered his mouth with his hand so as not to laugh out loud. He knew, as did everyone in town, of the nature of Leona's relationship with Señor de Assíz. But still he could not understand how even her husband could ever tire of screwing Leona. Rivera himself had been with her twice, and those were two nights he would always remember. They were the nights, he told himself, whose smoldering memories would keep him warm through his old age.

On both nights Leona had been drinking heavily. She had telephoned and said that a fuse in her electric box had blown, and could he please hurry out and replace it? The first time this happened he had told her that a fuse was a simple thing to replace, and gave her instruction over the telephone on how to do it herself. But she was very persistent. It was obvious from her slurred speech that she was drunk, and from the fact that she offered him an exorbitant amount of money if he could get there within fifteen minutes. So in the end he had agreed to hurry out by taxi and rescue her from the darkness.

When he got there he found every light in the house ablaze. Alecia met him at the door and said that he was to go upstairs to the mistress's bedroom. It was necessary to go through the bedroom to get to the lavatory, Alecia explained.

"The lavatory?" he had said. "Why do I want to go there?"

"It's clogged up," Alecia told him. "That's why she called you, isn't it?"

"I thought she said a fuse had blown."

"There's nothing wrong with the fuses. It's the lavatory."

The second time this happened he knew better, of course, than to question whether it was the plumbing or the electricity that needed attention. Nor was he surprised the second time when, as he knocked lightly on the bedroom door and then stepped inside, Leona pounced on him drunkenly and dragged him to the bed. In fact on the second such episode they did not make it as far as the bed, but fell in a writhing heap to the floor.

She had clawed and bitten and scratched him on those nights until he felt scraped raw. But what a glorious rawness it was, and how sweetly his flesh tingled the next morning! That first time, however, he had made the mistake of remaining with her in bed after she had passed out. When she awoke in the morning, surly and fuzzy-headed, to find him kissing her breast (a breast which, by the way, in his opinion bore not the slightest resemblance to a shapeless glob), she had thumped the back of his head with her knuckles and ordered him out of her house. For the second such encounter he had been wise enough to steal away while she was still unconscious.

The last of these two episodes had occurred only a few months ago. Ever since then Augusto Rivera had been hoping that she would telephone again with a plea that he come to unclog her plumbing. In fact he had hoped that even tonight, after a hectic day of shopping, she might seek relaxation in too much wine and later invite him to her room to have a look at her lavatory.

But for now it appeared that fate did not hold such a fortuitous adventure in store for him. He sat with his head against the thin partition and listened as Leona anathematized all men, as she told Alecia how much better off the world would be if every single penis on the face of the earth would all of a sudden drop off like rotten fruit shaken from a tree. The mere thought of such an occurrence made Rivera ache between the legs. He squeezed himself just to make certain that it had not already happened.

Then Leona said something that came as a complete surprise to Rivera. "For six years the sonofabitch has had me whenever he wanted me," she told Alecia. "In six years I never denied him once. I've let him screw me in my own house, in every room in his apartment, in the back seat of his car. He's even screwed me inside his office while other people were lined up outside waiting to beg for a loan. It was *my* money that got the sonofabitch promoted to manager, and now he has the nerve to announce his engagement to that whore of a dancer!"

Rivera nearly choked on a mouthful of food. Sputtering and coughing, he pressed a napkin over his mouth to muffle the sounds. As soon as he was able he gulped coffee and washed the mouthful down.

Rivera's shock, however, lasted for only a few moments. Because he was a fatalist almost nothing could surprise him for long. He had heard rumors about his friend Simón and the Señora de Assíz, but so had he heard rumors about Leona and a dozen other men. He did not doubt that Simón had slept with her. What surprised him was that she seemed to attach so much importance to their relationship.

The dancer to whom Simón de las Gracias was engaged, and to whom he had publicly announced his engagement only last night, was a lithesome young woman on tour with an amateur troupe from the University of New Mexico. Rivera had gone to one of their performances three weeks ago because he had been told by a friend that the sheerness of the bodysuits worn by the dancers left little to the imagination. But he had found the modern dance routines distracting. Each of the six dancers lept and bounced and rolled across the floor apparently at whim, with no uniformity of rhyme or reason. If this was art it was an arcane, inaccessible art. It was like trying to understand someone who was speaking to you in a foreign language. Rivera had found their movements so upsetting, in fact, that his sense of confusion permitted him very little sexual arousal.

But apparently Simón de las Gracias had been able to transcend that confusion. Every night during the week of performances he had waited backstage with a bouquet of long-stemmed roses in his hands. The dancer to whom the roses were offered was named Tina. She was a shy and attractive nineteen-year-old of Japanese extraction. To Rivera's way of thinking she was too short and her legs too thick, but it appeared that Simón de las Gracias did not share these prejudices. Several times that week he and Tina were seen having breakfast together on the terrace of one of the more popular cafes. Although there had been a great deal of speculation concerning those two, the general consensus had been that Simón was simply enjoying a bit of fun, engaging in yet another of the lighthearted, frivolous romances for which he was so widely known.

But yesterday it had been made clear that the townspeople had underestimated Simón's involvement with the girl. Two weeks after she had left Popayán with her dance troupe, Tina returned to town alone, only to be escorted back from the train station by Simón de las Gracias. She had strutted down the street like a prima ballerina, people said, and not merely a short-legged college dancer. The banker walked beside her, barking at the overloaded porter who hurried behind them, struggling with her bags.

De las Gracias had then supervised Tina's installation in the Lindbergh Hotel. He had even gone as far as to bribe the resident of the finest suite to move to another room, and had tipped the bellboys in advance with instructions that they attend to the dancer as though she were the Virgin Mother herself come to enjoy the festivities of Holy Week.

That evening, at the most expensive restaurant in town, Simón de las Gracias had stood at his table and, tapping his butter knife to the water glass, ordered the entire room silenced. He asked that everyone's glass be filled with champagne, and then announced that he had persuaded the dancer, "the most talented and beautiful woman ever graced by the hands of God," to abandon her "whirlwind tour" and return to humble Popayán to become his wife.

"He made an ass of himself," Leona said contemptuously. Even through the partition Rivera could hear the hiss of venom in her voice. "He didn't even have the decency to tell me about it beforehand. I had to hear it at the same time as everyone else, right in the middle of my strawberry torte. And that whore of a dancer—she just sat there like a dumb cow staring into her plate. Whirlwind tour my foot! He only wants her because she's a North American and has those slanty exotic eyes. She's not even a god-damn professional!"

In her anger Leona's voice had risen above the clatter of dishes and the murmur of the breakfast crowd. Alecia reached across the table and patted her mistress's trembling hand.

"Shhh," Alecia warned. "You mustn't let anyone know how you feel." Then Alecia began to weep. "I can't stand it when you're unhappy. It makes me feel so miserable that I want to die."

"Well," Leona said, whispering again in her frozen, tightly controlled voice, "you're not going to die. And neither am I. But somebody else is."

It was at this point in the conversation that the idea of robbing Simón de las Gracias began to take shape in Rivera's mind. Simón had no living relatives, so why should all of his riches—not a great wealth when compared to de Assíz's estate, of course; but certainly a sufficient amount to be regarded as riches by a man like Rivera— be wasted on the state?

And it was obvious from the resolve of her voice that Leona would not be talked out of her decision. Fate was fate; destiny, destiny. It wasn't wise, Rivera told himself, to get your fingers entangled in the cosmic cogs. He could have argued with Leona— and quite persuasively, he thought—that it was unreasonable for her, a married woman who was obviously unwilling to sacrifice her own social status and wealth, to demand fidelity from a young bachelor. It was unreasonable for her, a woman whose promiscuity was well rumored if not well documented, to expect a virile man six years her junior to affect an almost priestlike abstemiousness. Besides, what difference did it make if he got married? Marriage need not necessarily diminish his affection for her; on the contrary, as was so often the case, it might even enhance it.

These were all valid arguments, but arguments which Rivera knew would be to Leona like snow on the Sahara. She did not mind so much that the banker had added another filly to his stable, so to speak. What bothered Leona was that he had not enlisted her collusion, he had not come to her and said, "Listen. Why don't I get married so that no one will have cause to suspect that we are lovers? Why don't I make a big deal out of it, so that it will seem as though I don't even care that you exist?" What bothered Leona was that, for the moment at least, Simón de las Gracias truly did not care that she existed, that he had without hesitation publicly turned his back on her monetary and social influence, that he had sucked and pawed her breasts into shapeless globs and then without a moment's notice had moved on to breasts so firm the nipples still pointed upward like tiny banana tips.

For these reasons, Simón de las Gracias had to be killed. It would teach him a valuable lesson. "No one can use me the way he did and get away with it," Leona told Alecia. "If there's any using to be done, I'm the one who's going to do it."

She planned to shoot the banker early the next morning in the almond grove outside of town. That way the shots would not be heard, and several days might pass before his body could be found. Several days during which his firm-breasted, short-legged fiancée would suffer terrible anguish and concern, unsure of whether or not she had been abandoned to fend for herself in a country whose language she could barely speak.

"Tonight," Leona told her maid, "you will telephone him and say that it is urgent that he meet me at dawn in the almond grove. Make sure you impress upon him how important it is that no one knows whom he is meeting. Tell him that my life and his future depend upon it. He'll think it has something to do with my husband. If he refuses to come, remind him of what will happen to his bank if I decide to withdraw all of my money."

"I'm not sure I can carry it off," Alecia said. "Just looking at him I get weak and confused in the head."

"You won't have to look at him over the telephone. Just picture him in your mind as what he truly is—a shit, a pile of opportunistic walking slime. Think of what he's done to me, of how miserable he's made my life."

"All right," Alecia said. "I'll do my best."

"Good. And when he drives into the almond grove tomorrow, you'll be there to meet him. You'll direct him through the trees to

this little gully I know of, then you'll stand watch and let me know if
anyone else comes near. He'll know the place where I'll be waiting;
it used to be our meeting place whenever García came home. But
this time that little gully will be his grave and not his bed. I'll be
waiting for him with one of García's pistols hidden in my purse.
And when that lying banker comes up to me with his arms out-
stretched, giving me that shitty smile of his and his line of flattery
and bullshit, I'm going to give him just enough time to get nervous,
and then I'm going to shoot his pecker off."

Alecia gasped. Augusto Rivera, despite the wave of melancholic
sadness he felt at the thought of losing a boyhood friend, clamped
his hands over his mouth to restrain his laughter. One thing he had
to admit about Fate: it certainly had a good sense of humor. Rivera
could even picture the startled expression on Simón's face when he
looked down to ascertain the extent of his emasculation, his manhood reduced to a throbbing, blood-spurting stump. Imagining
such a scene might even have made Rivera gasp and shudder, as it
did Alecia; but, being a fatalist, he was able to accept the inev-
itability of such a tragedy and to appreciate the humor in it as well.

"I'll let him howl for a minute or two," Leona said, "while he
contemplates a life without his manhood. Then after he's experienced the total horror of it I'll finish him off. We'll bury him in the
gully underneath brush and dried grass, then I'll drive his car, with
you following in mine, to a place where no one would ever think of
looking for it."

"But I don't know how to drive," Alecia said.

"In that case you'd better drive his car. I wouldn't want you to
have an accident in my Buick."

Augusto Rivera ignored his breakfast, which by now had grown
cold anyway. More important than food was this opportunity that
had been thrust in his face. Briefly he considered running to his
friend Simón at the earliest possible moment and warning him of
the conspiracy. Surely the banker would find some suitable way of
expressing his gratitude.

On the other hand, dire consequences might befall anyone who attempted to interfere with the machinations of fate. Rivera had once read somewhere that the community of mankind was in fact one single large animal, and it was necessary for parts of that animal to be sacrificed at times so that other parts could evolve and survive. Death and tragedy were integral elements in the natural scheme of things. Look what had happened to the islands of Hawaii because they had been fiddled with: imported sheep and goats and pigs ran wild, exterminating native plant life; erosion turned once lush mountainsides into hummocks of dirt; a tropical paradise was slowly becoming a wasteland. There was little left to do with Oahu, in fact, except to pave it over with concrete and put up a giant Ferris wheel.

And all because someone had thought to improve upon the natural scheme of things. Rivera certainly did not want that kind of blame laid upon him one day. Besides, there was another important factor to be considered, and that was the safe which Simón de las Gracias kept in his apartment. Frequently the local merchants brought bags of money to de las Gracias' safe after the bank had closed to be kept there until the following morning. It was even suspected, because of jokes about the instability of government-backed banks which de las Gracias was heard to make when he had been drinking, that he kept all of his own money, including the collection of foreign gold coins he had been augmenting since childhood, in his own safe.

So all Rivera had to do, he reasoned, was to wait until de las Gracias drove off to meet his fate in the almond grove in the morning. Rivera would then gain access into the banker's apartment and go to work on the safe. That way he could not be accused of interfering in even the slightest manner with the destiny of the banker. And since tomorrow was Holy Thursday the banks would be closed; Rivera would have all day, and all night if he wished, to get the safe opened and emptied. As a personal challenge, however, a kind of testing of fate, he would allow himself only three hours. If after three hours the safe refused to yield its fruit, Rivera would simply sneak out of the apartment, walk down the street and refresh himself with a glass of beer. Nothing would be lost or gained. He would accept such a stalemate as his preordained destiny.

This, then, was the plan Augusto Rivera formulated while Leona Carneiro de Assíz and her maid Alecia perused the boutiques and clothiers of Popayán—and gradually filled the front seat of the Buick with their purchases. Throughout the day Rivera dozed behind the steering wheel, waking out of his somnolence when his name was called, then driving ahead two or three blocks only to park the car again, jump out to retrieve the packages thrust upon him, load the packages into the front seat, and then climb in behind the steering wheel again to nap until the next advancement.

By the end of the day Rivera's neck and spine were stiff, his muscles cramped and taut. But later, as he carried the purchases into Señora de Assíz's house and thought about what the morning would bring, he felt his energies renewed. It was not often that he was given the opportunity to watch fate from the sidelines and to know all the while which way the play would go.

In the foyer of her home Leona handed Rivera his salary for the day. In addition she presented him with a hand-tooled leather belt with a turquoise and silver buckle.

They stood alone in the cool shadows of the foyer, Rivera with his back to the door. "I had to guess at your size," Leona told him, "but I'm sure the belt will fit you. My hands have a pretty good memory for the size of your waist."

Rivera felt a tingling flush in his chest and between his legs. "Maybe you'd like me to unclog your lavatory tonight," he suggested.

Had Señora de Assíz not been in such a good mood she would have rapped him on the top of his head and pushed him out the door. But with the excitement of tomorrow morning warming her blood, she merely laughed and gave him an affectionate pinch on his buttock. "Too bad you're such an ambitionless man," she told him. "You and I would have made a good pair."

For the first time in his life Augusto Rivera wished he had made something of himself. Maybe Leona would have a different opinion of him if he came to her with a suitcase full of Simón de las Gracias' money. Unfortunately, Rivera realized, he was a fatalist, and as such was not entitled to any elaborate speculations of what might have been. He would simply have to allow things to happen as fate saw fit. Otherwise he might inadvertently cause Popayán to go the way of Hawaii.

An hour or so before dawn on Holy Thursday, Augusto Rivera rose from his bed and splashed cool water on his face. He brushed his teeth, shaved, and dressed. Then, traveling along back alleys and narrow paths frequented only by neighborhood dogs, he walked toward the heart of Popayán, toward the apartment house in which Simón de las Gracias lived.

The morning was dusky and cool. Rivera thought he could detect a strange scent in the air and inhaled deeply. He imagined that he could smell the ocean, though the ocean was over the mountains and more than four hundred miles away. But rather than being refreshed and revivified by this aroma, as he would have been on any other morning, Augusto Rivera felt peculiarly agitated. There was a tension, he imagined, in the air itself; a force or pressurization like that which exists before a thunderstorm explodes and rattles the sky. But the humidity was low and there was no chance of rain.

Rivera attributed this disquieting sensation to his own nervousness. "Calm down," he muttered, and reassured himself that he was fated to do whatever he did, that even his smallest movement was already programmed into the cosmic design. Finally he blamed his edginess on his empty stomach. He promised himself that later in the morning, whether he had cracked the safe or not, his fate would include a sumptuous breakfast of at least five courses.

On the outskirts of town Leona Carneiro de Assíz had already deposited her servant girl at the mouth of the almond grove. Then Leona drove on through the rows of trees, the dirt lane barely wide enough to accommodate her gleaming black Buick. The Buick crept along at little more than five miles per hour, softly purring, slinking, it seemed, like a huge sleek cat crouched low for a pounce. The interior of the car still smelled of perfume and pine-scented air freshener from the day before.

After emerging on the far side of the almond grove, Leona parked her car only a few yards from the bowl-like declivity in the earth where she and Simón de las Gracias had coupled on several occasions. She could even pinpoint by the flatness of the grass in the gully the exact place where they had last spread their blankets. She switched on the car radio, tuned to a local station, and waited.

The radio announcer was giving the daily weather report. Too nervous to pay attention, Leona heard only fragments of his report. She got out of the car and went down to the grassy gully, squatted and urinated. She carried with her a red leather purse in which was the twenty-five caliber revolver she had taken from her husband's den. Then she returned to the car and climbed inside again, but after a few minutes she nervously switched off the radio and climbed back out. She stood at the front of the car, drumming her fingers on the hood, the purse with the pistol inside resting on the bumper. Unconsciously she leaned into the curved eye of the headlight and rubbed her crotch against it. Her vagina itched. The nipples of her breasts felt swollen and sore.

At the other end of the almond grove Alecia was so nervous she could not stand still. Already she had hidden behind a tree three times to squat and piss. When she remembered the telephone call she had made to Simón de las Gracias the night before, her heart beat so feverishly that she felt compelled by the sudden weakness in her knees to sit down. She had had to telephone him five different

times, for it was not until well after midnight that he had answered.
When finally she heard his voice on the other end of the line she
felt as though her lungs had collapsed, her chest a vacuum, and she
had hung up without uttering a sound. For this Leona slapped her
on the top of her head and then gave her half a glass of brandy.
After a quarter of an hour Alecia tried again. This time the banker
answered sleepily. Alecia had then closed her eyes, drew a deep
breath and mechanically recited her lines:

"Be at the United Fruit and Nut almond grove at dawn tomorrow morning. Your future happiness and the life of Señora de Assíz
depend upon it. For your own sake don't tell anyone where you are
going. I will meet you at the mouth of the grove to direct you to
her. Considering the help she has been to you over the past six
years, you cannot deny her this one small favor." Without waiting
for his response, Alecia hung up.

During the next half hour Leona's phone had rung almost inces-
santly. Leona sent Alecia, who by now was nearly in tears, to bed.
Each time the telephone rang Leona would pick up the receiver and
then slam it down again, breaking the connection. Finally at about
1:00 A.M. the telephone fell silent. Leona spent the remainder of the
night dozing fitfully in the cowhide-covered chair in her husband's
den, the loaded pistol in her lap.

Now Alecia paced uneasily between the trees in the almond
grove, in and out of the shadows. The top of the sun was peeking
now above the horizon, throwing a broad stream of pink light well
into the rows of trees; shining, it seemed to Alecia, like a powerful
spotlight searching her out. She felt more ugly than usual and
wished she could burrow beneath the mat of rotting leaves and drift
into an unconscious stupor. It seemed that even the insects and
birds resented her presence there. They flitted about, buzzing and
chirping in greater agitation that Alecia, who had grown up in the
countryside, could remember having ever witnessed before. It was
as if they knew of the crime she was about to help commit. She felt

herself losing control of her bladder and hurriedly squatted behind a tree.

Augusto Rivera squatted in the morning dusk of an alleyway and watched as Simón de las Gracias emerged from the front door of his apartment house. The banker paused momentarily on the sidewalk to stretch and yawn, to cast an appreciative glance toward the brightening sky. He then walked to his automobile parked at the curb. Simón was dressed casually in a short-sleeved shirt and tan slacks. He looked as though he were on his way to a picnic. Perhaps he expected to engage in a bit of early-morning adultery. In any case he moved with a graceful nonchalance one would not expect of a man who was about to have his pecker shot off.

Alecia saw the dim glint of the headlights of the banker's car from a quarter mile away. "Oh God," she mumbled, arching up on her toes. "Oh sweet Jesus, here he comes." She shivered, although the morning had already warmed, and, pressing her legs together, tightened her sphincter muscles. Simón drove up to the tree behind which she cowered. Winding down the window he leaned out, his armpits over the sill, and smiled at her.

"Hey there," he said, his handsome grinning face making her dizzy. "What's all this silliness about?"

Alecia feared that she could not speak, but to her surprise the words came out anyway, though they sounded to her as clumsy and faltering as square wheels. "She's waiting for you through the grove at the little gully. You know which one?"

He arched his eyebrows suggestively. "The gully of love?"

She did not know whether to giggle or cry. The banker looked at her homely face, the mouthful of crooked teeth and the wall-eyed, pole-axed expression, and shuddered involuntarily, thinking to himself how fortunate he was to be so attractive.

"What does she want to see me for?" he asked.

Alecia ducked behind the tree and pressed her forehead to the trunk.

"Is she upset because of my engagement?" he asked.

She dug her fingernails into the bark and, curling her toes, stifled a frightened squeal.

Getting no response to his questions, Simón de las Gracias pulled his head back inside the car. "Well," he announced, "I guess I'd better go talk to her. If I know Leona, she's probably angry enough to skin me alive." He laughed when he said this, then lifted his foot from the brake to the accelerator and drove away. Alecia slumped against the almond tree and, whimpering like a puppy, felt incapable of voluntary movement as she involuntarily wet her pants.

Getting into the banker's apartment presented Augusto Rivera with very little difficulty. He simply walked up the three flights of stairs to the top floor, encountering no one along the way, and at the door to Simón's apartment used a stiff piece of wire to pick the lock. This was a method he had perfected several years earlier, before he had had the foresight to borrow his landlady's house key long enough to have a duplicate made. Not that he ever stole anything of value from Doña Carmela. But sometimes, especially late at night, his stomach growled so loudly that he could not sleep. It was on these occasions that his stiff piece of wire and then his duplicate key had come in very handy.

In fact, once safely inside the banker's apartment Rivera began to suspect that his empty stomach might prevent an effective campaign against the safe. Besides, today was Holy Thursday and people would be sleeping late, so perhaps he could expand his three-hour deadline to allow for a light breakfast.

In de las Gracias' kitchen Rivera ate two bananas while preparing himself a sandwich from a plate of leftover chicken in the refrigerator. While he munched on the sandwich he explored the three rooms.

The living room and kitchen were of the kind you might expect in the home of a banker—practical and neat, neither overly plush nor austere. The bedroom was of another sort entirely. The bed was huge, a massive four-poster with a blue Persian-tassled canopy. There were stereo speakers mounted on each of the walls, the two side walls tiled with squares of gold-veined mirrored glass, the other two walls adorned with handwoven Indian tapestries, a print of Picasso's "Rites of Spring," and an original abstract painting of geometric figures which seemed to suggest that the sexual union of a square and a trapezoid would produce an infant triangle.

The dresser and its matching nightstand both had thick white marble tops. There was a ceiling fan with cherry-colored blades tipped in copper, and the carpet was of two-inch snowy shag. The room itself smelled so thickly of after-shave and sex that the odor tainted the taste of Rivera's sandwich.

Even so, Rivera thought the bedroom a wonderful place. He lay on his back on the soft bed and stared up into the blue sky of the canopy. Turning his face to a pillow he smelled the unmistakable odor of the short-legged dancer. It was a musky, healthy, exotically rich scent, an odor of ginger and nutmeg and oranges. The mere scent of her gave him an erection. Maybe her legs were not so bad after all, he thought. Besides, he should be more charitable in his assessment of her now that her fiance was destined to be killed. Maybe, Rivera told himself, I should call on her tonight to offer my condolences. A woman caught in the inexorable squeeze of grief is certain to respond enthusiastically to a sincere offer of solace.

But first there remained a safe to be cracked. As he finished his chicken sandwich Rivera searched the rooms for the safe. He found it after only a few minutes in the bedroom closet. It was much smaller than he expected it to be—perhaps as little as one foot square. It could not have weighed more than thirty-five or forty pounds. It was not so much a safe in the typical sense as a fireproof box with a combination lock. Rivera picked it up and tilted it sideways. Something slid heavily from side to side—a bag of money, perhaps; or at least a cigar box full of gold coins.

Now Rivera wondered whether he should attempt to crack the safe there in the bedroom or, since it was so portable, sneak it back to his own place. He finally decided on the latter because, at only a few minutes past 6:00 A.M., he could still quite easily make his way home again unnoticed. Anyway it was obvious that fate intended for him to take the safe home, otherwise fate would not have put such an idea in his head.

With bath towels from the banker's linen closet Rivera wrapped the metal box so that it looked more like a bundle of laundry than a stolen safe. And had he not at the last moment returned to Simón de las Gracias' kitchen for a bottle of cold beer, Augusto Rivera, with the towel-wrapped safe in his arms, might well have made good his robbery and escape.

When Simón de las Gracias drove his car up beside Leona's in the clearing outside the almond grove, then got out and walked toward her as she stood in the middle of the shallow depression with her back to him, the banker's thoughts were sympathetic and solicitous. Poor thing, he told himself. She's probably been crying her eyes out and can't bear for me to look at her.

Gingerly he made his way down the smooth wall of the gully. He kept one hand behind himself because he did not want to slip and get a grass stain on his trousers. Leona remained with her back to him, her hands held as though clasped in fervent prayer beneath her breasts.

"My Leona," Simón de las Gracias murmured as he approached her. "My fragrant little orchid. Why are you acting like this? You don't think I'm going to abandon you now, do you? Things might change a little bit but not so much that . . ."

Feeling his hand on her shoulder Leona pivoted and faced him. The barrel of the pistol she held struck him in the stomach. "Umpf!" he said, and jumped back half a step.

Leona lowered to her side the hand in which she held the pistol.

Stepping forward, she jerked her arm up again, ramming the pistol into the banker's crotch. He froze, only rising up on his toes a bit. Through his thin trousers he could feel the black eye of the pistol staring into his anus.

Leona stood with her face only three inches from his. She smiled. Simón de las Gracias trembled from the effort of balancing himself on his toes. Leona leaned forward and flicked her tongue across his lips. His head jerked back as though a cobra had hissed in his face.

"Do you think your dancer will still love you if I turn you into a girl?" Leona asked softly.

Simón's neck muscles twitched as he tried to speak. He looked as though he were trying to work out a bone that was lodged in his throat.

"After today everyone will call you Shorty," Leona said. "You'll have to sit down to take a piss."

Very cautiously the banker began to raise his hand, but as he did so Leona pushed the pistol barrel deeper into his crotch. He lowered his hand to his side again.

"This," he finally managed to say, "this isn't necessary, Leona. This is craziness. What good am I to you if you shoot me?"

"None," she answered. "Nor to anyone else. And that's the important thing."

Unable to hold himself on his toes any longer, Simón de las Gracias eased his heels to the ground. He looked into Leona's eyes and forced a frightened smile. "You'll always be my one true love," he told her.

"You'll always be a shit," she said. He saw her eyes narrow to a slit, her jaw tighten. He leapt into the air just as she squeezed the trigger.

What happened next would, in literature, be called an example of the literary device known as *deus ex machina*. This is an old trick employed by tired authors in which the supernatural powers of God are called upon to alter an unresolvable conflict. But this story is not literature, so we should try to keep God out of it. This is merely the account of a few of the minor incidents surrounding an historical fact. In historical terms, what happened next would be called the great Popayán earthquake of March 31, 1983. Over two hundred people were killed by this earthquake, and five hundred more injured. (The number of casualties was extraordinarily high for this size quake because thousands of people who did not live in Popayán had come there to celebrate Holy Week; so it seems that God will have his influence whether we like it or not.) Millions of dollars in damage was incurred, including the destruction of fine old colonial cathedrals and monasteries. The quake registered a 5.5 on the Richter scale and was felt even in the mountain villages of Cajibío and Piendamó, where windows cracked and dishes rattled in china closets.

In Popayán, however, in the apartment of Simón de las Gracias, a handyman by the name of Augusto Rivera was standing beside the refrigerator and drinking a bottle of beer when the ceiling began to splinter. Plaster dust scintillated down from the network of splitting veins and fissures. The building itself then began to sway from side to side, shuddering as though an angry giant were attempting to wrench it free from its foundation. Augusto Rivera went to the window and looked out. Buildings had begun to tumble. Great wounds opened up in the concrete, wounds from which gases, steam, and water were spewed. People ran into the street still wearing their pajamas and nightclothes only to become rubber-legged drunks who wobbled to the ground. Those who managed to rise could take only a few steps before their feet were swept from underneath them again.

Augusto Rivera stood dumbfounded, the bottle of beer foaming in his hand. From the sound of the explosions, the wail of the fire siren, the splintering crunch of wood and metal and concrete and the moaning of the earth, he thought that Popayán was under attack by an unseen enemy. "It's World War Three," he said to himself.

Then he heard the four-poster bed crash through the floor to the rooms below. He stood back from the window in the middle of the living room and watched the mirrored bedroom wall fall away to reveal the morning sky, now hazy with rising clouds of dust. Flinging down his beer bottle, Rivera started for the door. He stooped to pick up the towel-wrapped safe, but before he could straighten his legs the floor caved in beneath him.

Near the mouth of the almond grove, Alecia, who had been sitting against a tree, jumped to her feet at the sound of the gunshot. Like a nervous chipmunk she took three steps this way, then three steps that way. Finally she turned and started running back through the almond grove, needing to reassure herself that her mistress was safe. But halfway through the grove almonds began to fall from the trees. They plunked around her, plopping like heavy rain, some of them bouncing painfully off her head. The trees themselves began to shake, the leaves hissing at her, the limbs creaking ominously.

Shrieking with fear Alecia spun around and retraced her steps back toward the mouth of the almond grove. Coming into the open she did not pause but hurried down the narrow lane, the sky jaundiced and frightening now, the almond grove behind her alive like the evil forest of a child's horror story. Several times she felt the road pulled from beneath her feet like a slippery carpet, and tumbled forward, rolling in the dirt. After this had happened four or five times she no longer tried to rise but lay face down curled like an armadillo and dug her fingernails into the ground, certain that at any moment she would be tossed off the face of the earth to go sailing into the cold black emptiness of space.

Only a few hundred yards away Simón de las Gracias lay at the bottom of the grassy gully, his hands clasped over his scrotum while blood oozed between his fingers. Leona Carneiro de Assíz had, for the first few moments after the shooting, stood over him smiling, thrilled by his moans and his disbelieving look. She was about to shoot him in the head when suddenly she pitched forward as though someone had pushed her from behind. When she tried to stand she was thrown to the ground once more. She tried to scramble up the side of the gully but slid on her stomach back to the bottom. She could only assume that someone—God or Satan or the patron saint of bank managers—was coming to de las Gracias' rescue. She forgot about wanting to finish him off and, at the sound of Alecia's bloodcurdling scream, even tossed the pistol aside as evidence of her good intentions. But the ground continued to rumble beneath her like a mammoth whale attempting to flip her off its back. She crawled on her hands and knees up out of the gully, stumbling and knuckle-running to her car.

As Leona drove through the almond grove her Buick pitched from side to side, almonds plunking off the roof like hailstones. She veered too sharply to the right and grazed a tree, smashing a headlight. Pulling away she overcompensated and veered to the left, smashing the other headlight. By now the quake had subsided, but Leona was trembling so violently that she failed to notice any change. Through the shadows of the almond grove she could see blue sky and headed toward it as if for salvation. Clear of the trees and the raining almonds she pressed the accelerator to the floor, not even slowing as she sped past her maid who lay curled in a ball at the side of the road.

The Popayán earthquake lasted approximately eighteen seconds and was followed by two minor tremblers. The earth had lapsed into a relative calm by the time, a quarter of an hour later, that Simón de las Gracias struggled to his feet and made his way to his automobile. He steered with his left hand and cupped his scrotum with his right, unaware that a major natural catastrophe had come and gone. He found puzzling the number of almonds crunching beneath his tires as he drove out of the almond grove, but in reality was in far too much pain to give it more than a passing thought. A mile from the almond grove he came upon Alecia, who was trudging along lethargically. When he pulled up beside her she looked at him as though he were a corpse and assumed that she was supposed to ride with him into hell. She crawled into the back seat and curled up on the floor. She whimpered and moaned but would not speak.

Only after he had passed the ruins of several houses and other small buildings did Simón de las Gracias realize that the earth had truly moved beneath him earlier, that the tremendous shuddering he had experienced had not simply been the result of his own pain and shock, and that Leona had in fact, and not merely in his imagination, fled from him in fear.

Coming into Popayán was like coming into Dresden or London after an extensive bombing attack. Destruction was everywhere. Citizens moved about mechanically, numbed zombies, dragging bodies and bathtubs alike from the rubble. Simón de las Gracias drove as close to his apartment house as he was able, his progress for the last fifty yards blocked by deep craters in the street. Abandoning his vehicle and the moaning girl inside it, he walked with both hands cupping his crotch, his legs splattered with blood. No one, however, took notice of him, for blood was an insignia worn by many.

Near the pile of rubble that had once been a part of his home Simón de las Gracias found Augusto Rivera. Rivera lay amid fragments of sheetrock and lumber, a jagged laceration across his forehead, the flow of blood staunched with plaster dust. He was half-sitting, half-reclining, his legs buried in rubble, de las Gracias' safe tucked under his right arm. The banker looked up at that portion of the building that had remained standing. He saw his kitchen sink, its drainpipe exposed like a splintered tibia, hanging in the air.

De las Gracias made his way through the debris and slipped his right hand under Rivera's arm. "Let's get you out of there," he said. His voice was flat and emotionless.

"Better not," Rivera told him. "My legs are broken. Just let me stay here where I'm comfortable."

The banker nodded and backed away. He looked up at his kitchen sink again.

"This is your safe I have under my arm," Rivera said.

De las Gracias looked at it. "How did you get it?"

"I was stealing it from your home when the earthquake hit."

The banker only nodded. Then he said, "Hang onto it for me until I get back."

"Where are you going?" Rivera asked.

"The Lindbergh Hotel."

"The Lindbergh Hotel is down," Rivera said.

Now for the first time since his shooting a pained expression darkened the banker's face. He felt himself getting sick to his stomach, pain swirling about inside him.

"But your fiancée made it out," Rivera told him. "She was here already looking for you. I sent her out to the almond grove."

"I just came from the almond grove," the banker said, his brain fuzzy with shock. "She must have started out over the hills on foot."

"She was very worried about you."

"She's a good girl," de las Gracias said.

Rivera nodded. "Did Leona shoot your pecker off?"

"I jumped," de las Gracias said. "But she got one of my balls."

"I would have warned you but I didn't want to interfere with fate."

Simón de las Gracias stared up at his kitchen sink. "I guess I'll go see if I can find a doctor."

"Did anything happen to Leona?"

"She ran off after she shot me. She's probably all right. What could happen to Leona?" The banker turned and walked away. He was trying to recall in which direction to find the San José Hospital. As he stood in the middle of the street, holding his crotch and looking to his left and then to his right, he heard a prolonged creak like that of a tree falling and looked up just in time to see his kitchen sink tear loose and come crashing to the ground.

"Are you all right?" he called to Rivera.

"Sure," the fatalist said. He smiled crookedly through the cloud of dust. "It missed me by a mile."